Ripple

D1713205

Tui Allen

Ripple

DEDICATION

This story is dedicated to the dolphins of Taiji,
and the spirit of every cetacean,
ever killed or imprisoned by man.

Ripple

CONTENTS

ACKNOWLEDGMENTS

Tui Allen

ACKNOWLEDGMENTS

Dr Ewan Fordyce of the Geology Department of Otago University, who gave me paleontological and geological information, showed me fossils from Ripple's era and introduced me to the fossil itself.

Carolina Loch and Gabriel Aguirre of the Geology Department of the Otago University, who were as interested in my fictional information as I was in their factual information about the fossil.

Daphne Lee of Otago University, who also helped me to find paleontological and geological information I needed.

Mark Simmonds, International Director of Science, Whale and Dolphin Conservation Society for checking facts and contributing guidance beyond all expectations.

Jeff Tucker – for preventing my death by starvation while I wrote this book.

My son Leith Simpson – for motivating me to continue when I was discouraged and proving that you are what you think you are.

My daughter Heather Simpson - for inventing music of her own, having the willpower to pursue goals in the face of adversity and doing her bit to help the dolphins of Taiji.

My stepfather Jack Allen for giving me access to the open oceans in childhood and teaching me the names of the stars.

Gregar Haycock – for surfing information and descriptions of the physical sensations of surfing.

James Gurney for information about tides, currents and wind directions affecting the surf and the link between surfing and creative energy.

Steve Thompson for answering scientific questions.

My cousin Heather Thompson of the NZSO for assistance with musical information and terminology.

Shaun Cooper of Massey University – for mathematical assistance when I needed it.

Barbara Else for her three assessments of the story of Ripple.

Raymond Huber for editing the manuscript.

My literary friends who provided ruthless criticism to help me refine the text: **Hilary Boyd, Rod Fee, Shauna Bickley, Ted Gibbons, Katie Henderson, Pauline Herbst, Bronwen Jones, Jeannie Mclean**

My niece Nicole Adams for providing critiquing from a young person's viewpoint.

Chrystene Hansen, mind adept, for the healing journey that got me started.

Ripple

PROLOGUE

Remember, you humans, this is not your story, though it's high time you heard it. Mother Sterne herself suggested I tell it to you.

'The humans need to know, Father Clement,' she said. 'Why don't you tell them?'

'But they are humans! How does one communicate with them?'

'I'm sure your sublime skills will cope with the challenge of human verbal languages, Father. You know there is no deity, including myself, in the entire Divine Hierarchy who appreciates and understands the story better than you.'

It is true that I appreciate Ripple's story so much more than Sterne, yet she was the one who made it all happen – I was only ever there to act as her mentor. If I'm honest, she did it in spite of me; not that she gained much from it herself, poor thing.

Mother Sterne forbids me from being rude to humans. She has high hopes for you and is almost as obsessed with you now, as she was with the dolphins in the old days. She knew what she was talking about back then as it turned out, and her powers have only improved since.

However, before I start on all this "politeness to humans," please excuse me for explaining slightly snappishly, that Azure is the true name for your planet. 'Earth' is just dirt.

~~~

Was it really over twenty million years ago? Is it even possible for you to imagine your planet as it was then? ~~You humans hadn't come down from the trees.~~ I mean to say, your ancestors were still living their simple arboreal lifestyle…

1
DEITIES AND DOLPHINS

It began exactly twenty million, three thousand, two hundred and fourteen years ago as we were traversing the outer universe together.

'Sister Sterne, this spirit, has failed in too many lives to achieve the purpose you speak of,' I said. 'Surely you do not intend to let it try again?' Sterne was still only a sister back then.

'But I believe in this spirit, Father Clement. I most respectfully request to be allowed to give it one more chance'.

The spirit in question hovered beside Sister Sterne, secured by a curve of her aural wing. It was only faintly visible, an ellipse of soft light, shimmering against the darkness of space.

'Look at it,' I said, 'It's clearly tired and has grown disillusioned with its task. Don't you think it needs an aeon or two in the great Hereafter to recuperate, before you send it back to the struggle?'

Her evergreen eyes flashed.

'I'm sure that is what the spirit itself might prefer, Father, but it has an important contribution to make to a planet and perhaps to the entire universe. I am not ready to let it give up.'

We slowed briefly to admire the interplay of light and colour within a nearby globular star cluster.

'But why is it that even you, as its deity, are unable to guess what it is this spirit has failed so repeatedly to discover?' I asked.

'I believe it is destined to ignite something so new in the universe, not even we divine beings have yet any concept of what it is to be.'

'I'll admit it is often the mortal creatures of the universe who initiate the most immortal trends.'

Sister Sterne raised the spirit before her. We could both see how its glimmering faded when even the faintest of competing light sources, such as a small distant nebula, passed behind it. It was certainly tired.

'Can't you see that tiny spark?' she said. 'It's easy to miss but I have a feeling that it contains a strength that transcends even such deep spiritual tiredness.'

I groaned inwardly – not this 'light of the spirit' nonsense again.

'You're too hard a taskmaster, my girl. You must realise that some souls cry out for a little fun!'

We floated on at light speed, allowing a kaleidoscope of glittering star systems to spin by us. I paused and admired the intense colours pulsing through the incandescent veils of gas-clouds in the Tayili galaxy.

'Supposing we were to agree to your request, Sister Sterne. Have you any idea what kind of life-form might allow this spirit to succeed with its one last chance?'

She coughed. 'I have given it considerable thought. Perhaps you've been correct all along about . . . er . . . certain things, so I have concluded that this spirit may indeed require a little laughter, to help it reach its full potential. I also consider that sound and hearing are crucial to its purpose. Finally I believe it needs to be consigned to a life-form which is as intelligent as possible without being so far advanced that it has "Past-Life Memory".'

She fidgeted with her spectral aura and I noticed a beautiful elliptical galaxy wheeling by beyond her left aural wing.

'Perhaps, Father, I've made an error by always sending it into more superior life-forms that do have that faculty. I did this because I felt this spirit had a high purpose. But now, it has suffered so much, its memories are unhelpful. It needs a fresh, uncluttered beginning.'

'Well there are many life-forms in the universe fitting your criteria,' I said. 'However, I'm a little concerned at your proposing to send it in at a lower level this time; it seems unusual to step backwards with one who is supposed to make a contribution to the universe.'

'You may understand my thinking better if you saw the life-form I am considering.'

'I will look, Sister Sterne, but I warn you I shall take some convincing that this exhausted spirit needs anything further than several aeons of solid rest.'

'See that beautiful spiral galaxy on the far side of the universe?'

'You mean Koru Maelstrom,' I said. 'A very sweet barred spiral. It's within a family of galaxies I was quite active among myself, once upon a very long time ago.'

'You may recall then,' she said, 'floating deep within that galaxy, among millions of other stars, a small star known as Sol? Orbiting Sol is a planet which could be very suitable, although it can be a savage place.'

'Where is your compassion Sister Sterne? Ought you not seek out a gentle home for this spirit? Savagery has never encouraged it to achieve in the past.'

'Please humour me, Father, while I explain. There is much beauty on this planet and beings of great intellect have begun evolving there over the last few million years. Let's cast ourselves in its direction now; sweep with me across its surface. What do you see?'

'I see brilliance, purity, and blueness, – a wonderful azure colour - but of course, this is Azure. I haven't visited it for at least an aeon. I had forgotten what a jewel it is. Good gracious! Look at the life that has evolved since I was last here. You could be onto something with this my girl. I wonder you didn't think of it sooner.'

'Yes, I thought that liquid surface could prove perfect. Note the friendly, intelligent creatures cavorting there. Surely this spirit may thrive here at last, if it can inhabit a body like those. I notice their intellects are highly adapted to process sound. They are perfect in that respect. Even their colours are glorious.'

'But look at them enjoying themselves, Sister. That's the big thing; they're having fun! My goodness, it makes me feel like jumping in the water myself and joining the frolic.'

I stared eagerly down at the streamlined, leaping bodies of the dolphins, every colour of the rainbow, spinning and skipping from wave-top to wave-top. I knew Sister Sterne would be rolling her evergreen eyes at me behind my back, impudent minx that she was in those days.

'Fun is all very well, Father,' she said, 'but I like the souls under my care to fulfil themselves. At the end of their lives they're not likely to be appreciating all the good times they've had, they're going to be thinking of their achievements.'

'When you've observed as many souls as I have, Sister, you'll soon see that these things can be all tied up together.'

Sterne waved towards a pod of whales. 'You see that much larger species? They have even greater intellect and advancement, but they do have Past Life Memory. The dolphins have none, so I deem them more suitable. But look deeper now, Father, down into the water. It's worrisome is it not?'

'Hmm yes, I now see the savagery you speak of. However, these creatures you've chosen seem well adapted to survive the dangers of their world. There is always risk.'

While Sister Sterne floated above Azure, anxiously pondering, I circumnavigated the planet at a leisurely pace observing the various life-forms before returning to her side.

'How are beings on Azure communicating these days?' I asked. 'There was little happening last time I was here, but it is clear even from a quick glance, things have progressed well since then.'

'No land-based creatures have progressed beyond grunts or squawks,' she said. 'But the Azuran "ocean mind" long ago adopted the telepathic communication methods in use throughout the developed universe; they call it thought-streaming.'

'I'm pleased to hear it. Communication could prove useful to this troubled spirit. So often it turns out to be the key.'

'I've tried hard to think of the best for this spirit's next phase, but I can't make a better suggestion than this I have shown you.'

'I think you have chosen well Sister. In fact, to my surprise, you have convinced me.'

'Then we are agreed? There is to be another chance?'

'One last chance. But if this spirit meets with failure again, I must insist we let it rest until all the worlds of the universe have mellowed an aeon or two.'

Shortly afterwards, I departed from her to return to other business. Sister Sterne remained close to Azure, staring down into its sapphire seas, awaiting the perfect moment, while the problem spirit hovered beside her, shimmering softly.

But my mood had been so lifted by my glimpse of the dolphins of Azure, I placed the planet and Sister Sterne's problem spirit under permanent observation watch, along with all the others I was keeping within my fields of special interest, so I'd always be aware of events surrounding them. I returned often in person and spent much time with Sterne, supporting her in her work with the tired spirit, in its last lifetime of chance and so between us we watched its story unfold.

2
UNBORN

A baby was conceived shortly afterwards among the dolphins of the Northern Islands School on the planet Azure. A few days later the embryo dug itself firmly into the wall of the uterus of its mother, a rainbow dolphin called Pearl.

Sterne and I were pleased to observe the cells of the embryo dividing and developing at a healthy pace. The problem spirit had made a powerful beginning to its sentence on Azure.

~~~

As was usual with dolphins, Pearl suspected the pregnancy from the moment of conception but she noticed nothing different about this one. No strange tinglings. No premonitions; only the usual sense of fulfilment of a new life beginning; as though every blue seemed bluer and every wave danced for her alone.

Late one afternoon, a few weeks into her pregnancy, Pearl swam with a group of old friends across a glittering ocean. They'd hunted well, and now cruised in anticipation of sunset while quietly discussing a mathematical conundrum of interest to the group. They swam parallel to a line of small islands just visible to the west. The western horizon was rising up towards the sun and would soon hide it altogether leaving the ocean in darkness. The eastern sides of the islands were already in shadow although the sun still blazed above them. The sea was almost too bright but looking east, all was smoothly luminous.

The dolphins perceived another group of their own kind ahead, swimming unusually slowly. There was no alarm shown by any of the dolphins in either group. Not all those in the slower group were even aware Pearl's group was approaching. She guessed they were a team of practical astronomers at work. The vocation had always interested Pearl, and she might have chosen it for herself, had its demands not conflicted with her standards of motherhood.

The astronomers in the group were lost in their work, and would have been unsafe without the team of minders who guarded them. Pearl noticed how rarely the astronomers breathed. She wondered where exactly they were in mind at that moment. Were they still within the Koru Maelstrom home galaxy? Or visiting one of its millions of near or distant cousins? Were they still spinning along their thread-like paths between the galaxies listening for signals that called them in? Or were they already conversing with the inhabitants of an alien world?

She noticed one minder fussing more and more anxiously over one of his charges, before finally gently nudging him to the surface to remind him to breathe. The sound of the exhale was like an explosion in the minds of the watching dolphins, communicating the intensity of the work in progress. He who had just breathed, rolled slowly down and meandered into the increasingly inky depths. The minder, calmer now, cruised in his slipstream. Pearl recognized the golden-bodied dolphin who had breathed. He was Rigel, leader of the astronomers, and father of the baby she carried.

~~~

Rigel is not what Pearl called him of course, but that is the name you humans have for the mighty star whose name he bore, so it's the closest translation we have.

~~~

As Pearl and her group swam on, they continued the discussion that had so absorbed them before seeing the astronomers. Pearl listened to the glittering thoughtstreams of the friends around her.

Here we all are, she thought, enjoying sharing our knowledge of mathematics, but it wouldn't be ours to share, if not for our astronomers, who brought the seeds of mathematics from alien cultures to enrich us.

~~~

'Look at the spirit lights of those parents!' said Sister Sterne. 'Surely they will provide this baby with the genes for the task.'

'Spirit lights?' I said. 'What are you talking about Sister? We're looking at physical bodies, surely.'

She sighed. 'With respect Father, we are deities – it's possible to train our immortal eyes to see and assess the light of any spirit, whether or not it is under life sentence. Focus with the ultra-vision of your divine inner eye on the female Pearl swimming before us now; try to locate her spirit-light and tell me what you see.'

'Can't see a thing except a shapely-looking dolphin body. Beautiful colour isn't she? Iridescent, like the sea-jewel she's named for.'

'For a dolphin of Pearl's nature, Father Clement,' she insisted, 'focus near the heart. After a while you get the feeling for where each character type is most likely to display its light.'

I focused again and to my surprise I did see a glimmering there.

'Hmmm, perhaps you're right. I fail to see how it tells me anything though.'

'Can you see our problem spirit there within her also?'

'Yes, I suppose so. Its looks much as it did before you sentenced it; faint and tired.'

'Now observe the male, Rigel, who is fathering our problem spirit in its new life. He carries his light in the upper brain, just above and forward of centre. Can you find it?'

'Vaguely.'

'Now compare his with our mother dolphin. Can you see the difference? His light is so powerful, so physical, so focused. Hers is a softer light, calm and multi-directional. But can you sense the will they both share?'

I saw the lights and I supposed there were differences between them. It seemed too slight a signal to base a whole new life upon, but Sterne was so absorbed by her light-readings, she deserved some encouragement.

'Sister Sterne, I am far from convinced of the worth of this method of yours, but if this spirit lives up to your assessment, I'll recommend your skill to the Sacred Council for closer analysis. It could help your advancement in the Divine Hierarchy.'

Sterne's aura expanded suddenly with uncharacteristic warmth, emitting great streamers of magenta light into the space surrounding her.

'Thank-you Father! I would be honoured to be recommended by a deity of your standing.'

I sighed with concern for the spirits of the mortal creatures frolicking before us, while the soft dusk deepened to night across their ocean and the starlight glimmered on the waves of their home.

But let us forget for now, the ambitions of deities and focus again on the Azurans whose story resumes a few months later . . .

~~~

Inside Pearl the baby woke and began to think. The first thought was a question.

Where is it?

Then came a command from herself to herself.

Listen!

The baby listened to her own beating heart and her mother's. She heard another sound, a sudden rush out and in, from her mother's body. It only happened now and then. The baby did not understand that sound and she puzzled over it.

There was another kind of rushing; something big, outside and around all the time.

Is there liquid out there? Is my mother jumping and playing in liquid, just as I do here inside her?

My mother is thinking of me again. Listen! I can hear her thoughts. She is soothing me. I am safe. I am warm. How great she must be to carry me here inside her. I must think my love to her as she thinks hers to me.

Again and again the baby commanded herself to listen. She sometimes felt her mother sending thoughts out away from her. The marvellous thoughts went on their way and she wondered what they meant.

Are there others like her out there? Others, who she sends them to? Listen! I can hear some of them. Their sounds show me that they are the same shape as me, but bigger, like my mother.

The baby heard sounds coming from every direction and she spent all her waking hours trying to work out what each one meant.

One day she heard a wild high cry from high up in the world outside.

Are there others out there who are different from us?

'Mother. Mother. Can you hear me?'

'Yes my baby. I can hear you.'

'What makes that crying sound?'

Pearl saw the tern calling as it flew above. She thought-streamed the picture inwards to her baby.

A pretty creature, thought the baby. I like the sound it makes.

But where are the sounds I am waiting for? Are they in here or out there? Listen! Listen!

~~~

Over the next few weeks, thoughts, questions, and pictures passed between Pearl and her baby in an increasing stream. Pearl did all she could to help the child make sense of her new existence. She was a 'mind' mother, more interested in what was in the child's mind than in its physical self. Most dolphins could communicate efficiently at birth, but few with the fluency of Pearl's children.

~~~

It was about this time that Sister Sterne and I noticed the presence of seraphim in unusual numbers. Something seemed to be attracting them to the Solar System of Koru. I found this strange since I didn't recall their having any presence or interest in Sol or Koru during my previous sojourns there. Sterne regarded them forbiddingly whenever they dared enter her presence. She tended to discourage the annoying familiarity for which these 'groupies of The Hereafter' were notorious.

~~~

'What am I?' asked the baby one day when Pearl was swimming up the windward side of a large wave in a storm. A group of seraphim surrounded her – their transparent energy fields clearly visible to us, though no dolphin would see them.

'You're a baby dolphin.'

'What is a dolphin?'

'A being of the oceans of the planet Azure.'

'Oceans? What is that?'

'Water. Just like the water you are swimming in now. But oceans are vast, deep, blue, clear, and beautiful.'

I understand 'vast' I think. Deep too. Beautiful maybe, but . . . 'Blue? Clear? What is that?'

'You'll understand when you are born.'

'What is being born?'

'When you come out to live in the big world out here.'

'I will go out there?'

'You will.'

'What is it like out there?'

Pearl watched the wind sweep the tops from the waves, pulverize them in the air and fling them across the surface in boiling streaks.

'You can swim as far as you want and never reach the end.'

'I want to be born now!'

Not far off, in deeper water, Pearl sensed the stealthy movement of a hunting shark.

'You'd die before you swam two body-lengths if you were born now, especially in this storm. The world out here is dangerous for a baby, especially one that's been born too soon.'

A few weeks later Pearl received the message again.

'Mother, I need to be born as soon as I can.'

'You can't be born until you are ready, so you must be patient.'

A deliciously stupid mackerel cruised past her nose. She reached for it lazily. This would be an easy catch.

'But Mother I need to find something. Can I just pop out for a minute?'

Pearl missed the mackerel.

'No dear. It doesn't work that way.'

Her next target wasn't quite so stupid, but she eventually caught it, stunned it with a well-placed bite to the head, deftly turned it in her mouth so that it would slide down easily and swallowed, savouring the oily richness of the meat.

By this stage of her pregnancy, an older female relative called Breeze constantly shadowed her for support. Breeze and Pearl shared in the delicacies surrounding them.

'The baby seems restless. Breeze, can you check on it please?'

Breeze scanned Pearl's womb. 'It's twisting and turning a bit.'

'What's the matter baby?'

'I'm trying to find something.'

'What on Azure could you be seeking?'

'I don't know what it is. I don't know where it is. But I have to get out of here so I can find it!'

Pearl felt the baby thrashing.

Breeze sent soothing brainwaves to calm the child. It helped, and Pearl called upon Breeze often after that to calm the searching baby who couldn't wait to be born.

~~~

Weeks passed.

'Mother, am I male or female?' Pearl and her daughter Echo received this question together.

'We don't know yet but Breeze will know very soon. I think you're a female and perhaps one day you will be a mother like me.'

'I hope so. I want to be just like you.'

'Do you know your older brother and your sisters, my baby?'

'I know about Aroha and Rev because you think of them so much. I know Echo because she is always with you and she is watching me now.'

'And is Echo your favourite sister?'

'Yes. She will be my friend forever.'

Pearl and Echo laughed.

'Now rest and sleep,' Pearl soothed. 'We must hunt. Then I can eat so you can grow.'

Pearl, Echo and the other dolphins of the school continued hunting and feeding, while the baby rested at last.

~~~

A few days later, Pearl, Breeze and Echo, swam west together through a narrow strait between two islands. Pearl noticed Breeze studying her womb.

As though aware of Breeze's scrutiny, the baby asked, 'Mother, does Breeze know if I am a girl yet?'

Breeze herself answered, 'Yes, I am sure now that you're a girl,'

'I'm a girl! Just like my mum.'

All the dolphins including the baby, cavorted in celebration.

'My little sister.' said Echo, 'Look at you – stop bouncing around in there. You'll make my mother sore.'

'What's more important is that you are healthy and of fine size and shape,' said Breeze.

Pearl was well satisfied with all of Breeze's information. The three dolphins emerged at the western end of the strait and veered left to head down the western side of the southern island.

'What name shall you give me, Mother?'

'I'll give you the name that seems to suit you when I see you swimming for the first time.'

~~~

The weeks passed and the little female grew.

'Mother, Mother! Once I was able to move and swim about but now I can hardly roll over. I feel trapped.'

'You're growing so quickly you are filling up the space I have to hold you. That is good. It means you will be born soon and be as free as the birds in the sky. This is your time to rest, grow, and be patient'

'But mother, what is it like to be born?'

'It may be a little frightening, but it's worth it.'

'I want it so much, but I'm afraid too.'

Next day, Pearl and Breeze imparted the information the baby would need to survive the coming ordeal.

'There are things you must know about the world,' said Pearl. 'It has both air and water. You'll be born underwater but you must quickly find the air and learn to breathe. Breeze will help you. Can you feel the little hole on the top of your head? That's your blowhole. Exercise it. Play with the muscles surrounding it so when you reach the air for the first time you'll know what to do. It'll feel very strange at first. Air will rush in and out your blowhole, whenever you ask it to. You can breathe out anywhere but air can only come in when your blowhole is up above the surface.'

'What's the surface, Mother?'

'It's the place where the air meets the water; a beautiful shining expanse.'

'I think I can hear it.'

'That is very likely. Now listen carefully. I have instructions for your birth. You'll be born tail first. Once your tail is out, it may take a long time for the rest of you to be free. I'll go on swimming as usual. The moment you feel your whole body is free, you must swim up to the air and take your first breath. Breeze and Echo will be there in case you need help.'

Breeze explained.

'When you are born, swim up towards the light. It's at the surface too, just like the air.'

'What's light, Breeze?'

'It's hard to say, because it's silent. Light will seem powerful and huge. It's much stronger above the surface. But you must swim towards it, even if it hurts your eyes.'

'I hope I haven't forgotten how to swim. It's so cramped in here.'

'Not long now my little one', Pearl re-assured her. There was silence from the baby. Then one more question.

'Breeze, what are my eyes?'

'Rub your head against your mother and you'll feel two little bumps, one on either side of your head. The light will dazzle them at first. You might need to keep them half closed until they get used to it, especially if it's sunny.'

'Thank-you Breeze, I'll try to remember everything.'

'Don't worry, little one – I'll help if you forget. Do what we tell you at the time, and all will be well.'

'Whatever it is, wherever it is, I'll find it, once I am born. I know I will.

3
SEARCHING

Pearl's contractions started two days later, one cool and sunny morning. Rev, Breeze, Aroha, and Echo, swam near for extra protection. The baby's tail soon appeared. Breeze swam closest to Pearl to observe and reassure the baby, and communicate with Pearl as required.

'Echo,' said Breeze, 'Can you do lookout duties please? Let us know about any sharks or predators the blood might attract.'

'Can't Rev do that? I want to see the birth!'

'Rev, do you mind?' asked Breeze.

'Any shark that comes in range will feel my rostrum re-arranging his insides.'

'Just make sure you let the school know before you take it on single-beaked!' his mother warned.

'Alright, I'll tell them . . . if it's a big one.'

'Rev! Do as you're told!'

Breeze watched carefully throughout the entire birth, checking on distress levels of mother and baby. Pearl pushed hard into the final contraction and the baby arrived in a cloud of blood. Breeze, shadowed by Echo, was ready to provide any assistance the newborn might need. But, to everyone's delight, this baby needed little help, her tiny flexible body undulating to the surface as naturally as the ripples that spread on a calm sea when a fish leaps. So Pearl named her new baby 'Ripple'.

~~~

Ripple gasped as the air rushed into her lungs. So this was air! A thunderbolt to body and brain. She scanned the world by vision and sonar; looking, listening, searching. The cold clawed at her.

There's too much air. Too much water. Too much space. Too much light.

It must be here somewhere . . .

'Where is it, Mother?' she said.

'Where is what?'

'Perhaps I left it behind in the warm. Can I go back and find it?'

'You can't go back, dear.'

They swam on, the adults guiding Ripple to keep her near the surface.

'Now breathe again,' Pearl ordered.

'I already breathed!'

'It's time for your second breath.'

'Must I?'

'You must,'

'Pouuff! There, I did it. I will never get used to that.'

'You will – I promise.'

Ripple was already swimming smoothly in her mother's slipstream like a tiny living shadow of the adult. By now the cold was digging its way towards her innermost organs. Pearl injected the first milk into her mouth. Magical! It drenched her with warmth. The icy needles mellowed into cool caresses.

For the first hour or two Pearl and Breeze patiently reminded her to return to the surface and breathe regularly, until she'd accustomed herself to this strange new task and made it a regular habit.

Soon, she was recovered enough to start enjoying her freedom.

This was a world worth seeing. The space, the light, the blue and white sky! It was beyond anything she could have imagined before she was born. After the first shock of it she quickly learned to appreciate the air pouring into her eager lungs. She loved the cool softness of the sea enclosing her; the warmth of Pearl's rich milk, sliding thick and cheesy down her throat; and the colours of the dolphins glowing in rainbows against the one intense colour that gave the whole world its name.

And the movement! The freedom! The beautiful sounds! With such stimulation, Ripple's race to learn accelerated like the wind of a rising gale.

But why can't I find what I am looking for? It's everywhere around me. I'm certain of it.

~~~

There was much to frighten her in the outside world: a sudden shadow from a cloud passing over the sun, a noise she did not yet understand, the first glimpse of an unfamiliar creature such as a large ray.

'Whistling whitecaps!' she would say and cling closer to her mother's side.

'Jellyfish!' Echo teased, when she noticed Ripple taking fright at every new sound and shadow.

'She is a jumpy one,' agreed Breeze.

~~~

But what if I die before I find it?

Was that it? No, it was a gust of wind breathing on the ocean.

What about that one? No, it was that bird; his wingtips brushed the face of the wind.

Some huge booming thing, deep down in the sea. Is that what I seek?

'Echo, can you hear that booming? What is it?'

'It's the heartbeat of a blue whale, Ripple, but he's far away.' Echo thoughtstreamed a picture of him to Ripple.

'What's he doing?'

'Eating krill by the million.'

He's magnificent, thought Ripple, but he's not what I'm looking for.

It hums in every atom of this beautiful world, but still I cannot find it.

~~~

One stormy night, Ripple swam with her mother and Echo, near to a windward shore.

What cataclysm is happening here? So many sounds - I must see what makes each one, in case it has the clue. Now, that's just the waves as they topple and crash on the rocks and the sand, and that's just the wind whipping the crests into foam and hissing them out across the surface. But what's that great rumble coming up from the bottom? Whistling whitecaps! The currents are pushing boulders about down there, the way I push little bubbles.

But none of these sounds are the ones I'm looking for.

'Mother! Echo! Are you hiding sounds from me?'

'Are you crazy Ripple? How could we hide sounds from you?'

Still Ripple sought for something that stayed hidden and beyond the roaring of the world around her, she heard a silence that seemed to be waiting . . .

Silence is emptiness, she thought.

I'm searching for something to fill that emptiness, before it sneaks up on me and pounces. Is silence my enemy? Is it my friend? Is it both?

It's both, but it is deepening. It's laughing at me. I can smell it waiting in dead bones and empty lobster shells and black holes in rocks. When we swim over the deep I hear it roaring from the abyss. Who's it waiting for?

She screamed. Not a thought-scream, a loud audible scream.

'The silence is waiting for me. Mother! Mother! Save me!'

'What's the matter now, Ripple? What silence for Azure's sake?'

'The waiting silence.'

'What are you talking about?'

'I'm frightened of it mother. It's waiting in the deep. Make it go away!'

'Ripple, there's no silence, there are a thousand sounds to listen to. If the deep bothers you, just think of the wonderful food it produces for dolphins to enjoy, or look up into the sky instead.'

Ripple looked up at the stars and sensed a silence beyond the galaxies that was deeper and darker than the sea itself.

No-one can help me. Not even Mother. I must find what the silence is hiding and show it to everyone. Why does it frighten me so?

The silence threatened Ripple until Echo swam by in the morning with a strip of seaweed draped across her dorsal fin.

'Ripple, catch!' she cried and dropped the seaweed. Ripple forgot her fears, claimed the seaweed and raced away with it. Echo did not rest until she'd won it back. The game lasted an hour and gave way to hunting games that took up the rest of the morning.

Rev joined in occasionally, but grumbled at having yet another sister to put up with. Aroha was not around as much as the other two but Ripple saw her from time to time, admired her from afar and thought her almost as great and beautiful as Pearl.

'Aroha has a mate called Matangi. Imagine having a mate!' said Echo.

~~~

Conversations between mother and baby continued as before:

'What should I do, now that I'm born mother?'

'You should study the grown-up dolphins to see what they do with their lives. Every dolphin should contribute something worthwhile to the school.'

'I see them eating fish and leaping about and having fun.'

'Yes,' laughed Pearl, 'They do plenty of that! But their days are long and they need more than food and fun to fill them. Some dolphins decide on their vocation within just a few weeks of being born. Your sister Echo is two years old and still has no idea what she wishes to become.'

'Tell me about your vocation mother.'

'I'm a natural historian. I carry knowledge of life on Azure from down through the ages. Your father, Rigel, is one of the greatest of all astronomers. He's discovered many worlds and penetrated deeper into the universe than any astronomer before him.'

'When will I meet him?'

'One day, my darling. He is very busy and none of us see as much of him as we'd like.'

Ripple swam in silence for a while, wondering about her father. From time to time, Pearl delivered her delicious milk into Ripple's mouth, and she felt it sliding down, warming her and strengthening her growing bones and muscles. Mother and daughter dived under the surface and watched the rays of sunlight shafting down, brightening the blueness of the deep. Above them the surface stretched as far as she could see - a heaving sheet of light and movement. Ripple chased the silver bubbles escaping from her mother's blowhole, hunting them as though they were tasty anchovies, sometimes snapping them up when she caught them, sometimes following them all the way up so she could hear the tiny pop as they reached the surface.

'Could a dolphin become a sound adept?'

'Not really. All dolphins are adept in sound. It's a bit like asking if you could be a breathing adept. But if you're particularly interested in sound, perhaps you could have a vocation as a health adept using your ultra-sound to study the anatomy of dolphins, or an animal adept echo-exploring other sea creatures.'

Thinking of the insides of bodies only reminded Ripple of the trapped feeling she had before her birth.

'Ugh I'd hate that! Why would anyone want to look inside bodies when they could look up and out into the blue?'

She shot up through the surface into the sky as though she would leap right over the sun. Her wake glittered on the breeze like a trail of uncut diamonds.

'Well I just hope you won't be like your silly sister Echo, unable to make up your mind about anything.'

~ ~ ~

From Ripple's first existence on Azure she attracted seraphim. She was not the only dolphin they followed but she was their favourite. Sometimes groups of them haunted her as she rode her mother's slipstream or played with her sister. Seraphim are creatures of the Hereafter, so we knew they were there but the dolphins did not. But why were they so interested in this dolphin? I asked Sterne for her opinion on the reason for their presence.

'Perhaps their prescience allows them to guess at the possibilities I've read in her spirit light,' she replied.

'But why might immortal beings like seraphim be interested in the capabilities of a mortal dolphin?'

'You should ask them, Father Clement.'

I did ask the seraphim but their response was as I expected; a jumble of nonsense delivered as though it meant something sensible, while staring adoringly at me and flickering impudently in and out of my aura. Their telepathic mess trailed off into a hotchpotch of chanted poetry in praise of my sublime perfection. It continued long after I would have liked it to stop. Such tiresome creatures, although harmless enough.

4
ROUGH START

My interest in the spirit within Pearl's baby had now intensified to match Sterne's.

The savagery of Azure lay at the heart of her concerns about consigning the spirit there. Those concerns escalated on the day of Ripple's birth when, later in the afternoon, I observed a different group of dolphins dealing with the daily dangers of the blue planet.

If a dolphin swam south and slightly west down the island chain from Pearl's Northern Islands School for five or six days they would come across the Southern Islands School of dolphins. This was another of the zones on Azure that mysteriously attracted seraphim at that time. In fact it was seraphic presence which first drew my attention to the area. I looked to see what had attracted them and found myself gripped by events unfolding there.

~~~

Kismet and Mimosa of the Southern School had a two-day-old baby called Cosmo. Cosmo's parents were young, perhaps too young, but they shared a love that seemed capable of transcending any problems their inexperience might cause during the trials of parenthood.

Unlike many dolphin couples, these two refused to be physically separated. Where Kismet led, Mimosa followed.

On this particular day, Kismet led Mimosa and Cosmo far from the main school. The family were unaware of the cloud of seraphim floating above them.

Kismet wished Mimosa to feed splendidly today, to help her recover and to ensure she had all the nutrients she needed to provide rich milk for Cosmo. Hoping to bestow every treat she could desire upon her, he led her to a favourite hunting spot, where a rich supply of flavoursome sea life welled up from the deep ocean and could be effortlessly collected.

The food proved all he could wish for, and as Mimosa fed, Kismet swam a little way apart to get a better view of her and Cosmo together. Cosmo shadowed his mother, drawn along by her slipstream, following her every move. Sometimes, when her moves were too complex, his imitative antics were hilarious to Kismet. Watching his family and feeling the bond that linked them, Kismet knew he had arrived at the sweetest time of his life.

He was in the act of laughing at some comical manoeuvre by Cosmo when a shadow passed over his spirit. His laughter faded. What danger was here? He darted back to swim close beside Mimosa. She picked up his alarm. They scanned the ocean and quickly located the danger. Shark! A big one; too big for Kismet and Mimosa to manage between them. It was not far off to the south-west and heading in their direction.

'That shark's hunting us!' cried Mimosa.

'I won't let it hurt you.' he reassured her.

At first Kismet believed there was still time to get back to the main school for protection. If they left now and swam at top speed they should outpace the shark. They set off and Kismet quickly realised his dire miscalculation. In his newness to fatherhood, he had forgotten to allow for how much slower a baby would swim, especially over such distance, even with the slipstream of his parents to help him.

Kismet thought-streamed the main school with an urgent cry for help. He received a reply saying fighter dolphins were on their way, but the school was far off and the shark too close. Kismet knew the fighters could not arrive in time. The family was alone with its peril.

'It's my fault we're in this danger,' he said, 'I should never have brought you so far from the school. Swim away from me. Take him home! I'll do what I can to delay the shark.'

~ ~ ~

I could see how difficult it was for Mimosa, but she did obey Kismet. I saw him watching his family fade from his view to the north-east, knowing he would never see them again.

~ ~ ~

The shark was closing in, stealthily but speedily. Even with his eye-vision now, Kismet could see its massive shape approaching through the hazy water. It was four times his size and weight — a heavy missile of efficient muscle propelling a jaw that gaped to reveal row on row of murderous teeth. Kismet intended to do everything in his power to stop this monster from reaching his family. He knew what it would take and did not hesitate. He swam towards the shark, aiming to attract it. All too soon, the lidless eye of the predator focused on him and the jaw gaped wider. The shark sensed that its prey had split into two groups. It hesitated over which to choose. Kismet twisted in front of it and then rammed the shark from below. It turned to follow the other two dolphins, perceiving them as the easier option.

Kismet sprinted after it and crossed in front of the open jaws, swimming irregularly as though he were injured. The shark made its choice. It lunged at Kismet. Its eyes rolled back leaving blank white walls. The great jaws crunched down. Kismet was quicker and more manoeuvrable than the shark.

He darted aside at the last moment but allowed its outermost teeth to rip him near the tail. Red clouds bloomed. Kismet tasted his own blood in the water. The taste excited the monster enough to make it forget the other two and stay where the blood was flowing.

'Because of my error,' thought Kismet, 'all three of us might die today. I deserve death. They do not. But it's hard to die, not knowing if it will be enough to save them.'

The shark bit again and again. Kismet used his fading strength and all his skill and cunning, to evade as he could and delay the process to buy time for Mimosa and Cosmo. A quicker death would have been less painful, but that would not help them escape.

~~~

Mimosa strained to judge the greatest speed she could maintain without allowing a tiring Cosmo to drop out of her slipstream. Even at this distance, she knew everything that was passing through Kismet's mind, so tuned was she to his thought-streams. She felt his ordeal blow by blow, as though the monster was ripping at her own flesh. As she led her son away from the place where his father was dying, she sent thoughts of her own back to Kismet to help him through his last moments on Azure.

She promised him she would save their son, and because she knew he blamed himself for their peril, she told him that she did not blame him. She thanked him for their time together and sent messages of love.

Her final farewell to him was the last thing he received before his mind closed down.

She recognised that moment. Shortly afterwards, she felt his passing from Azure. It was as though the ocean had evaporated and left her swimming in emptiness. There was nothing left, except the tiny body struggling in her slipstream. He was all she had of her lost love.

'I won't let Cosmo die,' she vowed. 'I won't let my Kismet die in vain'.

They swam on but baby Cosmo was exhausted and slowing. He whimpered for food. She knew he would fade faster without it, so she slowed again and let him suckle. She forced herself to contract her lactation muscles and eject the milk into his mouth, while every other instinct urged her to leap for the moon to escape the approaching danger. Cosmo took the milk and then surfaced to breathe. By this time she could feel the deadly rhythm of the shark's approach. The nightmare was beginning again.

She thoughtstreamed to the rescue team.

'Where are you? Come quickly!'

'We're coming, we're many, but the distance is great.'

'Then swim as you've never swum before and save my baby at least.'

The shark had arrived, hunting them down. It loomed into view. When the first strike was imminent, she urged Cosmo to continue without her and swam towards the monster as Kismet had done before, determined to prevent it attacking her baby.

She thrust her fin into the gaping maw, just far enough for it to be slightly ripped on the first row of teeth. The teeth were still flecked with Kismet's blood and now the blood of Kismet and Mimosa mingled there. She skipped aside quickly. Like Kismet she intended to delay her own death to make time for the rescuers to arrive. Once again, the taste of blood persuaded the shark to choose her as its prey. Soon, billowing red clouds were staining the sea as before.

But Cosmo had not swum away. She saw him still swimming dangerously close to the shark and she heard him crying, 'Mother! Mother!'

'Swim away Cosmo.' she called. 'Some dolphins are coming for you! I cannot come with you. Leave me now! Swim away!'

But he did not obey and she knew he was too tired to swim on alone. She heard him call to the shark.

'Stop! Stop!' cried Cosmo, but the shark would not have listened even if it could.

~~~

I noticed that Cosmo ceased to breathe when he saw the shark hurting his mother. The non-breathing Cosmo charged, as though he was no longer exhausted. He darted like a wriggling sprat straight towards the side of the great grey body that rose like a wall before him and drove his tiny rostrum into it with every ounce of force in his body and soul. The impact almost knocked him senseless but fortunately for him the shark didn't notice and continued feeding.

Dazed, half blinded, short of oxygen, and with his rostrum bleeding from contact with the shark's gritty skin, Cosmo continued attacking the unheeding monster. In one almost accidental glancing contact with its mouth, three of the shark's outermost teeth ripped through the skin of Cosmo's left side leaving a deep triple gash bleeding freely.

~~~

Mimosa was fading fast. She had lost too much flesh and was finding it difficult to move quickly enough to slow the process. But the shark was not as hungry as it had been before, so Mimosa managed to stay alive for several minutes more. She felt the hits of the shark as a series of dull thuds; she was dragged through the water, then released. The clouds bloomed around her, exactly the shape of clouds in the sky but faster expanding and dreadful in colour. As with sky-clouds there were gaps between them, where she saw the deep Azuran blue of the sea. All colours were fading for Mimosa now and darkness crept in from the edges of her vision as though all of Azure was receding. But something moved there; she caught a last glimpse, in a gap between the red clouds. It was her baby. He was still whole and what were those large shapes surrounding him?

The fighters had come! One of them spoke to her.

'Mimosa, your baby is safe now. Go in peace.'

They'd take him away. He would live!

'Goodbye my baby. I'm sorry I cannot see you grow. Keep my love within you always.'

I saw him receive that love she sent him. It was a powerful gift; the last gift of a dying mother to her baby, and it settled deep inside him.

Mimosa relaxed at last and began to come back to us; Azure became a speck of light in the distance and then it vanished as the darkness closed in around her.

~~~

We allowed the spirits of Kismet and Mimosa to enter the Hereafter together as this was all they asked.

~~~

Back on Azure the team of skilled fighters easily drove off the now-replete shark with a few good hits to its belly, but had to quickly turn their attention to Cosmo who was losing consciousness from lack of oxygen. They held him at the surface and stimulated his breathing reflexes by intense thoughtstream and echo-vibration until they heard him take his first half-choking breath. Once breathing was re-established, they waited until full consciousness returned; then tried to take him into their slipstream to begin the journey back to the main school. But Cosmo would not leave the blood-stained waters where his mother had died. In the end, they took turns to work in pairs and almost carry the baby home, supporting his tiny weight from below.

Fortunately the school elders were aware of their need and moved the school towards them to minimise the distance. Cosmo was soon in safekeeping. Lactating females lined up to provide milk for this newly orphaned one, but it was many hours before he was in any state to receive it and even then took much persuading.

Cosmo was scarred for life. The triple slash was long and livid. It bled freely, slowing his recovery.

~~~

We deities, watching from the Hereafter understood that the scars on his skin were not his only scars.

~~~

The shark returned a few days later. It had developed an appetite for dolphin flesh and showed signs of further intent to prey on the school. A group of carefully trained fighter dolphins, including some who had been in Cosmo's rescue mission, were despatched to remove the threat. The team chose their spot carefully, approaching the monster by echolocation in clouded waters and from many directions at once, to confuse it. It fought back hard, but while dodging its razor-teeth, they attacked its gills and its ribless body with their hard rostrums, mashing its internal organs until it was dead.

Once again the small Southern Islands School had proven their reputation for training the best fighters in the oceans.

~~~

Baby Cosmo remained uncommunicative for many days after his parents died. He was never without milk, thanks to the many lactating females in the school, willing to provide for him. He was valued as all young dolphins were and well-cared-for by friends and relatives, but still he was alone in a way that was rare among his kind. He was bereft of parents but also doomed to life without siblings, though there were cousins and friends aplenty to partially fill this void.

My own mother's milk, thought Cosmo, was sweeter than any milk from other mothers. I want to catch my own food.

So, before he was three months old, Cosmo was hunting and catching his own small prey. He freed himself early from other dolphin's mothers, and freed them from him. He carried his mother in his memory; every detail of her appearance, every shade of her personality, every thought she had ever shared with him, both before and after his birth.

But his father was no more than a shadowy shape on the edge of his early memories. To Cosmo, Kismet was just a loss; the loss that had ravaged the last few minutes of his mother's life.

~~~

Sister Sterne and I now took as much interest in the famous fighter dolphins of the south as we took in those of the northern school where Ripple swam with Pearl and Echo.

5
TENTACLES

Rigel appeared only twice in the first three months of Ripple's life. He swept through with barely time to notice his latest offspring. Each time, Ripple's awe of the God-like golden stranger, sent her scurrying into her mother's shadow. She hid there and peeped at Rigel from under her mother's flipper.

On the second visit, Rigel spoke briefly with Pearl and then stroked Ripple absently with his flipper before leaving. Ripple expanded with pride and basked in the glow of his touch for days.

By now Ripple had developed the independence to venture from the safety of her mother's slipstream, usually in the company of her sister Echo. The two would race off on side trips to hunt or play-hunt for small fish, play with bubbles or seaweed or to meet up with other young dolphins of the school. They gradually increased the time and distance they strayed from Pearl's side as the months passed and Ripple's confidence grew.

Echo proudly showed her new little sister to all her friends in school and looked forward to the day when Ripple could join her there for lessons.

Once, when the two young females had ventured off together, Ripple felt a strange vibration in the water.

'It's the Shade, Erishkigal.' warned Echo, 'She's trying to attract you so she can eat you.'

Ripple leapt twice her body-length out of the water. She crashed back to the surface and cowered behind her sister.

'Take me away. I don't want to be eaten.'

Echo laughed. 'You jellyfish! She can't hurt you unless she touches you. She can't reach us here and even if she tried, we'd be long gone. The only dolphin she could catch is one who's alone and careless.' Ripple calmed a little but stayed close beside her sister.

'I'll teach you how easy it is to keep safe from her. Look down. What do you see?'

Ripple peered down at a shadow in the water.

'Nothing, just a funny dark patch. Is that the Shade? What's that smell?'

'The stench of Erishkigal and that shadow is her ink. She's hiding inside it so the fish can't see her. But we can see her with our hearing. Look inside that shadow now.'

Ripple scanned the cloud of ink, and clung closer than ever to Echo.

'She's the size of a whale! But she has no bones - just teeth ripping fish to pieces, and wriggling snakes of muscle. She is like . . . many creatures, not just one.'

'Those 'snakes' are her tentacles; she's one creature with many arms,' explained Echo. 'But you're right in a way. Each tentacle thinks for itself and each one is tipped with poison. Keep watching and listening.'

Then Ripple noticed that fish were swimming straight towards the shadow in the water. They were disappearing into the cloud of black ink.

'She's stuffing fish in by the ton, but why don't they swim away?'

'They can't see her by listening as we can. Her pleasure signal is stronger to them than her death stench. You'll know her by the ink smell and her vibration in the water. She's at her most dangerous to dolphins when she does not give off ink and when she does not make vibrations. But since she always does both when she's hungry, the danger's rare.'

Ripple, still keeping her sister's body between herself and the monster, peeped around Echo. She saw more fish swim willingly towards the shadow and never re-emerge.

After a long time, the stream of fish slowed as Erishkigal satisfied herself.

'She's so gorged she's stopped drawing them in,' explained Echo. 'Now, watch carefully.'

Ripple saw the gentle current dragging at the cloud of ink, wafting it away in veils of black, like clouds at midnight blown from the face of an evil moon. The monster was soon visible, her red eyes glaring up at them. Ripple noticed the soft pulsing of electric blue at the end of each writhing tentacle. Erishkigal's body was a great bloated bag stuffed with rotting fish bodies. A few live fish were still dying in agony on her tentacles, and she seemed to be enjoying their pain even though she no longer needed them as food.

Ripple looked into the monster's mind.

Her silence is blacker than the silence of the universe. Perhaps she's swallowed what I seek and silenced it.

'Where's her sound, Echo?'

'She's deaf as a stone.'

'Deaf?'

'She can't hear,' Echo said.

How can she live if she can't hear?

Ripple's fear attracted Erishkigal. The monster moved slowly towards them.

Ripple nudged her sister, imploring her to come away.

'She can't hurt us,' repeated Echo. 'She may be intelligent, and she may dream of eating warm flesh, but we know the names of all her tentacles.'

'I want to go home to Mother.'

'Calm down, Mummy's girl. Trust me.'

The Shade moved closer, staring up with red eyes blazing. Ripple clung closer than ever to her sister.

Echo coolly blasted the monster and her eight minions with one scorching thoughtstream:

Erishkigal - Shadow Queen
Vipa, Venga, Malevine,
Lucifina, Sadistine,
Fera, Lashette and Clawdine,
Go down now!

There was one mind-splitting thought-scream from the monster, but, at the command of one young dolphin, she turned and sank into the depths, dragging her slithering servants, lashing and silently howling behind her.

'Nothing to it,' said Echo,

Then Echo taught Ripple the names of the tentacles to give Ripple power over Erishkigal. Ripple repeated them until she could never forget.

It was a long time before she could stop thinking of the Shade. She stuck to Echo as they swam back and would not leave Pearl's slipstream for two days after the encounter.

~~~

'Look at your stomach Ripple. It's bulging with milk and fish!' laughed Echo one day. 'No wonder you're growing so fast. How does my stomach look?'

'I don't want to look in your stomach!' Ripple did a quick back-flip to avoid seeing it.

A light breeze from a blue sky covered the sea with glittering ripples. Lazy swells left over from the stronger winds of a day before heaved the ripples up and down. Echo whacked into the side of a swell scattering sheets of spray over her sister.

'Go on. Have a look! Tell me what I had for lunch!'

'Disgusting! You had squid. I can see the poor things all munched up and half digested. Can I look at the birds in the sky now instead of at your insides?'

'Insides are more interesting than outsides. Brains, hearts, skulls, kidneys; I love them all.'

Ripple, turned her back, leapt a passing wave and changed the subject; 'What're you going to be when you grow up? Mother says you ought to know by now.'

'Don't you start, Ripple! Why does she worry about it so much? It's not that I don't want to do anything; it's more that I do want to do everything and I can't settle on just one. Last week I thought I'd be a home planet adept and study the volcanoes and tides. The week before that I wanted to be a natural historian like Mother. A month ago I wanted to be a mind adept like Aroha. Before that a gymnastics teacher, a poet, or a fossil adept, a weather adept, a plant adept, a mathematician, an animal adept, or an astronomer. . . . Ripple I don't have a clue! How will I ever decide? Aroha knew her vocation when she was much younger than me. Did you know our father is a famous astronomer?'

'Yes, mother told me. I've seen him twice now. He stroked me . . . just above my flipper.'

'Mother says we are all as clever as we are because we've inherited his brains, but Mother is the cleverest female I know, so it could just as easily have come from her. Do you have any idea what you want to be, Ripple?'

'All I want to do is listen to sounds and arrange them in my head,'

'A sound-arranger huh? That's a new one. You'd better think of something quick before Mother decides you're as bad as I am.'

~~~

A few weeks later we were again observing the Northern Islands dolphins from directly above them. As usual seraphim drifted in the vicinity.

'Ripple, shall we play with seaweed today?' suggested Echo.
'We did that yesterday.'
'How about animal seaweed?'
'How can seaweed be animal?'
'Can you keep a secret?'
'Maybe.'
'Follow me.'

They swam towards the nearest island and Ripple followed when Echo dived. Rocks tumbled steep and jagged to the west. The sea filled the void to the east. The water was so clear, that from our viewpoint, the two dolphins looked to us like birds flying in the air beside a mountain. A fantasy of seaweed decorated the rocks beside them. Eels lurked and crabs scuttled into holes and crannies.

Echo slowed, scanning a dark hole in the rock-face.

'Shhh,' said Echo, 'He's in here . . . Wait.'

Echo turned around until her tail pointed at the hole, flukes positioned across its entrance. Ripple hoped no moray eel lived in there. They waited.

'Time's passing,' she thought. 'We'll need to breathe soon.'

Then she noticed green seaweed drifting from the hole. But while all the surrounding weed was bending northwards in the current, this weed flowed first south, then east, then in all directions around her sister's waiting flukes. There were suckers on it! It was not seaweed but tentacles.

'Echo. It's alive. '

27

'It's an ordinary octopus.'

'It looks like the Shade. I'm scared of it.'

One tentacle touched Echo's fluke and sucked on firmly, then another. Ripple backed off, about to dart away. How could Echo let it touch her?

'Ripple, you're being a jellyfish again. It's only Squelch; he's harmless.'

The octopus climbed on while Echo held herself steady. Its weight dragged her down slightly at the tail.

Ripple kept her distance. The octopus flowed like a cloud-shadow over Echo's tail and up onto her back. It wrapped itself all the way around her body just behind her dorsal fin. Echo headed for the surface with the load attached.

About time too, thought Ripple, She burst through the surface and breathed.

'Ooh - that air's sweet!'

'Meet Squelch!' He's a five-day octopus. Squelch this is Ripple.'

'Hi Squelch. What's a five-day octopus?'

'An octopus with a five day memory,' explained Echo. 'That's pretty good for an octopus. Want him to remember you? You've got to visit lots.'

Ripple stared inside its body seeking audio-processing functions. She squealed at it in high frequency, but saw no reaction.

'Is he deaf like Erishkigal?' she asked.

'He can hear very few frequencies and not the one you just used.'

His silence is not evil like Erishkigal's - only calm and blank. How sad to miss so much sound. But those eyes of his! Are they reading my heart and soul? Perhaps he can see as deep as I can hear.

He thought-streamed a question, as efficiently as any dolphin.

'Are all you dolphins female?'

'We have a brother —boys are nuisances.'

'I'm male.'

Ripple saw waves of opalescent colour shimmering over the creature's skin as it writhed and swirled on her sister's body.

His colour changes every second!

As though encouraged by her admiration, it dazzled her with colour changes from bright orange to dappled blue-green to black to soft pink to burgundy to brilliant gold spots on green to mottled red with purple stripes and finally back to speckled seaweed green.

Then he lifted each tentacle one at a time and waved at her, flooding each with a new colour as he did so until every tentacle was a different colour.

'A rainbow of tentacles! How does he do that?' she asked.

'He's like the Shade in more than just shape. Each tentacle can think separately from the main brain – his nervous system's so different from ours, he's really closer to some aliens than he is to dolphins. If he loses a tentacle, he can carry on his life while growing a new one. If you lose your tail, you're shark fodder.'

Ripple shivered. 'Don't say that Echo.'

Ripple watched the rainbow tentacles swirling in air and water. Squelch's great eyes stared at her, as though awaiting his moment. Suddenly he reached for Ripple with one tentacle, attached himself and flowed from Echo's back to hers. She felt the suckers latching and unlatching on her skin as he moved himself into position. By now she was brave enough to giggle at the tickle it made. A powerful octopodean command swept through Ripple's brain,

'Let's go!'

'Shall I take him?' she asked.

'Go! I'll follow,' replied Echo.

Ripple swam away with the octopus, with Echo in her slipstream. The bulge on her back altered her hydrodynamics and slowed her slightly, yet she was surprised at how easy he was to carry. The girls could feel the pleasure he took in riding them. When Echo took her turn in front to allow Ripple a rest in her slipstream, Squelch immediately transferred himself to the leading dolphin.

'Jump higher!' he commanded, 'Go faster! More cartwheels!'

~ ~ ~

We smiled down on them and I wished I too could ride a dolphin over that dazzling ocean. Inspired by what they saw, the seraphim moulded the electric particles of their bodies into octopus and dolphin shapes. The seraph-octopuses mimicked Squelch by leaping on the backs of the seraph-dolphins who imitated the real dolphins' cartwheels and leaps. I found the seraph-antics mildly entertaining. It was true that they diminished the decorum of the Hereafter, but a little laughter is good for one. Sterne of course, soon tired of their nonsense and banished them from her presence so she could concentrate on observing the dolphins below.

~ ~ ~

Two days later, I watched Squelch 'cloud-catching' with Echo and Ripple. The seraphim were mimicking the action again. Ripple aimed for the clouds with Squelch aboard.

'Up . . . up.' Squelch commanded. 'Higher . . . higher!'

Squelch could go higher than his mount by jumping upwards off her back when Ripple was at the highest point of her leap. They tried positioning the take-off at the top of a large swell to get even more height.

'I'm a flying octopus. I'm truly alive.'

SPLOOSH! He and Ripple crashed back into the sea.

'Your turn, Echo,' said Squelch.

~ ~ ~

Sister Sterne could see little point in such diversions and did not join us. I left the seraphim engrossed in impersonating the three playmates and rejoined

Sterne who was observing a group of twelve dolphins, swimming near Akarana Island, not far off to the west.

A storm had recently tossed a lot of land debris into the sea there. The younger ones among the dolphins were playing with tree-branches, pushing them through the water and admiring the strange stiff shapes, so different from seaweed.

A baby dolphin called Whirly took fright at a sudden shadow and surfaced quickly in the middle of the debris. He inhaled a scrap of bark deep into his blowhole and tried to eject it but it was wedged in tight. His panic spread through the group at once. The adults, including his mother, surrounded him, supporting him at the surface. He writhed and struggled to breathe.

'Call for help!'

'What help can anyone give?'

'Whirly can only help himself.'

'Cough it out Whirly.'

Whirly tried but it would not budge.

Seconds became minutes and his mother knew that Whirly's time was running out. He was losing strength by the moment. If he'd been unsupported he would have been sinking by now. The dolphins prayed for help and Whirly's mother turned her spirit to the Hereafter and begged the universe to intervene.

Sister Sterne was ready and waiting, and the obvious solution was not too far off . . . if Whirly could just manage to hold on long enough.

Whirly weakened as the minutes passed. His mother urged him to hold on, but he was sliding into unconsciousness. For Whirly the sunny day was growing dark and the dolphins surrounding him watched helplessly, as he faded before their eyes.

~~~

Ripple and Echo, still swimming with Squelch, had no idea there were dolphins in distress nearby.

But Squelch suddenly lost interest in the cloud-catching game.

'Stop,' he ordered.

Echo braked with her flukes and swirled her flippers to hold position.

Squelch sat motionless on her back. His eyes scanned the horizon; then fixed on a spot to the west.

'Something's wrong,' he said, 'Swim to Akarana Island.'

The island grew as they swam towards it.

'Faster,' said Squelch, 'Go faster!'

'Get hydro then,' said Echo, 'and hang on.'

Squelch spread himself smoothly for better hydro-dynamics. Echo accelerated.

'Why Akarana?' she asked as she swam.

'We're needed there.'

'Who needs us? I heard no call.'

'Just shut up and swim.'

Echo swam as fast as the load she carried would allow. She raced through the sea, smashing every wave in her path. When Ripple took her turn at leading, Squelch transferred himself to the leading dolphin as always.

~~~

Whirly's heartbeat was faltering and he was far beyond suffering. But every muscle in his mother's body was tense as she raked his body with her teeth, scarring him in her efforts to stimulate him back to life. Since Whirly's fate now seemed irrevocable, the other dolphins were as concerned for the mother now as they were for her son.

~~~

Sterne and I could see Whirly's spirit loosen itself from its Azuran bonds as it prepared for flight.

~~~

Squelch arrived in a dazzle of flying spray. He was still aboard Ripple, and many seraphim followed in their wake. As they entered the bay, Echo took the lead and Squelch transferred himself to her. Fortunately, the problem was so clear in the minds of all dolphins in the bay, the new arrivals needed no explanations.

'Take me to him!' insisted Squelch.

Echo swam alongside the group where Whirly lay unconscious. The octopus reached across them to Whirly's back, inserted one whip-like tentacle into his blowhole, gripped the piece of bark, and tugged it out.

'Easier than pulling a periwinkle!' He waved the tentacle high in the air so that all could see the bark, still attached to a sucker near the tip.

The dolphins glanced in amazement at the octopus and the bark, before returning their attention to Whirly. He convulsed once, then lay motionless for a seeming eternity, before his blowhole fluttered weakly.

Had air gone in?

Perhaps a little. They supported him, more firmly, keeping his blowhole always above the water.

'Breathe Whirly, breathe Whirly, breathe . . . breathe . . . breathe.' His mother's thoughtstreams were arrows of energy plunging into the breathing zones of his brain. The others echoed her. Ripple and Echo added their strongest thoughtstreams to the team effort.

Only we divine beings could see Whirly's spirit hovering and dithering above him. The spiritual thread linking him to his body stretched, longer and thinner as Whirly's spirit moved towards the Hereafter. To us, it seemed the connection must surely break. But slowly, slowly, the thread thickened and shortened again as the spirit drew back towards physical life. Hope grew.

Jaws gaping, eyes still closed, Whirly's blowhole pulsed again as he dragged in one huge draught of air. Then he seemed to give up, and lay as though dead against the bodies supporting him. His spirit drifted higher again. His mother continued scraping his skin with her teeth and pouring her energy into him.

He lurched once more; lay unmoving again for another age . . . then convulsed again. It was hard to tell if he was struggling towards life or death. However, we saw his spirit drawing closer until it was almost inside him again.

Echo maintained her position near Whirly, holding Squelch. Ripple swam round and round the outskirts of the group, peeking in from the edges to see if Whirly had woken, unable to keep still.

More team thoughtstreams.

Whirly took another agonised breath. Oxygen seeped into his blood from the shocked but recovering lungs. Gradually the blood enriched with oxygen. The heartbeat strengthened, pushing fresh blood into every corner of his flesh. His spirit re-entered his body and seated itself firmly in its usual place to the left of his spine. It glowed weakly. Within five minutes, he was conscious but groggy and had no idea what had happened.

Meanwhile Squelch remained in the same pose, mounted on Echo, with the piece of bark still raised. A moment came when Squelch looked about and saw that the dolphins, having become confident of Whirly's survival, were all now looking at him, providing an awed audience.

Slowly he moved the raised tentacle tip backwards, stretching it further and further back until it almost touched the sea behind him. When the tentacle was at full stretch, he paused, holding that pose, enjoying his moment, watching the gaping dolphins before him. Then he lunged, flicking the tentacle forwards. The tip whipped through the air with the piece of bark still attached. He released the bark when it reached maximum velocity, so it curved through the air, with every dolphin eye following its path, straight towards Ripple on the far side of the group. She saw it coming and delivered it a perfectly timed whack with her tail, sending the bark on a second trajectory. This time it landed high on the nearby beach on Akarana Island, where it rattled on the pebbles.

'Out' called Squelch. There was a moments' silence, then hysteria: jaw-clapping, tail slapping, squeaking, whistling, leaping, breaching, mega-splashing and corkscrew-spinning. Ripple raced up to Echo and Squelch. Squelch flowed on over from Echo to Ripple who carried him in a high-speed gyrating circle around the whole celebrating group before returning him to Echo. All around us in the Hereafter the seraphim applauded, spinning and flashing their electric particles.

With fear fading from their minds, the dolphins thanked the octopus with grateful thoughtstreams and flipper-caresses. Echo too was a heroine for her part in the miracle.

The younger dolphins picked up other pieces of bark from the flotsam in the bay. They whacked these from tail to tail to see how long they could keep them airborne.

Whirly was himself again quite quickly, a little dazed but puzzled by the excitement. His mother didn't try to explain, but caressed him and swam close to him. Her eyes switched back and forth from her son to the octopus who had saved him.

Seeing them all staring at him, Squelch thought, Hmmm, Yes. I am alive right now. Might as well prove it to these dolphins. So he pirouetted, swirled his tentacles, formed himself into a big golden star, swiftly re-arranged into a pink and purple flower, dazzled them with rainbows of colour changes and swept himself smoothly from one delighted dolphin to the next. He could hear little of the dolphins' applause, but their appreciation was obvious to his powerful eyes and mind. Finally, the entire group, carrying Squelch, moved off in procession towards the open sea. Their mood spread into the surrounding ocean attracting others who came in twos and threes and bigger groups until hundreds of dolphins from many groups and families had arrived to hear the story and join the procession.

Rev arrived, bouncing up like a leg-fin frogfish. (Leg-fin frogfish are sometimes called 'psychedelica' Even Sterne finds them humorous.)

'I hear you've brought a heroic octopus into the family,' said Rev.

As it happened, Squelch was back aboard Echo.

'Go away!' Ripple ordered, 'This is none of your business. Squelch is our octopus!'

'There goes the secret,' muttered Echo.

'Squelch eh!' Rev said. 'Cool name. Hi Squelch!'

He poked Squelch with his rostrum. Squelch squelched. He transplanted himself to Rev without a backwards glance at the girls.

Rev swam in the leading wave as they rejoiced their way across the glittering blue. Every dolphin was eager for a turn to carry the octopus, who was fed like a king on morsels brought to him throughout the afternoon. Periwinkles were popular, giving Squelch plenty of opportunities to re-enact his life-saving skills, by displaying the clever use of his tentacles. Squelch could only remember the last five days of his life, but even if he could have remembered all of it, this would still have been its brightest moment.

'I'm alive, I'm alive! I'm truly alive now,' he said, over and over.

The seraphim joined the procession, unseen by the mortal creatures. They trailed through the air and sea surrounding the Azurans and I noticed that one of them had made himself resemble a fragment of bark. He was allowing himself to be flicked from one temporarily tail-shaped seraph to another, in imitation of the new game.

Ripple and Echo followed more sedately in the middle of the crowd.

'Rev and Squelch are made for each other,' Echo warned. 'Those two will be insufferable now.'

~~~

Over the next few weeks, Squelch's tentacles were put to work on creative projects, like weaving nooses from seaweed, useful to drop over a passing sister's tail at inconvenient moments, such as while hunting. Ripple found herself towing a very dead and smelly stingray attached to her by a rope and noose of Squelch construction. Ripple was a favourite victim because she reacted so perfectly, chasing and charging at the perpetrators in uncontrolled fury. The power of his little sister's temper impressed Rev and he bragged about it to his classmates.

'Goes as mad as a starving tiger-shark,' he told them proudly.

6
ANGER

Cosmo and a dozen other young dolphins darted after a school of pilchards. Imitating adult hunting tricks, they formed a high-speed carousel enclosing the fish and herding them into a ball at the surface. Some dived under the fish to prevent them escaping downwards. Some ate a fish or two. Others played along for fun.

Cosmo was the hungriest. He snapped at a pilchard and missed it. Enraged, he grabbed another, cracking its spine in one bite. He darted in and out of the fish-ball, crunching down fish after fish. Their oily flesh recharged him. He ate ravenously and satisfied his hunger.

The other dolphins played around him, more intent on fun than food.

One youngster called Storm soon tired of the fish-ball game. Hoping to invent a new one, he entertained himself by rocketing into the air straight through the middle of the fish. The fish-ball disintegrated.

'What'd you do that for, Sponge-Brain?'

'Who wrecked our fish-ball?'

'Storm did!'

'Chase him!'

Storm darted off merrily but found himself pursued by friends pretending he was a predator and they were grown-up fighter dolphins. One of the bigger girls lightly walloped him with her tail in passing. Several 'attacked' at once from many directions. None of them hurt him. Storm was soon playing along.

Maram, the oldest dolphin in the group, kept out of the play-fight. He was a trainee fighter, there mainly to guard the younger ones. He watched from the outskirts of the mêlée.

Some of the others, including Cosmo came to Storm's defence, creating two opposing teams who 'scored' against one another; the kind of game which prepared them for fights against real predators. Storm's team played well, squawking loudly and often as though in distress, encouraging their 'enemy' to more displays of fake aggression.

However, Cosmo had ceased breathing from the moment the game started. He flashed in and out between the others, happily enough to begin with. But as the game progressed, the jagged triple scar on his left side began to glow a strange dull red. The play-fighting continued around him, but a coloured mist drifted in from the edges of his consciousness, obscuring logic. Looking upwards through the clear water, he saw Storm's older brother, Cirrus, prod Storm playfully in the belly with his beak. Storm squealed as though it had been a mortal hit.

It ignited a flame in Cosmo. He shot upwards to attack Cirrus with a fury that shocked them all. He plunged his rostrum savagely into Cirrus's belly. Cirrus gasped, stopped swimming and began to sink.

Maram and two of the bigger girls swam quickly down and supported Cirrus back to the surface, where he lay against them whimpering in real agony. Maram left Cirrus in the care of the two females and returned to find Cosmo.

Cosmo still had not breathed. His internal fires blazed, driving him to attack. He lunged, snapped and bit one young dolphin until he bled. He whacked another on the head with his tail, and drove his beak into two or three others hard enough to hurt. The young dolphins scattered in alarm. Cosmo raced after them at the surface, but Maram overtook him.

'Stop!'

Maram's order smacked into Cosmo's brain. At the same time, Maram's much-heavier body shoved Cosmo physically off course. Cosmo whirled in a dazzle of spray and charged straight back, but Maram's weight and superior skills easily deflected him.

'Cosmo! Calm down! What's the matter?'

Cosmo stopped and stared around, blinking in confusion. He was dazed from lack of oxygen.

'Breathe!' ordered Maram.

Cosmo breathed at last. The mist began to clear. Maram herded him forcefully away from the others while the fire within Cosmo cooled and the red glow on the external scars faded. Soon Cosmo was able to take in his surroundings more clearly. A short distance away, the two females still supported the injured Cirrus. A couple of others had gone to help them. The rest circled beyond watching Cosmo from a safe distance.

~~~

The story of Cosmo's frenzy spread quickly. Cirrus's internal bruising took many days to heal. None of the others attacked by Cosmo was as seriously hurt as Cirrus, but from that day other youngsters were wary around him. Although Cosmo apologised to all the ones he'd hurt, he was never able to explain his behaviour.

~~~

The school elders invited Maram to meet with them later, to share his view of the incident.

He described it as accurately as he could and the elders recognised that the shadow of Cosmo's violent beginnings must have triggered the attack.

'But the behaviour is inexcusable whatever caused it,' said one. 'If it happens again, we may have to banish him from the school, for the safety of our other children, although it would be hard on an orphan to be isolated even further in this way.'

'It shows that he has a powerful aggression,' said another elder. 'He could be a useful fighter some day.'

'Perhaps, but the best fighters are those who temper their aggression with calm intellect. They're never hotheads driven by rampant emotion. Attacking his own playmates? That's bizarre. Does he have the mind of a shark?'

'No, but we all know he carries the scars of one. Who knows how deep those scars may run? Careful training in the physical skills and psychology of fighting, with its emphasis on controlling and channelling anger, may be the very thing that could help him.'

'Perhaps Alcyone could assist him.'

The elders indicated agreement.

Maram had already proven strong enough to control Cosmo when the need arose, so the elders requested him to watch and provide any training that seemed suitable. They asked him to assess the idea of steering Cosmo in the direction of a vocation as a fighter like himself, and consider using the services of Alcyone, the mind adept, should Cosmo's emotional instability continue. Maram was happy to comply.

I like the little rascal, he thought, and he's more alone than ever now this has happened.

'I'll help the child in any way I can,' he told the elders.

~~~

Maram began by building Cosmo's physical endurance through long-distance journeys to strengthen his cardio-vascular system. Through time spent together in play and hunting, Maram noticed how quickly Cosmo's natural co-ordination allowed him to pick up physical skills.

As Cosmo began attending regular junior classes with other dolphins his age, Maram encouraged him towards the same areas of study he'd chosen at the same age, such as gymnastics, the theory of defence and attack, and mathematics. There were also classes in poetry, the sciences and those historical subjects that all young dolphins studied, whatever vocation they pursued.

The Southern Islands School was famous for the quality of its fighters. Being a smaller school, they needed the highest level of protection for the fewest numbers of fighters. Fight training began at a younger age in this school than any other on Azure.

Once Cosmo had mastered sufficient theory of the fighting arts it was time for him to move on to his first practical classes in defence and attack.

Maram offered his services as an assistant to Cosmo's teacher so that he could attend the classes and observe. His presence re-assured the other youngsters who remained uneasy about Cosmo.

~~~

Maram watched closely as Cosmo took the defender's role with a young classmate called Zoid as his attacker. Zoid approached him from below in slow-motion. Cosmo responded with the correct slow-motion avoidance moves. They practised the slow version a few more times. Each dolphin took turns at both attack and defence.

So far there was nothing to alarm Maram in Cosmo's responses. When the teacher required them to advance to the full-speed version Maram was happy enough for Cosmo to be included.

The speed increased suddenly.

Perhaps too suddenly, thought Maram.

Spray flew, flukes thrashed and the water whitened with foam. Again Cosmo took the defender's role first. Zoid moved away to make room for his first full-speed attack. He turned and hurtled towards Cosmo.

Maram saw the shark scars on Cosmo's left side suddenly glow red as Zoid charged. Maram tensed and switched his attention to Cosmo's mind which lay unveiled.

'He's losing control,' thought Maram. 'This could be trouble.'

Cosmo moved into an incorrect position. It forced Zoid to change course at the last moment to avoid collision. Even so, he brushed against Cosmo in passing. Cosmo snapped his teeth and whirled, sending sheets of white water sky-high. He lunged at Zoid like a shark at its prey.

Maram saw what was coming. He darted between them in time to deflect the heavy blow Cosmo had intended.

He corralled Cosmo away from Zoid.

'Cosmo, back away! Breathe!' he ordered. 'Relax and breathe!'

Cosmo did not obey. He drove at Zoid from a new direction. Again Maram blocked him.

Maram continued acting as Zoid's protector until Cosmo began to weaken through lack of oxygen. The attacks slowed.

'Breathe Cosmo!' said Maram again. He arrowed the thought straight into the breathing zones of Cosmo's brain.

It worked at last. Cosmo dragged in a tortured breath. The scars faded and the attacks faltered.

It's over now, thought Maram. He apologised to a confused Zoid for removing his working partner, and gained the teacher's permission to take Cosmo out of class.

Away from the excitement of the class the younger dolphin quickly calmed.

Maram repeated the same move they'd been practising in class. He kept Cosmo at it, always in slo-mo, for an entire hour. Only then did Maram allow a slight increase in speed.

Throughout the afternoon the speed of their practice moves increased so gradually that Cosmo was hardly aware of it. By working with Cosmo in this way for the whole afternoon, Maram ensured that he finally reached the level his classmates had in a single one-hour session, but without the anger re-surfacing.

We are lucky, he thought grimly. Few his age would have the perseverance to stay on task as he did today but few would've lost their initial focus on such slight provocation either. Much patience may be required of his teachers if he is to become a useful fighter, unless we can find a solution to this problem.

Maram became Cosmo's special teacher for all physical aspects of the study of fighting. This didn't mean that Cosmo always worked without classmates of his own level, but it did mean that Maram was always close beside him when he did.

Over the next few weeks, whenever the irrational rage re-surfaced in practice combat, as it did from time to time, Maram withdrew Cosmo immediately and gave him however many hours of patient one on one coaching it took to overcome the problem. He designed his coaching programmes to focus on Cosmo's unique need to separate his developing fighting intellect from the dangerous rage that sometimes possessed him during conflict. Maram thus protected Cosmo's classmates and allowed Cosmo to keep up with them in a branch of his education that would otherwise have been impossible to pursue.

Maram, recalling the suggestion of the elders, also decided to take Cosmo along to Alcyone, the mind adept.

~~~

The thoughtstream arrived suddenly from quite close by.

'Alcyone! Alcyone!'

She rolled smoothly above the surface and down again. Who was calling her? Alcyone separated herself from her group and turned to meet the newcomer.

It was Maram.

Her muscles tensed, almost to the point of rigidity. She postponed a breath she had been about to take, then sank in the water to gather her thoughts.

Has his time come, she thought? Already? He is still too young, surely? But why else would he need me? She veiled these thoughts so Maram would not catch them and calmed herself before surfacing to greet him.

Maram was not alone.

Who is that even younger one in his slipstream, she wondered?

Her visitors arrived.

'Cosmo here has a problem,' explained Maram.

The tension flowed out of Alcyone's muscles and she took the breath she'd been delaying.

'He cannot control his own anger,' said Maram, 'It slows his training as a fighter.'

Alcyone looked harder at Cosmo, who skipped about nervously under her scrutiny. Then she saw the livid triple scar on the youngster's left side.

'Is this Kismet's child, the one who was orphaned by the shark?'

'Yes.'

'I'll see what I can do.'

~~~

When Cosmo first began to spend time with Alcyone it was only because Maram asked him to. Those early visits were short and usually in the evening.

Alcyone's last child had left her side a year ago, leaving her plenty of time to devote to troubled ones like Cosmo. When he visited, she would ask about his day and something he said would always trigger memories from long ago. She'd tell him a story about it. Often they were funny stories. He began to look forward to his visits and he spent more and more time with Alcyone. Sometimes they even hunted together.

When he learnt a new attack move, or saw a sperm whale fighting off a pack of blackfin, he'd think, 'I'll tell Alcyone about that when I see her.'

One night, a month after his first visit, Cosmo visited Alcyone during a series of westerly squalls, which sent banks of cloud charging across the sky, leaving wide expanses of starry sky between them. Cosmo opened his mouth above the surface and felt the wind blowing right down his throat.

'Where's my mother now?' he asked suddenly.

'She's with your father, up there among the stars.'

He lifted his eyes above the waves and took a good look at the stars. They were calling to him. He was sure of it. He could not take his eyes off them.

'What are those stars?'

'They're great burning balls of gas far away in space. If you wish to learn more of them you should attend classes with Zenith, the astronomy teacher.'

There were thousands of stars but they were all too far away. He leapt but came no closer. He leapt again and again, higher and higher.

'What're you doing?' asked Alcyone.

'I'm trying to reach the stars.'

He continued leaping until he could leap no more. How could he ever cover such distances? He yearned for the westerly to drag him closer to them where he could feel their heat.

'Why did my parents go there?' He flung the question out among the flying foam of an icy squall. 'Why couldn't I go with them?'

'They're dead Cosmo. You're alive.'

'Can live dolphins go out among the stars?'

'Dolphins can do anything they wish,' she said.

'Then one day, I'll go to the stars.'

~~~

In view of the traumas the child had so recently endured, Sterne and I were delighted to witness such positivity and decisiveness on his part and looked forward to observing him in action closer to our own environment in the future.

~~~

Alcyone's knowledge of the troubled minds of the traumatised allowed her to quickly diagnose the scars across Cosmo's psyche. Once the trust between them was established she introduced her vocational skills to their friendship. She did this so skilfully and openly that he saw it only as a new and higher level to their alliance.

She took him travelling inside himself. Such journeys could not entirely banish a rage which was now a part of him, but she used them to teach him how to recognise his anger by the reddish colours that swirled in the mist they generated. She swam through that mist with him until he recognised the colours flowing through it; the gleams of rusty crimson, the streaks of burnt copper and the hot sparks of poison carmine. She immersed him in those colours until he could smell the smoke of them and taste their acrid tang and they became signals pointing to the onset of rage.

Then she taught him how to breathe and work his lungs to control the swirling mists inside him and harness the colours to his own purposes; mixing them with other colours, creating what he wished, whether it be perfect calm, rational thought, lethal attack, or all three.

~~~

'How well did you know my parents,' Cosmo asked Alcyone one day.

Alcyone had been waiting for such a question. 'I knew them both well,' she said.

'Tell me about my mother.'

She gave him her memories of Mimosa as a girl; her birth and naming, her childhood playing with her sisters, making mischief on her brothers, tossing seaweed, befriending seabirds, learning to hunt, making friends. She described Mimosa absorbing her lessons, choosing and building her vocation as an adept of Azure's internal planetary forces. Finally, Alcyone described the memories that hurt her the most: Mimosa in love with the young weather adept Kismet and her excitement at discovering the presence of Cosmo.

She coaxed him to share his own memories of Mimosa, though she saw how difficult it was for him. Most of his memories of her were from before his birth – impressions of love, laughter, and reassurance. All he remembered of her after his birth was the taste of her milk, her sky-blue colour with its magenta highlights and her terrible death.

Alcyone noticed he did not mention Kismet at all.

One day she asked, 'Do you have any memories of your father?'

He was silent. She knew that he wanted to swim away. But he stayed.

'No,' he said at last, 'it's blank.'

He slowed and looked at her sideways.

He's afraid of my reaction, she thought.

'No baby the age you were has had time to build impressions of a father, Cosmo.'

They swam on for several minutes in silence. She sensed one of his thickest inner clouds evaporating and she knew he would ask her about Kismet within the day.

'Tell me about my father,' said Cosmo a few hours later.

'I feel his strength flowing through your veins; sometimes you seem like his ghost swimming beside me. But his spirit was as sunlit as yours is overcast.'

Tortured, she thought, privately.

Alcyone then sent Cosmo a detailed mental picture of Kismet showing the power in his flukes, the open friendship in his eye, as well as each scar and blemish on his body and the way the golden colour of his skin flowed to emerald on his flukes and fins. Over the next few days she gave him every Kismet detail she could find, just as she'd done with Mimosa.

'Like you he looked upwards to the skies but unlike you his interests lay more within the atmosphere than beyond it.' She told him of weather events that Kismet had predicted and described the ways his vocational activities had helped the school. She continued until she'd ensured that Cosmo knew his father as though he'd lived with him for years.

Thus she allowed the sunlight of his departed father to shine between the storm-clouds of Cosmo's spirit and reach him.

~~~

Just as Alcyone helped Cosmo to recognise and control his rage, the combat training taught him how to wield it as a weapon. The rage which had held him back now contributed to his swift development into a fighter of passion and power. Maram was soon able to leave Cosmo to his fighting lessons without any further concerns.

The elders of the school were well pleased with Maram's handling of the Cosmo case.

The other young dolphins lost their fear of Cosmo and once again included him with confidence in their games.

~~~

Cosmo's interest in the stars grew stronger with every passing day, so Alcyone arranged for him to attend classes with Zenith. He became the most motivated and capable of all Zenith's students.

7
UNREACHABLE

Ripple's search continued. She still had no idea what she sought and because it stayed hidden, she thought of it as a secret. But she found clues to the secret in everything she heard, everything she tasted, in every smell, and even in things she saw with her eyes.

There were clues that frightened her. Was she seeking something fearful? But there were so many more clues among the beauties of the ocean, that she was re-assured.

In steep-sided Cascade Cove a small waterfall tumbled over a cliff into the sea. The waterfall was alive with clues. She swam near it often, listening, and tasting the strange sparkle of the salt-free water.

'What is it?' she wondered for the millionth time. 'Where is it? I almost have it. I must think. I must listen.'

Sometimes the secret seemed close around her, pounding her from every side but still eluding her. She strained her spirit upwards towards the clouds and stars, downwards to the deep, even shore-wards to the dry islands – searching, seeking but never finding, except in whispers that came to her in dreams. She sometimes awoke feeling certain she'd found it, overcome with echoes ringing through her soul, but always within moments it would fade and she would reach out again with her spirit and try to retrieve it.

It was like trying to capture a moonbeam; impossible, though it glimmers from every particle of moonlit spray. She thought of her secret as a private moonbeam.

~~~

One morning Ripple found herself swimming through mist. There was no breath of wind; the heaving surface gleamed like living mother-of-pearl.

Sterne and I drifted invisibly observing her responses to her changed surroundings.

Her visual world had shrunk; she could see just a few body-lengths in every direction. Beyond that, the air thickened into dense white.

Creamy, like Mother's milk. I wonder what it tastes like over there where it's thicker.

She swam as fast as she could, her speed leaving a wake trimmed with white lace on the surface behind. But wherever she arrived she found the opaque whiteness was always a few metres away. Sometimes the clear air around her closed in a little and sometimes it expanded, but the clearest space was always close to her.

Wherever I go, I can never reach the milkiness, because it isn't really there. Could it be the same for my secret? Perhaps, like this mist, my moonbeam is unreachable.

She dived below the cheating mist and stared into the black abyss that yawned below. She soon returned to the silver light but the abyss stayed with her until Pearl came looming near, ethereal in the mist.

'Mother! What's this whiteness? Is it real? It's like . . . nothing!'

Pearl presented Ripple with the one truth in the world that she most needed at that moment.

'This is a cloud sitting down on the sea and we're inside it,' said Pearl.

I'm in the middle of a cloud! Mother says so. Clouds are real. They blow about and change shape and make rain.

She played and chased among the shifting veils of mist until the sun had licked the last wisps from the face of the sea.

Sometimes, rainsqualls strafed the waves. Clouds covered and uncovered the sun allowing gleams of sunlight to reach the water, changing its colour by the moment, from blue to grey to green and back again. Ripple saw a rainbow on the sea and swam towards it, desperate to touch it, sure that such beauty might hold the key to her secret, but the further she swam, the further away lay the end of the rainbow. Ripple wept. Finally, she knew that like the mist, its solidity was an illusion. She would never touch it, never hear its vibrations. It would not yield to her the key.

To Ripple it seemed that the secret was like all the other unreachable things in her world.

Thoughts of those things spun through her brain. She swam in ever-diminishing circles. The only outcome was a poem:

The cool rainbow slides away
the nearer I approach.
The creamy fog will never stay
for me to taste and touch.
~~~
When I watch the moonlight
Light the flying spray,
I try to catch a moonbeam
But the moonbeam skips away.
~~~
The line between the sea and sky

is always distant from the eye,
and if I swim to it all day
the line will only move away.

She giggled to think of herself swimming round and round the world endlessly trying to reach the horizon.

~~~

By now Ripple was hunting most of her own food, although she still sometimes took milk from Pearl. She even searched for her elusive goal in the taste of the fish she consumed. When she was hungry, squid was like a prize you might search for all your life; the texture clean and firm, the taste sweet and delicate, the nourishment complete. It was not the same as unveiling her secret, but it was fine consolation.

One day when Ripple was eight months old, she watched the older dolphin children in their gymnastics class as they worked on new techniques in hydro-dynamic wave-skipping. She memorised their moves and then practiced by herself for two solid hours, far longer than the class had spent at the task.

She only stopped when she noticed how hungry she was. Her first thought was to find Pearl and take milk but then she remembered a nearby reef where squid sometimes swam even in daytime, so she went there instead and began to hunt. Here and there along the reef other dolphins were also hunting including a few from the class she'd been watching. After a little searching, she located a squid about the length of her own flipper.

The perfect meal.

She stalked it carefully, anticipating the moment her teeth would sink into the succulent flesh. She was closing in for the kill when a sleek shape swam up from below and chased the squid into a crevice in the reef, completely out of reach. It was Rev, back to his sister-baiting game.

She squealed and flashed towards him, lunging hard into his body. It would have been a nasty hit if he hadn't evaded her. He scurried off, but she followed, charging at him again and again as if to bash him to pieces. It took all his speed and skill to reach a safe distance, finally escaping into the protective zone of his mother. Even so, Ripple had to be restrained by Pearl from harming her brother. Seeing the bruises already inflicted, Pearl became thoughtful.

Rev never teased Ripple in food-depriving ways again, although with Squelch's help there were other methods almost as annoying.

When Ripple had calmed down and had time to satisfy her hunger by hunting in peace, Pearl took her aside and spoke to her.

'Ripple, I know he provoked you, but you've left him with bruises. This is not how dolphins treat one another. Whatever made you behave in such a way?'

Ripple could hardly bring herself to reply – it was the closest Pearl had ever come to chastising her.

'I . . . I hope I didn't hurt Rev too much'.

'I'm more concerned for you than I am for Rev. I believe you intended to hurt him even more. Dolphins might behave like that towards a shark which was threatening us, but not towards our own kind.'

Ripple apologised to her mother and her brother. For a time after that, she ceased eating, ceased all play and laughter and spent time staring into the black depths. In the end Pearl chastised her again.

'Snap out of it dear. You've only had one little telling off. Every young dolphin gets told off at times. You must now begin to think of happy things again. Look up at the stars, catch some fish and taste their juicy sweetness, rejoice in leaping. Think less about yourself and more about the beauty that surrounds you.'

Ripple wished to please her mother so she obeyed. By an effort of will she turned her thinking away from her shame and concentrated on the glories of Azure. Within a few hours she was leaping, listening, hunting, eating and searching, as joyfully as ever.

Pearl thought, even when she is joyful she is more so than the rest of us, but I won't reproach her for that.

~~~

Echo called Ripple 'Jellyfish' because of her fears. Rev called her 'Tiger-shark' because of her rages. Even Aroha, the mind adept, noticed her youngest sister's oddness. She spoke of it to Pearl one day during a visit with Matangi.

'Ripple's unsettled,' Aroha said, 'I read anxiety in her mind, so Mother you must let me know immediately if you think she needs my help.'

'I will,' said Pearl.

There was a short silence. Pearl consciously switched the focus to Aroha and Matangi.

'It'd be lovely to see more of you two,' she said, 'I know you're both busy with your work, but perhaps there'll soon be a baby you may need my help with.'

'That's the plan,' Matangi replied. 'We hope it won't be too long before Ripple is an aunty.'

'And it might be useful' said Aroha, 'for me to be closer to my birth family if Ripple should worsen.'

~~~

Sister Sterne hoped that by choosing Rigel and Pearl as parents she had increased Ripple's chances of succeeding in her spirit's mission. To see how this would work out, we observed the relationship between Pearl and Ripple with interest. It was easy to see how much the child puzzled her mother.

~~~

Pearl noticed Ripple swishing the surface with her fins and passing her head back and forth through the bubbles in a rhythmical movement at varying speeds.

'Why are you doing that Ripple?'

'Listening to the bubbles.'

Pearl perceived contentment and absorption in her daughter's mind, but she also saw an unfamiliar kind of thought pattern. Even we deities were mystified. It was like nothing we or Pearl had ever detected in another dolphin. Because it didn't seem negative, Pearl considered it harmless, an attitude that pleased Sterne. However, Pearl did wonder what other dolphins would think when they noticed.

Such a dreamy child she thought, but there are worse faults, and she swam away to discourage Rev from amusing himself by spoiling Echo's hunting on purpose just because he was not hungry and he knew she was.

Pearl cruised back later and watched Ripple nosing in close to an island coastline. There were neither fish nor any other reason for such a close approach to land. When Ripple had spent many hours there, Pearl asked, 'Why did you stay so long? You know there is tide danger in shallow water.'

'I was listening to the shellfish under the mud.'

'Why? We don't eat shellfish!'

'I hear the mud oozing round them. See the ones that swim above the mud? They whistle as they swim; a pretty sound if you listen to their heartbeats at the same time. But don't worry Mother; I listen to the tides too. Such noise they make, roaring in my brain. How could I not heed them?'

She likes shellfish, thought Pearl, for the noises they make?

Another time, Pearl noticed Ripple holding herself upright in the water; head as still as possible above the surface. Her gently swirling flippers and tail balanced her body for a long time in one spot. Ripple again said she was 'listening' so Pearl listened with her. All she noticed were the usual sounds of the sea: the rushing of the water at the surface, the heartbeats and movements of a school of fish, the distant passage of a family of whales, the swoosh of a diving gannet, her own and Ripple's heartbeats and breathing and the slow pulse of the swells. Nothing that could cause alarm or excite curiosity.

'Why keep still?' she asked, 'when there's nothing you can't hear while you're swimming around like the rest of us?'

'Sounds are clearer when you're still,' Ripple explained.

Pearl understood that Ripple had some reason of her own for her unusual activities. She again explored her child's brainwaves by ultra-sound, looking for a clue, but saw no pain alarms, no emotional confusion – only a mild anxiety and that same intellectual 'disturbance' as she began to think of it. She tried to get Ripple to explain for herself.

'Ripple, there's something in your thinking that doesn't fit the normal patterns. Other dolphins may think there's something wrong with your mind.'

'Mother, remember before I was born, I told you I was trying to find something?'

'What more could anyone want to find here on Azure, that we don't already have?'

There was silence for a long moment.

'I need to find it!'

'Find what?'

Gannets dived. Fish jumped. Sunlight glittered on swells that heaved like the flanks of sleeping animals, tons of water rising and falling, driven by the whims of distant storms. Mother and daughter swam on together through sea and sky that glowed every shade of blue from palest dawn to deepest midnight. No comments passed between them for a time. As they swam, Pearl made a private resolve to keep a close watch over Ripple and to discuss her concerns with Rigel, if Ripple's disturbed thinking continued.

Pearl broke the stalemate.

'Darling, I think you should play with your friends more and just let sounds tell you what you need them to tell you. Dolphins don't play with sounds – we use them to help us live in the world.'

'For me, there is more to sound than that Mother. Sometimes I feel that all the audible treasure of Azure is surrounding me, throbbing at me, and I'm wasting it . . . wasting it! Something hidden in those sounds is calling me to set it free; it calls from deep inside me, and from far beyond the stars!'

Pearl saw a vast longing in Ripple, an emptiness awaiting fulfilment. 'Something is calling her? A voice calling? A vocation?'

Pearl knew, almost as well as we deities do, that not all creatures shared the dolphin's ability to understand the world around them by using their hearing, building pictures in the brain by analysing sound as you humans do with your eyes.

Perhaps, thought Pearl, it's Ripple's task to bring order to her own confusion.

~~~

Sterne responded to that thought.

'You see?' she said, 'I chose exactly the right mother!'

~~~

Another swarm of seraphim had gathered around us. They buzzed and glittered and they too had watched the exchange between Pearl and Ripple. They cheered at Sterne's statement, as though it mattered to them. Their numbers had continued increasing among the constellations of Koru, especially within Sol's planetary system.

A group of seraphim entertained themselves by unravelling my aura into tentacles of light and parading them around the galaxy like streamers. I put up with such frivolity, though I considered it undignified for someone of my standing. Sterne swatted them aside ruthlessly when they tried the same thing on her. It didn't bother them. They rolled over backwards laughing like nincompoops. (At least words like that allow me to have some fun with your bothersome human languages.)

'Why must we put up with these confounded seraphim?' muttered Sterne, batting aside another which had encroached on her aura.

She turned her attention back to Pearl.

~~~

Pearl found it hard to worry about a daughter so normal and healthy in every other respect. She knew that Ripple was among the best tumblers in her school. Pearl had seen her playing for hours with the other young dolphins, spinning, speeding, leaping, twisting, diving, chasing, racing. Ripple had even invented new moves and they copied her, though most of them were older. Recognition by older playmates was an honour and Pearl knew it.

8
THE FIGHTER

Alcyone's memories of his parents became Cosmo's weapon against loneliness. He spent many hours running over them, observing the way his parents had lived.

Sometimes he created new scenes to weave through the memories; scenes where he spoke to Mimosa or Kismet and they responded exactly the way he saw live parents speaking to their children every day in the school around him.

'What's it like out there in the stars?' he asked his father one day.

'Beautiful,' whispered the memory of Kismet. 'Mysterious . . . but dangerous. Take care Cosmo. Don't follow us too soon . . . too soon,' and the whisper faded back into the sky.

~~~

Though he charged ahead in the fighting-related subjects, Cosmo's favourite class was astronomy. He absorbed all available knowledge including the names of every constellation and every star whose magnitude or significance had earned it a name.

One night after his astronomy lesson, Cosmo spoke to his teacher, Zenith.

'How can I defeat gravity and reach the stars?'

The ocean jostled around them, its small waves slapping at their fins in the westerly. The waves were sharply black, but flickering with spears of light reflected from moon and stars.

'I wondered when you'd ask that,' replied Zenith.

He dived and re-surfaced with a small squid, which he swallowed neatly.

'It can be done using the power of the mind. But here we have no teachers skilled in the techniques. We call it Practical Astronomy because it involves actual travel in space among distant worlds. We had a practical astronomer here in the Southern School once. He departed Azure well before his time, about a year before your birth.'

'What killed him?'

'A blackfin took him while he worked. It's not safe to separate mind from body. But that's exactly how the practical astronomers work.'

Cosmo recalled the warning from the memory of his father.

'Is that why so few pursue it?'

'Yes. But there are other schools of dolphins, elsewhere in our ocean, with many specialists in the art. They've developed methods of protecting their astronomers from most of the dangers of the vocation.'

'I wish there were practical astronomers in our school, but perhaps they serve no useful purpose since we survive without them.'

Both dolphins paused to forage among a tempting array of sweet transparent creatures that welled up around them. The deep water had released its spoils.

'It's not true, Cosmo, to think practical astronomers serve no useful purpose. Most schools could survive without poetry, mathematics and history but it doesn't make those vocations worthless.'

'Our history teacher told us of the spiritual Hereafter. Has that knowledge come from the practical astronomers?'

'No, our spiritual knowledge comes from the whales. They have past life memory and have shared their knowledge of the Hereafter with us to alleviate our natural Azuran fear of death. But astronomers have returned from space with other knowledge of much value.'

'What kinds?'

'Some has been of purely intellectual interest. Some is of such practical use that those who discover it make sure to share it widely. It's truly an honoured vocation.'

Cosmo stared at the blazing stars riding the misty veil of the galactic arm. He tried to imagine communicating with a creature from a world out there.

Zenith continued. 'They have also brought back thoughts, ideas and information about arts on distant worlds which we cetaceans of Azure can barely comprehend. We have our own arts of course. But have you heard of visual art, Cosmo?'

'No. What is it?'

'It's when artists manipulate materials in their environment to create representations of their world in order to express creative ideas.'

While trying to work it out, Cosmo did two forward somersaults and three backward ones.

Zenith laughed.

'Imagine I took a block of rock and somehow gave it the shape of an octopus in pain, because I wanted to show how intensely octopuses feel pain. That idea could remain there for centuries, permanent in the rock, long after the artist was dead. That's visual art.'

'Impossible! I might be able to break a soft rock with my tail or teeth, but how could anyone change a rock to an octopus shape?'

'We on Azure do not create visual art, since we cannot manipulate materials in this way. But because of the practical astronomers there are historians in some schools whose entire vocations consist of memorising images of art from other worlds.'

'Do the astronomers give anything in exchange for what they receive from those worlds?'

'Certainly, though not always to those they received from. They may receive from one world and give back to another. Azurans have shared much of their own culture with others in the universe. Some of the arts of war, developed right here in our own Southern School, are admired and copied by aliens. They too must sometimes defend themselves from attack by other species.'

'Practical astronomy is the greatest vocation on Azure! Surely it must be!'

'However, it's not available to you here in this school. It's far too risky and likely to kill you before you get beyond our own moon.'

Cosmo glanced at the moon. It commanded him to soar beyond it. The wave he rode at that moment lifted him bodily. He shot upwards from its peak and rocketed towards the moon. But as always, gravity defeated him.

'I must find a way!' he cried and crashed back into the sea.

The westerly strengthened; a squall whipped the crests into flying spray.

'To do that, you'll need to leave this school and find a teacher who provides better for your educational needs.'

As though in agreement with the squall, a chill current from the deep arose and surrounded them.

'I could never leave friends like Maram and Alcyone to go among strangers.'

'You've chosen no easy calling Cosmo.'

~~~

A group of about forty dolphins hunted south-east of the main school. Three tiger sharks swam in the area but it was safe for the dolphins because the sharks viewed a large group as more trouble than it was worth. However, some of the dolphins, having eaten their fill, peeled away, singly or in small groups, to head back to the main school. The remaining dolphins, still feeding hungrily, failed to notice how quickly their group was diminishing.

The sharks now took an interest.

The dolphin group included some youngsters, who would certainly be the sharks' first targets. The eldest male dolphin recognised the danger and immediately thought-streamed the main school for help. Then he and the other adults herded the youngsters into the centre and circled them closely and rapidly. A shark glided closer. A fast male dolphin left the circling group, for just long enough to dive deep, rise swiftly, and strike the predator hard from below. It bought time. The sharks withdrew temporarily but did not depart. The dolphins continued circling their young ones.

~~~

Back in the main school, Cosmo accepted his first call to action.

He controlled the flow of adrenaline that charged into his bloodstream; then raced into position at the tail of the squad of fourteen picked fighters. Maram swam nearer the front.

Other dolphins called out as they passed.

'There go the fighters!'

'Bring back our friends.'

'Bring back my son!'

'Stay alive out there.'

If I stay alive, we'll win, thought Cosmo. If I'm killed, I'll go to the stars. I can't lose.

They swam out at top speed in V formation, regularly exchanging the lead for energy-economy. On arrival, they darted deftly between, above or below the sharks, out-manoeuvring them to join the circling dolphins. Moments later more sharks arrived. The enemy now outnumbered the fighter dolphins and most of the predators were larger than the biggest of the dolphins.

But time had run out; the sharks were ready to feed.

The fighters began their work calmly, with most remaining on guard in the defensive circle. Two or three at a time darted from the circle to attack where they could. They struck at the enemy in short bursts, returning to the circle to let others take a turn. Cosmo glanced inwards at the frightened young dolphins – friends he swam with daily. He looked outwards to the shadowy monsters who cared nothing for the warm hearts and clever minds among them, seeing them only as sweet, warm flesh to rip apart and gorge upon.

Unspeakable memories stirred within Cosmo and his scars glowed red. The red mist of his anger drew in from the edges of his mind. He recognised that mist, welcoming it as a familiar weapon.

He relaxed every muscle in his body, using techniques and patterns Alcyone had taught him. He breathed just once, swiftly, efficiently. He focused on his heart and lungs, relaxing even those deeper areas of his body, allowing all tension to exit like vapour through his skin. A deadly calm deepened over him. But still his anger grew, inside the calm. He let it build, but fluidly, dangerously, as pliable as his own muscles, fins, and flukes. As he watched the predators threatening his friends, he honed the weapon he had created within himself from the red mist.

He cruised the circle watching and waiting while the enemy circled closer. He saw Maram take his turn in attack, deflecting a shark with a heavy blow just as it lunged, open-jawed, at the old dolphin who'd called for help. Cosmo's flame intensified into a bolt of physical and spiritual energy, poised for the strike.

A group of sharks charged straight at Cosmo's section of the protective circle.

He took another breath and turned to meet them. In a split second, he calculated the speed and direction of each approaching shark.

He waited until he could count the teeth in their jaws; rows of white triangles with red throats yawning behind. He saw their eyes roll back, blank and evil, as their vertical tails lashed behind them, driving towards him.

Cosmo struck. His body flashed and flickered among them, diving below them and thrusting upwards, plunging his hard rostrum into their gills and the ribless flesh of their bodies. He moved with such speed it was as though he had split into several of himself. He stunned three sharks in rapid succession and they began sinking. He bit two of the stunned sharks while whipping between their bodies. They bled. The blood attracted other sharks who attacked the bleeding ones. Soon the water around him was a bedlam of teeth, blood and dying sharks. The placement of Cosmo's continuing bites and blows encouraged the bloodshed to escalate.

He had indeed developed into a useful warrior. And every now and then Cosmo surfaced and breathed. Each breath was a sip of freedom; freedom bought dear by the discipline of his training.

In the first throes of Cosmo's battle, the other fighters instinctively kept away from his zone, giving him more space and scope. Besides, no living thing could be safe to swim among the blood-soaked mayhem produced by such a fighter. His calm ferocity amazed the dolphins.

Leaving one or two to watch the group of non-fighters, the others now joined Cosmo's fray, working at the outer edges of his zone, with even the seasoned ones raising their game in affinity with him. As it became clear that the enemy was routed, the team co-operated in shepherding the remaining 'feeding frenzy' of sharks to a safer distance from those they had threatened.

The sharks were beaten, baffled, vanquished. Many of them were dead. No shark who survived that skirmish ever bothered with dolphins thereafter. Not a single dolphin was lost that day. As the dolphins moved away from the fight zone, the sharks fed on their own dead and injured. Cosmo spotted one big shark gorging on its own entrails, until a trio of smaller ones stopped its hunger forever. The victors escorted their vulnerable charges home.

The story of Cosmo's battle flashed around the school and many younger dolphins looked at him with reverence. The fighters now viewed him with new respect. Maram himself took special pride in Cosmo, knowing his own part in his development.

Even the true veterans wished to honour Cosmo's achievement. One of them approached him later as they were hunting in the darkness.

'You're young, but you've already found the vocation that suits you.'

Strangely, these words did not please Cosmo.

Fighting, he thought? Is it to be my only calling?

He looked up at the stars and wished for the hundredth time that he could get closer to them.

~~~

Fighting aside, it gave me great satisfaction to conclude that life for the dolphins of Azure in that era was more about fun than survival, no matter what Sterne's concerns may have been. As an example, let us follow Cosmo on one such exhilarating occasion. Here, as he so often did, Cosmo followed the lead of his older friend, the fighter Maram.

~~~

Cosmo was happily anticipating an uninterrupted night of stargazing with clear skies and no predators for miles. Then Maram corkscrewed in with a hubbub of young dolphins fizzing in his slipstream.

'Come on, Cosmo! Forget your stars and have some fun.'

'I'm watching meteors tonight.'

'You can do that any night. Tonight's for surfing.'

'But it's perfect for stargazing. Antares rises soon.'

'Antares schmarees! Feel that easterly? And that westerly storm-swell? It's been building for days. That means great surf on the west coasts. If we arrive at half-tide we'll have three hours of good waves before the tide turns.'

A reluctant Cosmo turned his flukes to Antares, promised himself some stargazing later and hoped it wouldn't cloud over by then. But like the other dolphins he forgot all else as they rounded the northern cape of the island and felt the first vibrations of those waves.

'Feel the thunder?' someone whispered.

Maram had rounded up a good crowd. Four teams of five or six. Even Cosmo was now ignoring the blaze of the galaxy sweeping overhead and leaping up to look over the tumult of water that roared between the dolphins and the black shape of the land beyond. In the touch of the water, every dolphin recognised the whisper of energy that had travelled the width of an ocean and was now driving the waves to destruction on the sand. They itched to harness that energy.

Cosmo was in Maram's bunch as usual. Out beyond the break they waited for Maram to signal his chosen wave so the ride could begin. Maram picked a huge wave, and they joined it on its journey to its death. The vast power lifted them, pushing them effortlessly shore-wards until the wave felt the bottom and it towered higher. When it reached full height, they leapt exulting from its crest. Cosmo leapt highest. He saw the five other dolphins of his team flying below him on the charging wall of water. He saw the full length of the wave they were riding. It was breaking on their left where the weight of the water curled forward onto itself in a perfect curve, which collapsed into a pandemonium of boiling foam and spray. They headed right, towards purity, and let the white thunder chase them along the wave.

Beyond their own wave, the lines of the surf stretched the length of the beach, lit ghostly white in the starlight. To the south Cosmo could dimly make out another team just finishing their ride and heading back out to sea again.

The roaring of the ocean deafened him and time slowed as he rode its thunder; leap, glide; leap, glide. How close could they dare approach the terrors of dry land?

The team bailed at the last possible moment when the wave reached dangerous shallows. They flicked out behind it, darting away, leaping and spinning back to the safety of the deep.

Maram was laughing in Cosmo's mind, 'I knew you'd forget your precious stars once you got into that surf. Ready for round two?'

'Yes, I'll admit it now; these waves are too good to miss.'

9
UNIVERSE OF PROMISE

Clinging to her sister's slipstream, Ripple followed Echo into Tuatua Bay where they were to meet the rest of the poetry class. Echo's classmates loomed up through the pre-dawn gloom and assembled in the bay awaiting their teacher, Tercet. They cruised with close friends, some quietly reciting verses to one another in last minute revision. Ripple was intrigued by the snatches of poetry.

Tercet arrived and they gathered around him.

'Today we welcome Ripple among us,' he announced. 'You need only observe today Ripple, but join in as you wish and feel free to ask questions.'

He led the group out of the bay and headed north, travelling at a gentle pace on the calm sea. The sky glowed like a pearl in anticipation of sunrise. The silver-grey surface hissed around them, cool and sweet as springtime. Tercet asked Echo to present first. Echo moved into the leading position and the others fell into formation around her. She had everyone's attention but no one attended more closely than Ripple, who was agog to see her sister perform.

~~~

As your divine narrator, I must interrupt to explain why telling this story gets difficult. Dolphin poetry is made of ideas, not words or sounds, but I am forced to use words to describe it to you. Why did I ever let Sterne talk me into relating a story to humans? However, I must do the best I can. . .

~~~

'As my model,' Echo began, 'I chose 'The Albatross' composed 125 years ago by the poet Altair.' She recited the verse. . .

> The spindrift of the Southern Seas
> He sleeps upon its westerlies.
> As round the globe he glides with ease.
>
> Descending from his airy home
> He dips a feather in the foam
> And soars aloft again to roam.

Ripple imagined sleeping on a bed of wind, softer than the calmest water, low clouds drifting past. Her mind conjured the sound of air rushing over feathers and the swish of a wingtip as it dipped into the sea.

Echo continued with stage two of her presentation:

'Because my version of the poem is about our pet Squelch, I called it 'The Octopus' . . . .'

> The smartest octopus we've met
> And he is our beloved pet
> The one I never shall forget
>
> His colours changing, so bizarre
> His body-shape is like a star
> He makes us carry him afar
>
> His clever tentacles that dart
> Are individually smart
> I hope we never drift apart'

The young dolphins applauded Echo's effort and discussed her work enthusiastically. Ripple broke formation to swim alongside Echo and caress her, eager to show pride in her sister. Tercet commended Echo on using the rhythms and rhymes of the original. One of the boys could not help adding another verse;

> He wriggles like a nest of worms
> Forgetting everything he learns
> Deaf as sand and rocks and dirt
> And everywhere his ink he squirts

Then it was the next dolphin's turn. Each student had chosen a verse of famous poetry to memorise and model their own work on, presenting first the original and then their own version. As they worked and swam, the clouds low in the east dazzled silver and swathes of crimson mist stretched and glowed. The sun rose, side-lighting the waves to translucent jade.

Ripple listened to the poetry and combined the poems with some of her memorised sounds.

Poetry feels like a clue to my secret, but poetry is ideas - not sounds. Perhaps my secret can combine sounds with ideas.

She played her sounds across her mind and mingled the poetry in to see what happened. The other dolphins noticed her unusual thoughts.

'What's the matter with Ripple?' they whispered.

'Is she sick or something?'

Tercet asked Ripple to see him after class. He wondered if something had upset her.

'Ripple, have you enjoyed the poems?' he asked. 'Do you have any questions?'

'I enjoyed them very much and I have a poem of my own if you'd like to hear it.'

'Go ahead,' said Tercet.

'It's called "Unreachable." I made it up one day when I was chasing rainbows.

'The cool rainbow slides away
the nearer I approach . . .'

Tercet listened attentively to the end.

'It's beautiful,' he said, and he clearly meant it.

He liked it. It's wonderful to create something that I can share with others to give them pleasure. Perhaps I shall become a poet.

She chased out of the bay after her sister so she could share the poem with her.

~~~

Pearl was on her way to meet her youngest class of natural historians when Tercet stopped her to tell her that he'd noticed strange thought patterns from Ripple. Pearl chilled to think that others were noticing something different about her daughter. She thanked Tercet for his concern.

I must see how Rigel views the problem, she thought. I'll ask Delph to summon him.

She hurried off to meet her class. Ripple was among them.

'Species are classed according to their methods of communication,' explained Pearl to the eager learners. 'Creatures with little communication of any kind, like sea-slugs and oysters, are classed in the lower levels. Species like ourselves are considered "higher" because we use thoughtstreaming,'

'Which other species do?'

'Whales do. Also many kinds of octopus. I'm sure most of you have enjoyed talking to octopuses from time to time.'

Everyone wanted to tell a favourite octopus story. Ripple told how Squelch saved Whirly. All knew the story, but enjoyed hearing it again. Pearl allowed each of them to tell one story before she continued the lesson.

'Many land creatures communicate by screeching or making a sound to attract their friends' attention or to warn of danger. These are the intermediate animals, lower than we thoughtstreamers, but higher than the animals who don't communicate at all.'

'What if they want to tell someone what their favourite food is?'

'The ones who live on Azure in this era cannot, though who knows how they might evolve in the future. There are some who can, elsewhere in our galaxy. Dolphin astronomers travelling among the stars have found planets with beings that have developed complex "verbal languages" – collections of thousands of different sounds to express different meanings. But sometimes they still can't understand one another.'

'Why?'

'Because they all have different languages. Sounds have different meanings in each different language.'

'Why don't they just use thoughtstreaming?'

'Some don't have the intelligence, others have the intelligence but don't know the techniques, and others just refuse to believe it's possible.'

Pearl set the class a practical task: stop all thoughtstreams at their source in the mind and communicate with your partner using only sounds. The children beeped and clicked and squawked until the cacophony brought other dolphins rushing to discover what was wrong. Only then did Pearl stop the task.

'Did you succeed in communicating with your partner?' she asked.

'No,' said the youngsters when they'd stopped laughing.

'Perhaps not with your partner,' said Pearl, 'but at least with someone.' And she reassured all the new arrivals and sent them away.

'Are dolphins the highest level of animal on Azure?'

'Of course not. We began using thoughtstreaming for communication a little under a million years ago,' she explained. 'We have some catching up to do on whales.'

The children asked Pearl to teach them more about whales. She promised to take them to visit some.

The trip took place two days later. They swam northeast for an hour until they reached the deep water where they heard the trumpetings and clicks of the whales resounding through the sea.

'These are sperm whales,' Pearl explained. 'They click so loud the babies waiting for them at the surface can still hear their mothers when they are hunting at a depth of fifteen hundred dolphin-lengths below them.'

Soon they could all see the dark whale shapes looming like islands before them. The pod was waiting for its other members hunting in the depths to finish and return to them at the surface. The young dolphins stared at the great blunt heads, huge flukes and ridged skin. A smaller, younger whale spotted the dolphins and came to greet them. Pearl led her group close to it.

'May we ride your wake?' she streamed to it.

'Go ahead,' replied the whale.

The dolphins followed Pearl towards the head of the young whale. It set off surface-swimming in a great circle around the pod with the dolphins riding the wave formed by its head-wake as they might surf a wave near a beach.

'I see you hunted well today,' said Pearl to the whale.

Its reply resonated in their brains, as it described the recent hunt which had taken it to depths unimaginable to young dolphins. Pearl told them to scan the food in its stomach. There was a medium-sized deep-sea shark and several squid that were bigger than the dolphins. One was twice the length of Pearl.

'That squid has eyes as big as my head,' said Ripple.

'Giant squid swim deep,' said Pearl, 'but these whales can catch them.'

Pearl directed the children to tune in to the thoughtstreams of the adult whales. They listened to the rich streams pouring from mind to mind. However, as Pearl expected, the children could understand even less of it than she could.

'What are they discussing?' Pearl asked the young whale.

'They love to compare their past lives on distant worlds.'

'It's not surprising we can't understand them then,' laughed Pearl.

Ripple became suddenly depressed and wondered why. Only Sterne and I knew the reason.

'But in all my own past lives,' said the young whale, 'I don't remember a home as beautiful as Azure, so for today, I prefer to leave them to their talk of other worlds and other lives. I'd rather speak with beings like yourselves who inhabit the world I live in now.'

He swam on with the dolphins riding his head-wave, until Pearl called her class to follow her home.

Ripple swam at the back of the group without her usual bounce. They were almost home before her mood returned to normal.

~~~

As he swam towards them, Delph saw the astronomers performing the acrobatics which signalled the end of a challenging work session. They leapt and cavorted, releasing energy built up during the hours of physical inactivity while their minds had been away in the distant Tectarius galaxy. Among them, he spotted his old friend Rigel, leader of the team.

Rigel welcomed him, performing an energetic double spiral back-flip.

'How are you surviving with those students?' asked Rigel. 'Ever miss exploring galaxies with your old friends, instead of being stuck on Azure teaching beginners, year after year?'

Delph laughed. It was an old match between them. Rigel could not understand how someone like Delph, capable of the most challenging of inter-galactic exploration, could relinquish the universe in order to set younger ones on their own courses towards it.

'Every new recruit is a universe of promise.' Delph replied. 'You astronomers miss much of life on Azure while you're zooming around out there.'

'Nothing compares with soaring through the universe discovering new worlds.'

'But how well do you know your own youngest child?'

'Who? Oh . . . Ripple. Perhaps I would've been more interested if she'd been male and likely to follow my slipstream into astronomy. Rev shows little enough interest.'

'Your daughter is half-grown. She's in my junior astronomy class and I can tell you she is unlikely to follow your vocation.'

'Daughters; very charming I'm sure.' He shook himself from beak to tail as though to rid himself of family concerns. 'But I'm grateful to you teachers. Someone has to make sure we've new astronomers to carry on the work.'

He performed another impressive cartwheel and smacked into a wave to stop.

'Can we eat? I haven't had a bite since returning from Tectarius.'

They swam to a nearby spot where birds indicated good hunting. There they dined on small but tasty fish swimming just below the surface. At first they spoke of work-related things such as planets Rigel had visited and the likelihood of some of Delph's up and coming astronomers to travel there. Meanwhile the setting sun ignited white streaks of cloud into crimson streamers stretching from north-west to south-west. Their colour faded as darkness settled over the ocean and the two old friends, now well satisfied with their meal, prepared to part. Delph made sure then to give Rigel the message he carried from Pearl.

'We spoke of your youngest child Ripple. I really came to tell you that Pearl has concerns for her and would like to discuss them with you.'

'What concerns could a she-dolphin possibly have about a female child?'

This provoked a short but stony silence from Delph.

'As your old friend,' he said, 'I feel it's my duty to tell you how dim-witted you are about things that matter here on Azure. Pearl has not told me of her worries for Ripple. She wants to speak to you about it. Make sure you visit her!'

Delph swam off, irritation visible in every flick of his flukes, leaving Rigel to return to his team. His team-members observed uncharacteristic agitation in Rigel. How could the revered astronomer who could fling his own intellect a thousand light-years, be so rattled by an ordinary schoolteacher?

~~~

Under starry skies with half a moon, Rigel approached Pearl in the main school. She felt the familiar tug at her heart and put out a call to bring the children to see their father. They came bouncing in with the special Rigel stamp of physical vigour showing in every leap and twist. Ripple held back, but the three older ones rushed to their father caressing him with flippers and flukes. They leapt beside him and Rigel joined in the frolic, his children following all his moves, their play swinging between perfect co-ordination and mayhem.

They're like a bunch of shooting stars, thought Pearl as her family cavorted around her.

'Don't think about stars!' said Rigel, 'I've come here to get away from them.'

'Then don't look up – they're all around us tonight.'

'Maybe, but right now I'm happier to be here on Azure with you all.'

The sheer physicality of Pearl's family, when they were all together, made her tired at times.

'They're all so big now,' she said. 'When they all start bouncing I can hardly believe they came from me!'

'I helped,' he laughed. 'They've certainly grown, but we have one not-so-bouncy I see,' he said, eying Ripple.

'Ripple,' said Pearl, pushing her forward, 'is feeling shy right now but is usually very bouncy. Play for your father.'

Ripple flew into action among her brother and sisters. She leapt and twisted like an emerald flame between them.

'She seems a fine daughter,' said Rigel. 'I see she has her mother's smooth curves and graceful flukes.'

'And she has your dazzling skill in wielding them,' laughed Pearl.

The parents moved away from their children.

'Delph tells me you have concerns for Ripple. I sense she's concealing much from us.'

'She is healthy in most ways but she herself cannot explain some unusual thought patterns that we sometimes detect in her mind. Aroha thinks there's nothing too serious yet but she is prepared to intervene if the problem worsens.'

'I find it difficult to imagine anything wrong with Ripple. She seems a true daughter of mine as far as I can see. But I'm curious to know her better and must try to spend more time with you all.'

'We'd love to see more of you, Rigel, but we understand the demands of your vocation.'

'Any sign of Rev taking an interest?'

'Not the slightest I'm afraid. He likes chemicals more than anything. Aroha is performing well in her field. Echo is as undecided as ever and Ripple speaks only of wanting a vocation in sound. She cannot explain further. So we do have some worries about our children's vocations, but other than that and Ripple's strangeness, we have the healthiest family in the school.'

'They are young yet. Don't bother yourself about them, Pearl. I'm a little disappointed to have no astronomer showing up, but if it's not to happen, I can accept it. They must find the vocation that most suits themselves.'

'You're right; I'll try to worry less about them.'

The parents rejoined the family and they set off together in the moonlight. Rigel led them directly into the southwest wind so they could expend energy smacking into oncoming waves, smashing them to spray and sending phosphorescence glittering in their wake like constellations. They played until the first magenta glow of dawn lit the horizon. Then they hunted to replace the energy lost. Rigel left soon after sunrise, leaving his exhausted family to rest at last.

10
DERANGED

Cirrus had put out a call to the surf. Cosmo declined to join in as he had sky-watching plans. He watched Cirrus's group heading off to the waves.

Strange, he thought, Maram's not with them and he usually initiates the surfing. Haven't seen him for a while. Wonder what he's up to?

He considered calling Maram in. Better not he thought, he might be with a girl. What else could explain his absence from surfing?

A few days later, Cosmo came across Maram and Alcyone hunting together. He approached, intending to share their meal of pilchard.

Alcyone saw him. 'Maram's not well,' she warned.

Cosmo swam up alongside and greeted them. Maram did not respond. He hunted on, feeding mechanically.

Cosmo detected garbled thoughtstreams swirling in the sea around them. It was difficult to work out where they came from.

'Is that Maram?' he asked Alcyone.

'Yes. It's the illness.'

'Shall I call a health adept?'

'I am the best adept for this kind of illness. I've known since his babyhood that it would strike him.'

Twisted thoughtstreams escaped from Maram's mind and drifted randomly like poison gas. Cosmo lost interest in feeding.

'Can't he control his own mind?' he asked.

'He cannot.'

Then Cosmo remembered when he'd been like that himself.

'Some psychological disturbances are easier to treat than others,' Alcyone explained. 'His intelligence is strong as ever, but it's deranged. He knows you're here and it bothers him for you to see him like this. It might be kinder if you left us.'

Over the next few days, Cosmo heard whispers circulating in the school: Maram's problem was serious; he needed full-time care from Alcyone; he'd never fight or ride the surf again.

As time passed, the whispers suggested Alcyone's task was not going well; that if she could not help, it was serious indeed; that it was an inherited insanity.

A few weeks later, on a clear night with bright stars, Cosmo swam with Maram again and could not recognise his old friend. Maram's thoughts squirmed inside his skull like giant worms. Once again, Alcyone allowed Cosmo only a short visit before requesting privacy for her patient.

'His mental state deteriorates when others approach.'

'Is he ever well?' asked Cosmo.

'He still has occasional lucid spells, but they're becoming shorter and less frequent.'

'What'll happen to him?'

Alcyone swam closer to Cosmo and gave him a short range message that Maram would not pick up.

'He won't survive this. I can't foresee the manner of his end but it can't be far away.'

'In the school the whispers say his ancestors had this illness.'

'The whispers are true. But reassure his relatives that the chances are one in hundreds of it striking one of them. I saw the signs in Maram from his babyhood but not in others of his blood. Tell the elders I will stay with him until the end.'

'Are you safe to be alone with him, Alcyone?'

'He suffers from rages sometimes but so far he's directed no aggression towards me. I can't guarantee that others would be safe from him. As for predators, I'll call for help if I need it.'

Cosmo turned and looked once more on the sick dolphin. Although it seemed that Maram himself was no longer there, he fired a message into the mind of his friend, hoping it would find a stable spot to stick.

'Maram, if you need me, call and I'll come.'

Maram did not respond. He lunged unevenly in the sea and writhed as though in pain.

I'm glad to go, thought Cosmo as he swam away, leaving Alcyone to her lonely task. I couldn't stay and be close to that chaos, though I'm not proud of it. She's heroic to stay with him and endure what he's become.

Cosmo looked up and allowed his spirit to align itself with the perfection of the stars. He let the names of the stars sweep the worm thoughts of Maram away from his brain.

Maram's illness shadowed the school. Cosmo delivered the messages and reassured the relatives of Maram as Alcyone had recommended.

~~~

About six days after his last conversation with Alcyone, Cosmo received a long-range thoughtstream from her.

'Cosmo, I'm at the Black Reef. I need your help. Come quickly! Come alone.' Cosmo swam towards her immediately but the black reef was half an hour away. After ten minutes, he received another message, a perfectly lucid thoughtstream from Maram himself. It contained the same command he'd just received from Alcyone.

Cosmo continued swimming at full speed. Several messages he directed to Alcyone and Maram went unanswered.

He arrived twenty minutes later. The reef jutted out from the north-eastern corner of the island at the northern end of a sandy crescent-shaped bay. Cosmo scanned the bay, but detected no dolphin heartbeats.

He found Alcyone wedged between jagged rocks on the reef, her head above the water. Blood flowed from dolphin tooth-marks slashing her skin. Cosmo scanned her body and saw broken ribs, ruptured lungs, a mashed liver, a dislocated spine, and a heart that would never beat again.

No sign of Maram. Cosmo called and called but received no response. Not a single sprat swam near. He lifted his head and one flipper from the water to stroke Alcyone's body. That was when he spotted the dark shape on the beach. At first he thought it was a piece of driftwood. He looked again and recognised Maram lying on the sand!

Cosmo swam in towards the beach until his belly and flippers were rubbing the sand. He raised his head and viewed the dolphin lying there. Maram was alive but every thought was indecipherable.

'Maram, I'm here.'

He calculated from Maram's position on the beach in relation to the receding tide, that Maram had beached himself moments after calling for him – perhaps during that same last lucid moment. Maram had made certain he could never return to the deep that had become such a hell for him.

Cosmo remained near the beach through all the hours it took for Maram to die. The sun beat down. No rain fell. The tide forced Cosmo further and further away and then allowed him to approach slowly again.

During this time Cosmo received glimpses of Maram's mind and saw how Maram's suffering allowed him to exchange his insanity for physical pain. To him it was a good bargain. Maram's spirit separated itself at last from his diseased mind and the prison of pain his body had become. He floated into the Hereafter. At first he was not at peace, but Alcyone waited there with peace to spare.

~~~

Maram was serene by the time we took Alcyone away from him to send her on her paths to new phases. He looked down upon his body on the beach and was happy to see the flesh he had so gladly forsaken already providing bounty for many small animals of land and shore.

Only Cosmo concerned him. Maram watched over his young friend as he swam back and forth between the body on the sand and the body on the rocks. It was difficult for us to draw Maram away from that scene.

~~~

11
TO THE NORTH

Stars were appearing when Zenith saw Cosmo approaching. He listened carefully as Cosmo described the events of the afternoon.

'What will you do now?' Zenith asked,

'I'm leaving,' Cosmo said, 'I'm not yet sure where to, but you've told me of the northern astronomers. I'll swim their way until I decide.'

'Do you want me to come?'

'I need solitude for this journey.'

'You may meet danger, Cosmo.'

'I am danger.'

'Avoid waste. You have much to offer any school.'

Oh for the skills of Alcyone now, thought Zenith.

But Alcyone was dead.

Zenith observed Cosmo's departure and saw that he did indeed head north.

~~~

Many of the Southern School tried to contact Cosmo in the days afterwards, but failed.

We observed Zenith taking steps to ease what he feared could be a hostile reception for Cosmo – should he ever win through to the School of the Astronomers five or six days hard swimming away. Meanwhile we followed Cosmo on his lonely passage.

~~~

Cosmo swam towards the Astronomers with only the vaguest intention of arriving. He could think of no reason to travel in any other direction, and only the north held something that had once been of interest to him.

He swam fast, causing the acids to collect in his flesh until his muscles burned. Icy squalls lashed the ocean through the first night of his journey. He watched the stars that gleamed between flying clouds and recited their names as he raced onwards. He ignored hunger all the next day, and his bloodstream gradually lost its richness until there was hardly a calorie left.

Towards the end of his second night, with a three-quarter moon riding a clear patch in the western sky, he sensed a shadow in the blackness ahead.

Rain swept the surface from a squall that had just passed. He scanned the sea and picked up full detail of a solid shape approaching, on course to cross his path. A tail-biter, triple his own weight. He knew its senses would detect his electro-magnetic fields even in the darkness.

It knows very well what kind of meal I'll make, he thought,

The tail-biter followed him. Cosmo sped up to test its intentions. It stayed close. Tail-biters were the fastest and most agile sharks in the ocean. He slowed again but it slowed too, stalking him.

Cosmo scanned its belly. Empty. Good, he thought. Come and get me.

He swam slowly and the shark circled below him, awaiting its moment. The rain moved away eastwards and the moon gleamed as it floated high in the west.

There's nothing left for me in the south thought Cosmo. And in the north? Only unknown dolphins with no reason to greet me kindly. Why do I go to them? In the hope they might help me reach the stars? But here's a shark offering me a quicker path to the same destination. Who'd care if I were never seen again on the oceans of Azure?

He stared at the shadow below. Are you my solution? Feel free to send my spirit where all the best dolphins have gone before me.

The shark could not reply but Cosmo knew it would be keen enough to help him out.

Tail-biters dealt a cruel death, but tonight he hardly cared if he died tail-less and helpless, as long as his spirit was released. The shark moved closer.

~~~

It was clear to us as we watched from the Hereafter that Cosmo had run out of hope. Since he didn't ask, we could not directly intervene. But I could send him a sign of hope. Wondering how I might do this, I studied the ocean, especially the weather and celestial arrangements, the rainsqualls sweeping through to the east, the moon high in the west, shining fitfully between the clouds. It gave me an idea. I discussed my plan with Sister Sterne and she agreed it would do no harm.

So, a little manipulation of pressure zones and breezes, just enough to re-arrange the placement of some falling rain. And . . . ah yes . . . well done Father Clement, even if you do say so yourself. But would I be in time?

Now if that young dolphin would just look east . . .

~~~

With the hungry shark circling nearer, Cosmo took a last look at his beloved sky from the perspective of the planet he knew. His gaze swung to the west towards a patch of clear sky displaying the moon and stars. Then drawn by the darkness, he turned slowly to the east, where thick cloud created a wall of blackness no star could penetrate.

And there he saw something he'd never seen before in all his hours spent studying the heavens – something so rare, many who sought it had passed their whole lives without ever finding it. For a moment it was enough to make him forget, his grief for Maram, for Alcyone, for his lost parents. He even forgot the shark below, and certainly it banished his wish to look upon darkness.

It was the moonlight rainbow, glowing huge across the eastern sky; a geometrically perfect semicircular pathway, every one of its thousand colours silvered by moonlight to delicate pastels.

It floated serenely, with Cosmo positioned exactly beneath the highest point on its arc.

There is no other dolphin within a day's swim of me, thought Cosmo. This vision shines for me alone.

A cloud drifted over the moon. The vision faded, but remained burned in his memory.

Suddenly he remembered the School of the Astronomers and thought, I'd like to tell someone what I've seen tonight. But who? A strange dolphin in a school of strangers? I'd rather tell Alcyone or Maram.

He became almost still, holding himself in place by gently swirling his flippers.

The shark was very close now. Shall I live or shall I die? Cosmo breathed . . . and made his decision.

He swam erratically to attract the shark.

The tail-biter positioned for attack, all its senses focused on the prey. Cosmo slowed and drifted, twitching. The shark circled closer. Cosmo rolled belly up and spiralled slowly down towards it, his tail dangling, vulnerable and inviting.

This will be easy, he thought.

The shark moved away to gain space for acceleration. It turned towards the target, jaws gaping. The curving teeth protruded. It charged. Cosmo knew the pattern. One bite to sever the tail, then it could feed with ease. A moment before the strike, the eyes rolled back, blank and savage. It struck. Cosmo flipped – head down, tail up. The jaws snapped shut on empty water. Teeth sprayed outwards in the impact. Cosmo's flukes slid along the top of its head; a gentle caress. He dived deep, spun round, rocketed upwards. Cosmo rammed its rib-less body at full speed behind the pectoral fin.

Whomp! He felt its liver pulping.

The shark limped away, hunger forgotten.

That felt good, thought Cosmo, and perhaps in future he'll choose cold blood over warm. He swam on through the night and into the light of morning.

As the sun rose he saw gannets working to the north-east. Cosmo heard the whizz-bang of their high-speed dives and suddenly his hunger mattered. He altered course. The gannets had found a school of sprats, anchovies and pilchards. While they preyed on it from above large trevally preyed from below. Cosmo took some of the small fish as well as a couple of good-sized trevally. He continued northwards at an easier pace than before, while the new supply of calories enriched his bloodstream.

He travelled for two more days without further hunting, making do with what little crossed his path. Late on the second day he caught sight of other dolphins; some in pairs, some in groups. A few noticed him and he detected their thoughtstreams alerting the school that a stranger was approaching. He sensed that the ocean in his path held thousands of dolphins. He could catch glimpses of them far off, leaping and playing in the afternoon light. To the north-west the first of the Northern Islands appeared, like frozen whales on the horizon. A scout patrolling the southern borders of the main school picked up the alert messages. He approached Cosmo.

'Who are you and why are you here?'

'I'm Cosmo from the Southern Islands, here to speak with your astronomers.'

'Delph has asked us to look out for you. I'll take you to him.'

Cosmo followed the scout to the main school. Soon the ocean around him was thick with dolphins. He'd never seen so many. The scout led him through the school. Dolphins stared cold-eyed as he passed. Cosmo did not expect or even wish for friendly greetings and he didn't receive any.

He followed the scout through the centre of the school where every dolphin belonged to a family, where mothers played with their children, where youngsters dashed about together, secure in groups of close-knit friends. They eyed him curiously, wondering why this lone stranger had suddenly appeared.

His eye slid to a misshapen male dolphin, covered with lumps of abnormal tissue that crawled and moved.

Is he deformed? Diseased? Cosmo slowed and stared. Stars of Dorado! He's carrying a live octopus. He stared briefly into the eyes of the octopus. It returned his stare with an eerie vision that made him suspect that this half-deaf creature could gather more information using those eyes than a dolphin could with its penetrative hearing.

He heard a voice, from beside the one with the octopus.

'Look mother. There's a strange boy dolphin. Why's he here?'

Cosmo turned to see who'd spoken – a dainty female his own age, emerald green in colour. There were two other young females; sisters perhaps. All three stared curiously at him while enjoying the comfort of one another and a lovely older female who must be their mother. Her opalescent colours reminded him of his moonlight rainbow.

'Hush, Ripple. It's bad manners to stare,' said the mother. 'He's with one of our scouts so he must have a reason to be here.'

The one called Ripple leapt. Her slender body curved through the air, and the setting sun sent liquid gold spinning from her fins and flukes. He received a thoughtstream from her while she was aloft; a message of welcome and reassurance. Among these hundreds of dolphins, all regarding him coldly, this one female had greeted him with warmth. Why? Did she think she knew him? Weird. He did not respond.

Cosmo shook off the image of the leaping girl and swam on behind the scout, preparing himself to meet those who could become an important part of his world. He screened every corner of his fighter's psyche. Fighters, he knew, were valued in any school. But he was here to travel the skies, not to fight. The stars were appearing above him, strengthening his resolve, when the scout brought him at last to Delph.

Delph had just finished teaching a group of young male dolphins. He hadn't dismissed them so they looked on curiously.

'You're Cosmo?' said Delph.

'How do you know me?'

'Once long ago I worked with your teacher, Zenith. Four days ago, he sent me a message telling me to look out for you. Things might not have gone so smoothly for you approaching our borders if he hadn't contacted me. I shall now reassure him of your arrival.'

'I come hoping to study practical astronomy. In the Southern School we have no astronomy teacher above Zenith.'

'And he teaches only the lore of astronomy,' said Delph, 'not the practical arts.'

Cosmo was aware of the young dolphins. Some were sniggering.

'You're young,' said Delph, 'How do your parents feel about your decision to come so far from home?'

'My parents are dead.'

There was silence and Cosmo knew Delph was measuring his mind, seeking insight. He kept his fighting zones barricaded, but made no effort to hide anything else, knowing Delph would find little beyond hunger and weariness.

'Tomorrow I teach the lore of astronomy to dolphins your age. You're welcome to join them. I'll also arrange for you to attend classes in other subjects required of all aspiring practical astronomers. If it's the practical that most interests you then you must work hard to earn the right. Not every youngster who aspires, succeeds.'

Delph dismissed his class and departed to hunt with his family.

Two or three of the boys hung back near Cosmo.

'A Southern astronomer?' they sneered. 'We heard you Southerners hardly know the meaning of the word.'

Cosmo said nothing.

'Why couldn't they have sent us one of their famous fighters?'

I wouldn't mind taking a jab at you right now, thought Cosmo privately.

The sun sat low on the western horizon partially hidden by cloud, but now Azure herself rolled up between the dolphins and the last blazing speck of Sol's uppermost rim. The young males left Cosmo, a stranger among a thousand suspicious dolphins. One final squall chose that moment to blast the ocean and Cosmo welcomed it for making him less visible. The light faded quickly, providing even more cover. He rested for an hour, then hunted, among dolphins who ignored him. Then he rested again, letting the power from the food flow into his bloodstream and flesh where it set to work repairing the tired fibres of his muscles.

He wished he were alone as he'd been during his journey. The company was better then.

As he rested, a picture came to him. The family with the octopus, the shimmering mother, and the leaping emerald female flinging her burning water-trail above the setting sun

~~~

Ripple watched as Cosmo swam by.

A dolphin we've never seen, she thought, has arrived out of nowhere.

He's my age, but seems to have lived too many seasons already. Perhaps his weariness makes it seem that way. How lonely he is! Why's he left his family to come among strangers?

She imagined herself swimming alone into a school of unknown dolphins and shivered. She surveyed his mind and found it veiled but sensed a resilience she'd never seen in a young male and rarely in any male, except perhaps her father.

The sight of him detonated a 'sound' in her mind, like something falling from the sky, deep into the sea within her, sending ripples that spread out from her core. The sound stayed inside her, ringing softly.

Everyone he passes stares at him coldly, she thought.

No-one welcomes him . . . I shall welcome him.

She sank in the water, then thrust powerfully with her tail, shooting herself skywards. The movement caught his eye. She flew higher and his eye followed her flight. From the height of her leap she looked back at him and streamed her message.

'Welcome stranger,' she said. 'We are kind. Do not fear us.' She descended in a smooth curve and re-entered with hardly a splash.

'Why on Azure did you do that Ripple?' said Echo, as soon as he was out of range.

'He was lonely. I was sorry for him.'

'Lonely? He was hungry and tired,' said Echo. 'There wasn't so much as a sprat in his belly. I'd say he's travelled far and eaten little.'

'He carries dreadful scars for one so young,' said Pearl.

There was eerie silence from Aroha. Ripple glanced at her eldest sister who had suddenly frozen, staring at the fading wake of the scout and the stranger.

'What's the matter Aroha?' she asked.

'We shouldn't trust that dolphin,' said Aroha, 'He reeked of anguish. Was he hiding violence? How could that scout allow such darkness to come among us?'

'Perhaps the stranger was expected,' said Pearl.

Rev and Squelch drifted alongside. Another squall whitened the surface and spray hissed.

'I must warn the elders,' said Aroha, beginning to swim away.

Squelch shot a tentacle around her caudal peduncle pulling her backwards.

'Don't go!' he said.

'It's my duty to warn the school.'

'The coming of that dolphin is a good thing for this school.'

Ripple said, 'Squelch knows things Aroha. I'd believe him.'

Aroha looked into the mind of the octopus and saw only truth. The squall passed; rays of sunlight touched the waves, reviving their blueness.

Aroha stayed.

Ripple was silent but deep inside her the sound she'd heard was still ringing and the secret was all around her; everywhere.

~~~

Delph introduced the newcomer in Ripple's astronomy class.

Cosmo, she thought, Cosmo . . . Cosmo. That's his name. Why was Aroha so bothered by him?

Delph asked Cosmo to describe his journey to the group.

Cosmo seemed reluctant. 'It wasn't too hard. It took five days. I swam as fast as I could.'

'Did you see any sharks?' asked one of the boys.

'I saw only one but it didn't harm me. And I saw a moonlight rainbow on the second night.'

'You were fortunate indeed,' said Delph. 'Few have had that privilege. I myself have seen one only once.'

Cosmo passed his memory of the rainbow to all of them.

Some had never heard of such a thing. Now they envied him his experience.

Ripple saw the picture of it glowing in her mind and immediately recognised it as a clue for her search. She mingled the picture with sounds just as she'd done in poetry class. But this time she noticed the other dolphins looking at her. She understood that her thoughts were unsettling them so she pushed the rainbow picture to the back of her mind.

'Your moonlight rainbow,' said Delph to Cosmo, 'is better than the one I saw. Yours is the complete arc. You've shared a great gift. Thank-you.'

He slapped the surface with his tail as a signal to begin applauding. Ripple applauded louder than the others. For them Cosmo was too mysterious to trust no matter how dazzling a vision he shared. There was a sudden flurry of questions.

'How'd you get the big scars?'

'A shark. I was just a baby. Some fighters stopped it killing me.'

'Did they kill it?'

'Not that day, but later they killed it.'

'Is it true they have good fighters in the southern school?'

'It's true. The Southern School is small so we train our fighters from a young age.'

'Are you a fighter?'

'I hope to follow astronomy.' He submerged.

He wants us to leave him alone, thought Ripple.

Delph then required them to resume their studies of the stars of Scorpius. He put the dolphins into debating teams and gave each pair of teams a referee and a Scorpius related topic. He did not place Cosmo in a team.

Once the teams were absorbed in their work, Ripple noticed Delph and Cosmo working quietly together. Delph is finding out how much he knows, she thought.

Later, Delph called the referees to report on the debates. Then he re-introduced a topic they'd discussed the day before, the Butterfly Star Cluster in Scorpius. He asked if anyone was familiar with the fuzzy object near it. No-one responded.

'Cosmo will describe it for us,' said Delph.

She glanced at Cosmo and saw him recover from the shock of being singled out.

'The Sister of the Butterfly? Its stars are mostly blue, like the Cluster itself. It's thought to be about 200 million years old and is 1000 light-years away from Azure. It has 100 stars including seven with inhabited planets in orbit.'

'Do you happen to know its estimated size?' asked Delph.

'We think it's about 25 light years across.'

'Thank-you Cosmo,' said Delph. 'Zenith has taught you well.'

~~~.

# 12
# POINT SAVAGE

Cosmo arrived a little early at the designated spot. The last daylight had faded and the sky was clear. Why had Delph summoned him? Delph arrived and wasted no time explaining.

'I'm preparing a small group of dolphins about your age for the early stages of practical astronomy. I've decided to allow you some trial sessions among them, but your astral travel will be restricted to zones within Azure's gravity. Are you happy to accept the limits?'

'I am,' Cosmo said, and Alpha Centauri seemed suddenly brighter above him. This was hardly the interstellar travel he dreamed of, but any out-of-body travel was a step towards it.

'I know no other young astronomer who would leave his home, swim for five days alone and face a thousand strangers for the slim chance of learning a vocation. You shared a shining memory, but surrounding your moonlight rainbow there were darker visions which you withheld.' Delph paused.

He hopes I'll respond, thought Cosmo, but he doesn't expect it.

Delph gave him times and locations of the sessions and Cosmo hunted with extra appetite that night.

~~~

Cosmo swam hard, into a powerful headwind pushing a short, steep chop. It was past midnight and thickly overcast; sea and sky were coal-black, nothing to see but blinding flashes of phosphorescence flying by.

They were all boys as was usual with practical astronomy classes. Delph was in the lead; Cosmo swam to his left and slightly behind him; the youngest, a dolphin called Flip, in similar formation on Cosmo's left. The three others in the class, Quin, Rush and Givan, had arranged themselves on Delph's right. Together they formed a V formation like a flock of birds in flight and for the same reason; to take advantage of the lift from the slipstream of the ones in front. They navigated the darkness by sonar alone.

'Hold formation when I accelerate,' ordered Delph, as he drove ahead.

Cosmo breathed out-and-in in a fraction of a second, pushed up to speed and held position. He kept the tip of Delph's left flipper in front of him and was aware of Delph's flukes thrusting strongly alongside.

They smacked forward into the chop.

Breathe. Smash! Smash! Smash! Breathe.

The minutes passed. Cosmo wondered how long they could keep up such speed. His muscles burned with the effort.

He must ease up soon, he thought, but Delph accelerated. Top speed was not enough. Something beyond was required. Cosmo breathed again. Alcyone had taught him how to relax his spirit for combat. He did it now, knowing that a widening gap meant failure. Nothing existed except the fin before him, waving effortlessly, goading him. The acceleration continued; he found new limits of speed and pain. When it became more than he could bear, he deepened his inner relaxation. His mind began sliding away, separating itself from his body, lifting him beyond pain. Cosmo swam until the acids seared his straining flesh, the microscopic fibres of his muscles tearing and ripping under the strain.

Delph slowed at last. It was minutes before Cosmo's mind gathered its homing instinct and drifted back to his gasping body, like a feather falling from storm-cloud and settling on a ruffled sea. He was alone with Delph. They had out-swum the others.

'You're young' said Delph. 'But your mind and body are strong. You could be great one day.'

They swam back side by side.

'Interstellar journeys,' Delph explained, 'are not unlike what you've just experienced: the blackness, the speckles of light flying by, the sense of speed, and the same separation of mind and body. I saw that you achieved separation tonight. It often happens for the first time during supreme physical effort. You've done well to reach that stage so quickly. Soon you'll learn to separate without so much as a swish of a pectoral.'

Rush, the fastest of the others, was the first they met on the way back, then Givan, Quin and Flip. Delph allowed each of them to turn and swim back with them. Rush had the grace to congratulate Cosmo on his fine swimming, in spite of his own surprise at being beaten. Givan was quiet for a time and Cosmo thought he had more difficulty in adjusting to the idea of Rush being thrashed than Rush himself did.

Cosmo ached for days, from beak to flukes, as the damaged muscle tissue healed. The muscles healed to a stronger state than before as is usual with hard physical training. Cosmo found that the training had permanently increased his top speed.

Speed sessions were not as common as endurance workouts. For these, Delph allowed the boys to swim at a more moderate pace but expected them to swim without rest or food for hours on end. All of them improved as the training progressed, but Cosmo kept a comfortable edge on them in speed and endurance and the others respected that.

~~~

In Cosmo's absence Delph asked the other four how they felt about the newest member.

'He swims like a demon,' Givan admitted. 'But who is he? What is he?'

'Physical score one hundred percent,' said Quin. 'Intellect one hundred percent. Transparency ten percent. Emotions unknown. Group loyalty unproven.'

'He's secretive, but the little we know of him is all good,' said Rush.

'He wouldn't hide the good stuff would he,' countered Givan.

'Wish I could be like Cosmo,' said Flip.

'You don't know what you're wishing for,' said Givan.

To Delph this continuing lack of acceptance of Cosmo was the chief reason he didn't allow Cosmo to join the boys on missions beyond the moon. Teamwork was too important, even at this stage of their training, though their journeys did not yet take them beyond the solar system.

But after that first speed session, when Cosmo achieved mind-body separation, Delph gave him astral travel experience on all missions within Azure and the moon, so his skills kept pace with theirs. He also allowed Cosmo opportunities to study the science and practice of navigation and noted his aptitude.

Delph thought about Givan's strong intellect and navigation prowess, Rush's physical power and co-operative skill, Quin's mastery of data collection and storage, Flip's ardent enthusiasm. The best leader needs to combine all those strengths, and yet have something more: a capacity to forge team spirit, the charisma to arouse courage, the ability to inspire trust. That last one alone, he thought, bars Cosmo from participating, let alone leading.

That night Delph swam away from all other dolphins into an empty stretch of ocean and made long-range contact with Zenith in the south.

'Young Cosmo,' he streamed, 'could succeed at practical astronomy, if he were not so veiled in mind.'

'He's known tragedy,' Zenith explained. 'Once in his babyhood when he lost his parents and again just prior to his departure from us, when he witnessed the deaths of his two closest friends.'

Zenith then sent a graphical thoughtstream. Delph received it like a movie playing out in his head; exactly the movie that Zenith himself had received from Cosmo, displaying his experience with Alcyone and Maram at the Black Reef.

'I understand why he wouldn't wish to have such matters discussed by strangers,' said Delph.

'There's something else Cosmo conceals from you, perhaps for good reason in view of his ambitions.'

'You can trust my discretion. I value any information which could lead to a better understanding.'

'It may surprise you to know that the Southern School has never, in living memory, produced a better fighter than Cosmo.'

'A fighter?'

'A good one.'

'If he's good by the standards of the south he is indeed skilled.'

'If ever his team-mates are in need of protection, they could not have a better defender.'

This explains so much, thought Delph. How could I have been so blind?

~~~

The call flashed around the main school.

'Surf's up on the western beaches.'

Lessons were finishing, so Echo, Ripple and some classmates abandoned their after-school hunting plans and headed west with hundreds of others. Ripple and Echo swam together until a large group of newcomers bounced in and separated them. Ripple swam among the newcomers. She imagined the roar of the waves and the bodies of dolphins dancing in the surf

~~~

I, Father Clement, senior deity of the Sacred Galaxy, looked forward to watching the surfing, as did the seraphim. I suspected they intended to join in as far as their disembodied state would allow. Sterne however, was not so keen.

'If Ripple is to waste time playing, my time is better spent elsewhere. I could return to Azure when she is more likely to be working at her task.'

I was inclined to forget how Sterne still sometimes required the guidance of those older and wiser. It was fortunate that I took such interest in certain species under her care.

'Surfing is more than just fun,' I said. 'It's the dolphins' celebration of the power and beauty of some of this planet's most wondrous phenomena. This is a chance for you to explore the relationship between the celebration of the physical universe and the advancement of the spirit. Someone with your spirit-reading skills might learn much.'

She rolled her evergreen eyes in that impertinent manner of hers. I urged her to observe the seraphim who had already heeded the dolphins' call to the surf. They swarmed above the western beaches, trailing their crystal veils through the water, testing the strength of the forces driving the waves, before the dolphins themselves arrived.

'I'm certain Ripple's task is a purely intellectual one,' snapped Sterne. 'Bouncing around in a lot of froth won't help her.'

However she had the grace to respect my advice, and stayed to watch the surfing.

~~~

His astronomy team headed west, so Cosmo followed. The call to surf had its usual effect on him, twisting his spirit with visions of the Maram of old leading the charge into the wild waves of the southern islands. He separated himself from the team as they swam so he could think for a while of friends he would never see again. He tried to think only of Maram as he was before the illness struck, and before the chaos raged. But always the memory of the blood of Alcyone clouded the sea, and the dry land where flesh boiled, skin cracked, blood seeped, and the beach pressed upwards, crushing . . . crushing. He swam faster to banish the visions. But it required a stronger physical battering than mere speed could provide. Fortunately help was at hand in the shape of big waves.

It was a couple of hours before high tide and the waves were building to fantasy proportions. Because of wide variations in the shape of the coastline and the contours of the ocean floor, every kind of surf was available. The dolphins could choose from waves ranging from gentle to brutal, according to their moods, and capabilities. They inspected the options, made their choices and caught their first rides.

Cosmo chose Point Savage where huge swells rolled in unimpeded from the open sea, smooth at first, until the seafloor, rising suddenly, pushed them into towering top-heavy ridges. These unstable mountain ranges of water raced ashore between misshapen reefs which reflected new forces into them, complicating their ruthless energy.

The few others prepared to ride here were all fighters. They chose Point Savage because only here could they hone their physical skills against waves that were worthy adversaries. Cosmo did not know these dolphins well, but he knew they were members of one of the school's elite-level fighting squads. He carefully screened off all the fighting zones in his mind so they wouldn't recognise him as one of them; then launched himself into the thunder.

'Sweet brutality,' thought Cosmo, as the first wave grabbed him and flung him shore-wards.

Cosmo was on his third ride for the day. Three other males shared the wave with him. They all swam ahead of the break. It imploded behind them in white pandemonium.

An emerald flash to his left. A female. Ripple! What's she doing here? If she needs help, the others can give it.

She swooped before him, at peace among the fury, like a gull in a storm.

He watched as she whipped along the wave then leapt before it. The curve of her body echoed the curve of the wave. Her movements flickered, he thought. No wonder they call her Ripple. And her mind? Strangely empty, as though she too was keeping certain zones hidden.

She flicked out the back of the wave. He followed, staying in her slipstream as they returned to deeper water to meet the next wave. A group had gathered beyond the break. He checked it for dolphins he knew. There were none. He stayed beside Ripple for wave after wave. Later, he checked again, scanning to see if any of the astro-team had turned up. That moment's inattention was all it took. She caught her next wave and he missed it. He took the wave behind but it lacked thunder and sparkle. He exited early, returning to the calmer water beyond the surf. He cruised quietly, letting several perfect waves pass. Then he caught sight of the emerald flash shimmering towards him through the surf. This time he made sure he caught the same wave.

All around them the thunder deepened, the blue intensified, the spray flew higher and dazzled brighter than he'd ever seen before.

~~~

Dozens of seraphim followed Ripple and Cosmo, trailing their particles in the waves. Sterne stared in absorbed silence, almost mesmerised.

I couldn't resist enquiring, 'Much to see in their spirit lights? Hmmm?'

'Remarkable,' she admitted, without shifting her gaze. 'Most remarkable.'

~~~

Eventually the tide changed and the best surf was gone. Up and down the islands' coastlines, dolphins thought of hunting. Cosmo saw Rush and Givan approaching with other groups who'd surfed further south. He dived, separating from Ripple before his friends arrived. The crowd of dolphins headed back towards the main school, picking up other groups on the way, including one containing Echo. Cosmo noticed Ripple race out to meet her sister so they could swim on together.

Why do I care where she is, he wondered?

But somehow, all the way back to the main school he knew exactly where, in this large group of dolphins, that one small female was swimming.

~~~

The seraphim had joined the dolphins in the surf, flown beside them on the waves and even followed after the surfing was over. Two groups hovered above the homeward-bound dolphins; one group swooped above Cosmo's team and the other followed Ripple and Echo. But as the exhilaration of the surf faded from the dolphins, the seraphim increased the distance between themselves and the ocean.

~~~

The sisters hunted in the dark. They'd located an uprising current delivering abundant multi-species food from the deep.

'Echo, something strange happened to me today. If I tell you will you keep it to yourself?'

Echo was snapping up delicacies in satisfying mouthfuls.

'I'll try,' she said, 'but I'm not so great at closing my mind off like you. What happened?'

'That Cosmo, the new blue Southerner; he surfed with me at Point Savage.'

'You surfed at Point Savage!'

'I surfed with Cosmo.'

'You're lucky to be alive.'

'He's not that bad.'

'I meant Point Savage, stupid. Did he say anything?'

'We didn't exchange a single thought. He was just . . . there . . . beside me all the time! I'm sure he was watching me.'

'I know where he went,' said Echo. 'Hunting with that astronomy team. Shall we join them?'

'No! I don't think he wanted to be seen with me. He left when they arrived.'

'In that case, he's not worth bothering about.'

Ripple scooped up three baby squid in one gulp and squished them between her teeth. Their chewiness soothed her and the sweet juice trickled down her throat.

The roar and dazzle of those waves haunted Ripple for days and she couldn't separate Cosmo's midnight blue shape from the memory. She could feel the secret all around her closer than ever, as though it was hammering on her mind trying to get in.

Is Cosmo the key to the secret?

He approached her after astronomy class.

'Great surf yesterday,' he said.

'It was loud.'

'Loud?'

'It wasn't boring.'

'Too tricky for some.'

'I liked the noise it made.'

'What's noise got to do with it?'

She could not explain and he swam away.

Why did I talk about noise? He'll think I'm crazy. He's the colour of the deep sea. There's nothing in his mind but planets and stars and galaxies. Why do I hear that ringing every time I see him? I heard it when we surfed together. Oh, the secret; it's here with me now. I can feel it everywhere. Is it Cosmo who brings it closer? Or is it the sound? I must hold the sound and find the secret.

~~~

13
SERAPHIC PRAISE

Early next morning, Pearl noticed Ripple slowing and pausing as she swam close to a reef, a large outcrop of rock whose crumpled surface lay exposed like a giant brown scab on the skin of the sea. She watched as Ripple drifted beside the rock. There were fish nearby, but Ripple ignored them. She swam as though trying not to disturb the water. Her eyes closed and she strained to be as still as she could without sinking. At times she was slowly sinking then rising, sinking and rising and occasionally breathing.

It occurred to Pearl that Ripple's mind was as far away as the minds of the astronomers had been on that day during her pregnancy when she had recognised Rigel. That thought caused a whisper of uneasiness in her spirit. She scanned the sea but found no danger. So Pearl stayed just close enough to safeguard her daughter, but far enough to allow her the solitude she seemed to need.

~~~

Pearl understood those needs of her daughter and partly because of that, the universe would remember forever that day Ripple swam alone beside the reef.

Like Pearl, we of the Hereafter were watching Ripple closely, though the seraphim were not helping our concentration. We could see and understand more of what took place in Ripple's mind than Pearl could, but in spite of all our advantages, Ripple made progress that day that even we did not then understand.

On that day she left all of us floundering in her wake, dolphins of Azure, seraphim and deities of the universe alike. I can only tell you what happened because we pieced it together afterwards. It's always humbling to look back on that time from here so far in the future remembering and viewing our own confusion as we watched the brain activity of one half-grown dolphin cruising beside a reef.

~~~

Ripple simply listened to the sounds the water made as it draped itself around the rock, racing up its sides and draining away, gurgling in pools, rattling on pebbles, sweeping the seagrass, sucking at seaweed and combing through pockets of sand, as wind, tide and gravity pushed and pulled it around that patient reef.

The Cosmo sound rang through her mind, enriching all the physical sounds surrounding her.

Yes! It brings the secret closer, she thought.

She concentrated then as never before.

Which is having more fun with this rock? The wind in the water below, or the water in the wind above?

She collected the sounds and thought about each one: arranging them, naming them, filing them away in her memory, letting them interact as though communicating. Her thinking at this time was methodical and mathematically precise. On and on she worked, while the wind played between clouds and waves and the sun inched across the sky.

But suddenly all that stopped, swept aside by chaos.

That chaos was the first musical chord drifting free from her subconscious.

Neither Sterne nor I could interpret it. We could decipher nothing in her mind except the chaos and one emotion – elation. How could she be elated in the presence of such intellectual turbulence?

We heard Ripple call from her spot on the surface of Azure and from deep within her own spirit. She called to herself. She called to the universe;

'Is this it? Have I found the secret?'

Sterne could not answer that prayer. We had no clue to its meaning. The shifting radiance of Sterne's aura stilled suddenly as she held Ripple in the forefront of her consciousness. Even the seraphim stopped their antics and focused on the young dolphin. All of us drifted through those long moments dangling in anxious uncertainty.

~~~

A cloud floated over the sun. Its shadow crossed the water where Ripple cruised. The sudden change in light swept the chaos from Ripple's mind as swiftly as it had arrived. Exasperation drove her to leap skywards, triple the height of her own length. At the top of her leap she emitted a physical sound, a long angry dolphin squeal.

'It escaped me!'

What happened next could only be described as a tantrum. She swam around the rock several times: smacking the waves with flukes and flippers, leaping, diving, squealing, squealing, squealing. She killed a fish with one snap and released it uneaten. She killed another innocent fish and another. She slowed at last, calming, relaxing. Swam around again, breathing as she swam. Once calm, she swam out over deep water and stared down, past the slanting green light, past the dimmer shadows deeper down, into the blackness of the abyss.

There are monsters that could rise up from the dark at any moment and snap me in two, as I did to those fish. Perhaps I should sink down and let them? I'm so tired.

Ripple turned and swam back to the sunlit shallows where she had lost the chord. Pebbles rattled, seagrass swayed, water gurgled on rock, a gull cried from the sky. She searched but the chord was gone.

She found a dead fish and discussed it with herself:

Who killed this fish and didn't eat it?

I did. I'm sorry now.

Eat it then. You killed it so you must eat it.

I'm not hungry.

You shouldn't have killed it then.

I'll manage one.

Ripple ate one fish and apologised to the others she couldn't eat. She left them floating and forced herself to concentrate once more on the sounds of the reef. We saw the effort that took in the face of her frustration. But as the sounds of the rock drifted back into her a miracle happened; the Cosmo sound returned. She felt it ringing once more.

~~~

And in the time since she had discovered that first chord something had shifted in the universe. I sensed a rapid increase in divine vibrations. It could only mean one thing; other deities arriving! All around us within moments their auras glowed huge among shifting seas of seraphic ardour surrounding them. Drawn in by energy emanating from the prescience of the seraphim, these august presences from the Divine Galaxy were gathering near Azure. They represented every level of the Hierarchy including some great luminaries from the Sacred Council itself.

'Why is the entire Hereafter focussed on this one little Azuran being?' I wondered.

~~~

Ripple watched the reef co-operating with the westerly to sculpt the sea into towers reflecting the mid-day sun. Peace returned. The Cosmo sound rang on. Lucid thoughts filled her mind and soon she was working as methodically as she was before the chaos. An hour passed. Chemical signals within her brain flashed from neuron to neuron, leaping the synapses between, like fish leaping from wave to wave, but faster and faster. The acceleration dazzled us. Millions of hormones and electrical impulses inter-reacted, germinating rational thoughts and ideas which flowered in her mind.

'Never have I been more convinced that I chose the best parents for this spirit.' boasted sister Sterne, 'The workings of her intellect already rival those of the great astronomer, her own father Rigel.'

The beauty and order of the thought patterns she generated had reached a peak of complexity when once again they vanished, swept aside in a flash of emotional chaos. We were appalled as before, but as on the first occasion, we saw that it didn't upset Ripple. There again was that overlay of ecstasy that revealed her to be enjoying the disturbance that had overthrown her thought processes.

This was the second chord. And it was the moment of her breakthrough. Right there on Azure Ripple discovered something that she had tried but failed to discover in all her previous lives. The chord melded into the Cosmo sound and stayed within her, ringing, ringing. This time no cloud covered the sun, no shadow passed, no dark tentacles stirred in the deep to distract her. The chord stayed. To us it was still only chaos.

She called again to the universe but this time she made a statement before she made a request.

'This is it. Let it not escape me!'

~~~

Sister Sterne, young deity of the Sacred Galaxy, heard Ripple's prayer. All the divine beings surrounding her were stunned by a sudden expansion and outpouring of glory from Sterne's aura. It knocked the seraphim flat. Entranced, they stared at the translucent streamers and veils of light in cerulean, magenta and silver radiating from Sister Sterne's presence near Azure for thousands of miles into space. Sterne granted the request. Ripple was allowed to hold onto the chaos which was her chord.

~~~

The sounds Ripple had collected had combined with the Cosmo sound to create the chord in her mind. But this time it stayed. She could hear it ringing . . . changing . . . lifting . . . falling . . . floating . . . growing in volume, staying before her, not like a picture that she could see all at once, but playing out along a timeline. It lasted several minutes. When it was over, she froze in the water and let herself sink, then swam slowly up again and breathed.

Afraid to leap, afraid to dive, afraid to move in case her moonbeam escaped again, Ripple centred herself and gathered courage to play it through once more. The chord played exactly as it had the first time but now straight from her memory. She changed it slightly to create a second chord and then a third. She took some pure sounds from her memory and let them play among the chords, rising and falling in a repeating pattern creating the first melody. Behind the chords, she allowed her own heart to beat the first rhythm. She played the music over and over re-modelling until it was perfect.

She put words of love into the melody, memorising as she worked. The first music of the universe was Ripple's love song for Cosmo.

Under a moonlit rainbow
Through the flying spray
Who did you leave behind
When you came my way?

Carried in the midnight silk
Of starry currents in the seas
I listen to the rising wind
That sings to you of galaxies

It sings to me of you,
Stranger from the blue.
And will you take my music
To the galaxies with you?

Under a moonlit rainbow
Through the flying spray
What were you fleeing from
When you came my way?

Her body moved in time to the first music. Those movements were the first dance. The first dance sent spray flying far over the sea. Every drop hit the ocean with a tiny 'ting'. Those sounds combined in their thousands and joined with the sound of the waves crashing on the reef to create a great up-rush. This was the first applause.

~~~

Our ancient friends, the visiting deities, bestowed celestial respect upon Sterne and myself. Then they de-materialised back into the distant reaches of the universe they inhabited. They had been there when it all began but even they were none the wiser as they left Sterne to her puzzling task.

Whatever our confusion, Ripple's tired and ancient spirit knew that it had found what it was seeking - a discovery with the power to change and enrich existence. Sister Sterne said suddenly,

'Look at her spirit!'

'Where? How? Do you mean her aura?'

'No, her spirit light. She carries hers just behind her head and slightly to the right.'

'I can see it but it's hardly more than a blur.'

'It's perfectly clear! Look, it's flashing like fire! Remember how tired it was before she was born? I hardly recognise it now!'

There was no doubt Sterne could see more in the light of a spirit on a distant world than most deities could see in one that was sitting within the space of our own aura. It was then I first understood that this talent of hers would one day take her to the highest levels in the Divine Hierarchy.

The seraphim had been strangely calm since Sterne's aura had knocked them flat. Now they began to make 'praise', as they called it. They surrounded Sister Sterne and babbled a cacophony of chaotic ideas in appreciation of her contribution to Ripple's mysterious achievement. Sterne let them express themselves for the very short time it took her patience to run out. Then she expanded herself until she towered over and around them, extended her aural wing into a vast celestial broom and swept them aside with a great swoop. Even as they were tossed and tumbled on their way, they stared adoringly at her, babbling garbled praises.

But then the seraphim did something that surprised us. They regrouped themselves in the space above Ripple. They formed phalanxes on both sides of her and stared down, babbling the same drivel. Seraphic praise for a mortal creature? Never before had we known such a thing. What had this dolphin done?

For days afterwards the seraphim behaved like supernova remnants whose excitement exceeded their confusion. They corkscrewed around the galaxy in unpredictable swarms, more distracting than ever. I tried to persuade them to visit other parts of the universe so Sister Sterne could work in peace, but they had become obsessed with Azure and would not depart from Koru. I took it upon myself to control them.

~~~

My search is over. The sound clues, the poetry, the Cosmo sound. All the clues were pointing to music! How could I not see it singing in my face? I must tell mother.

Mother? Maybe not Mother. The first song is Cosmo's song. He must hear it first. I'll make a special song for mother. And I'll make a song for Father and one for Echo and one for the sunrise and the mist and the scent of the landflowers. There are so many songs to make. My task has changed from searching for music to creating it.

Once Cosmo hears my song, he'll love me as I love him . . .

~~~

14
GLISSADE

Ripple sensed Cosmo among the crowd at astronomy class.

I must give him the song, she thought. She swam towards him.

Not now, dimwit.

She turned away.

It has to be a private thing. I should arrange to meet him somewhere.

Delph made them study the nebula in Carina. Ripple took nothing in. Never had a lesson dragged like this. The nebula remained nebulous in more ways than it ought. She kept watching Cosmo and sometimes she thought she caught his thoughts coming her way. Delph dismissed them at last. Ripple waited to see which direction Cosmo took. She prayed he'd swim away alone but he was still talking to the one called Rush from the practical astronomy group. He headed north-east. Great, she thought, he's alone. She swam after him but not hurrying. She mustn't seem too eager.

Rush passed her like a sou-west squall and braked alongside Cosmo.

Whistling whitecaps! What does he want now? She followed at a distance hoping the two would split up, but they were too busy discussing the nebula. She picked up snatches of their thoughtstreams glowing with celestial dust-clouds and newborn stars, enough for her to glean that Rush was picking Cosmo's brain, hoping to understand the complex energies of the nebula.

These dolphins aren't as hostile to him as they used to be, she thought, but it'd be easier for me if Rush would just leave him now.

Rush spotted his family, said good-bye to Cosmo, and swam to join them.

Now, thought Ripple.

She swam towards Cosmo. He saw her coming and slowed. She felt the song waiting inside her like a land-flower expecting the touch of the sun. But she screened every scrap of it from him, calmed herself and approached smoothly. He didn't seem unhappy to see her. Could this be the time to give him the song?

A group of five adults shot by heading for a hunting spot. They were not the only other dolphins in the vicinity.

No, she thought, not here. Too many stray thoughtstreams flying around.

'I need to meet you somewhere private,' she said.

He jumped over a wave, dived below another and surfaced alongside her. His flipper brushed her side.

His touch is like the breath of the nebula.

She explored his thoughts and saw nothing but curiosity.

'I can't explain what it's about,' she said, 'I can only show you.'

'Where and when?'

Her brain trolled and miraculously hooked answers to both questions.

'Cascade Cove,' she said, 'first light tomorrow.'

The waterfall will make it perfect.

'I'll be there,' said Cosmo.

Now I have to give him the song. He'll be proud to think that he helped to make it happen.

But what if he hates it?

~~~

At first light, Cascade Cove was full of blackfin hunting stingray. She heard them long before she reached the bay.

The sky is so clear, every star distinct. The light will be harsh when the sun rises. How can I give him the song? Thank the stars for hungry blackfin, but I must escape before he sees me, in case he names some other place.

She raced back to the main school without looking to see if Cosmo was in the vicinity.

He approached her two days later after a class.

'The blackfin made it difficult,' he said, 'Want to try again?'

Did he know I was there? Does he think I never turned up at all?

'We could try again tomorrow,' she said.

~~~

Ripple arrived first and Cosmo came soon after. This time there was not a blackfin for miles. The sky was overcast and a pearly morning light glimmered on the bay. The sound of the cascade seemed muted. Perfect.

He's happy to see me. He's wondering why I called him here. His skin is the colour of the planet itself. Oh, I'm ready to give him this gift.

Dawn was approaching and she believed that music was about to rise like the sun. She sensed millions of years of empty silence vanishing behind her. The future rang with music expanding and rolling down the millennia and it was all to begin here . . . now.

She positioned herself where the sound of the cascade was the perfect volume. Ripple's audience consisted of Cosmo, countless seraphim and we two deities.

She released the first song in streams of thought that soared into the air and sea surrounding Cosmo.

Her audience listened but not for long.

Music was sound. She was streaming it to us. Thoughtstreams are not sound. They are ideas. All we heard was chaos. Cosmo too, heard only chaos.

When her love song for him had hardly begun, Cosmo dived deep and turned away.

'I get the message,' he called back to her as he swam out of the cove, 'Good-bye.'

He never looked back.

Ripple stared after him, stunned. The music faltered . . . and stopped.

~~~

Sterne turned to me and said, 'I know this spirit well. I have watched her through many lives. Her will is strong but I cannot see her surviving this blow.'

~~~

Rain began to fall.

In Cascade Cove there was no breath of wind. The sea heaved smoothly and the ripples spreading from each raindrop collided on the swells. Ripple swam slowly out of the bay through the hissing rain. She picked up speed away from the island, veered right, swam for half an hour, then veered left so she would reach the deep sea without passing through the school. She swam eastwards, far from any other dolphin, to a place where the sea was empty. Empty and silent. The silence monster waited for her in the blackness of the deep.

You've won and I've lost, but I'll fight you one last time.

To defy the silence, she let the first chord ring faintly from the deep places in her mind. She let the chords grow and the melody begin to play . . . but much slower than before and sad as the grey rain. The silence monster waited, biding its time.

Under a moonlight rainbow
Through the flying spray

Ripple danced slowly to the music of the only song that had ever existed. There was no waterfall here; only falling rain.

When the song was finished, Ripple slid toward the silent abyss.

Cosmo didn't want my song. I can't give it to any other. I must hold it within me. Will it eat its way out through my flesh? Shall I die down here in the dark? I'm so tired. . . I must find the place where I can rest . . . forever.

~~~

Cosmo was not afraid to fight a legion of giant sharks but now he was afraid of Ripple and afraid for her. Her terrifying chaos had forced his retreat from the cove just as the rain began falling.

'Her physical beauty blinded me,' he thought. 'How could I have been so shallow? I thought she liked me, but that was rejection wasn't it? Or is there something wrong with her? Is she another Maram? Stars of Dorado! I must warn someone.'

He found Pearl and Aroha in the main school swimming in a mist of happy excitement. Their mood evaporated at his arrival.

'Something's wrong with Ripple,' he said. 'She was in Cascade Cove half an hour ago in a state of chaos.'

'I must find her,' said Pearl.

She sent a distance thought-stream to the outer scouts. One in the south had identified Ripple heading for the deep water. He gave Pearl the details.

~~~

Ripple's consciousness faded as her glissade continued. Meanwhile the seraphim whimpered and clung closer to my aural wings as they followed our divine gaze into the depths and saw a flesh and blood monster there, armed with razor fangs loaded with poison – the Shade Erishkigal, Nightmare of the Southern Seas.

She lurked below Ripple with her ladies in waiting. The eight tentacles – Vipa, Lucifina, Malevine, Venga, Sadistine, Clawdine, Fera, and Lashette – writhed around her like a nest of anacondas. Their squirming stimulated the suckers on each tentacle to a unique vibration which performed two functions to ensure Erishkigal's survival. The vibrations spread into the sea like a nectar which her prey could not resist. They also stimulated the muscles around a cluster of blue neon fangs sprouting from each tentacle tip. The constant working of the muscles sucked the fangs up inside the flesh one moment to load with venom, and disgorged them the next, clutching and straining for living victims to invade. The repeated sucking in and out of these fangs made the tip of each tentacle appear to pulse with blue flame.

Erishkigal discharged a stream of ink through a funnel protruding from the bloated bag of her body. This ink spread the stench of death and shadowed the surrounding water, hiding her from creatures lacking echo-locatory senses.

The Shade was feeding. Fish were drawn in by the sweetness of the vibrations which grew sweeter at their approach until each fish was a sensitive tongue that could taste all over itself, basking in honey. Near the end the pleasure became intense, then came a shadow, a flash of electric blue, the grip of a suckered tentacle strong as the jaws of megalodon. The blue tips skewered them, vomiting agony into their flesh.

'Bring me food my deadly daughters. Bring me any living creature you can entice with your piquant venom.'

'You are beautiful my Queen,' purred Lashette to her mistress as she fed her an overweight three metre tiger shark. Deftly she passed the struggling animal in towards the circular mouth at the junction of all eight tentacles. She forced it in headfirst where her mistress could rip the plump flesh from its bones with her double ring of dagger-teeth.

'Take this, my Queen. Eat! Eat!' she cried.

'My gifts for you,' screeched Venga, 'are always better than Lashette's. Accept this great tuna, my Glorious Queen!'

Venga clawed at Lashette until she bled, then smacked her aside and fed her own contribution into the mouth of the monster. Lashette whimpered and shrivelled from the pain, then rallied and slashed at Venga. The Shade ate everything they gave her and revelled in their conflict.

'My Queen you are the loveliest of all things,' cried Fera ripping the stinging tail from a ray and feeding the rest of its thrashing body to her mistress.

'But only I know how best to serve you, my Queen,' hissed Clawdine. 'My vibrations are most powerful; they attract the biggest prizes for your pleasure'

'What does size matter?' howled Vipa. 'Mine is the most subtle honey and it attracts the tastiest morsels for my lady's nourishment.'

Erishkigal's complex brain pulsed with the pleasure she took in ripping her victims. As she gorged, she enjoyed the agony of the fish awaiting their doom as they lay gripped in the suckers of her minions like jewels.

'Lashette is right,' she purred. 'I am beautiful and I am sweet. No one can resist my honey.'

'Stop! Be still! What is that I see above?' asked Sadistine.

'It's a dolphin,' said Fera.

'And she doesn't know we are here,' said Erishkigal. 'And she does not care. Stealth now my deadly daughters and we will eat warm flesh.'

The eight tentacles halted their telltale vibrations and slowed their movements to secretive slithering. Erishkigal ceased ink production. The Nightmare of the Southern Seas was closing in on Ripple.

~~~

In trying to catch up, Pearl was forced to swim as she hadn't in years. This daughter of hers was too much of an athlete. She streamed her calls far across the surface and through the deep.

'Ripple!'

Pearl echo-located her daughter in the dark, too deep for any dolphin, not swimming, just sinking. Pearl dived down and down until she was alongside. She placed a gentle flipper on Ripple's skin.

'Ripple, stop. Come back to us,' she commanded.

There was no response. Pearl knew this was too deep for safety and Ripple was unheeding; anything could happen to her here. She scanned the ocean around and below and discovered the monster rising towards them.

Pearl's thoughtstream arrived in the mind of the monster.

'Go down Shade!'

Erishkigal stopped rising but she did not go down.

'I desire dolphin flesh . . . '

There was a large squid still attached to her suckers. Without allowing her upwards glare to waver from the dolphins she ripped the tentacles from the squid.

'I will rip you like that!' she hissed and swallowed them.

'Not today you won't,' said Pearl.

She commanded The Shade by her true names:

'Erishkigal - Shadow Queen
Vipa, Venga, Malevine,
Lucifina, Sadistine,
Fera, Lashette and Clawdine,
Go down now!

Erishkigal found she couldn't resist the command. She slithered down and down to places so dark there was no need of ink to hide her. There she continued feeding on the cold flesh of deep-sea creatures but her tentacles writhed in thwarted lust at the thought of the warm flesh they'd missed.

~~~

Ripple and Pearl floated above Erishkigal, but still far too deep for dolphins.

But Ripple's glissade carried her still deeper.

'Ripple. Come back!' It seared into her brain, inescapable. This time she heard.

My mother is here. She's with me in the darkness, touching me.

Pearl waited, willing Ripple to drag herself back from the abyss, lending her all the support of a mother's love. But still they drifted deeper.

Pearl had to think of something, anything her daughter might respond to.

'Aroha is having a baby!' she announced.

Ripple heard.

Baby? . . . Baby . . . .

A new life called to her. The weight lightened. She stopped drifting.

'In the spring,' said Pearl.

An unborn baby drew Ripple back to the place in the deep where her mother waited.

~~~

Sister Sterne's aura blazed like a supernova and billowed through the Hereafter in clouds of magenta glory. Once again her energy overwhelmed the babbling seraphim.

'What did I tell you? A mother in a million!' gloated Sterne.

My respect for the work of Sister Sterne DS was expanding by the moment.

~~~

'Ripple dear, you must come back with me if you want to meet the baby.'

Would it be a boy or girl? What colour would it be?

Mother and daughter rose, slowly at first, then faster and faster, towards the light.

They reached the surface and breathed. To Pearl, the air had never tasted sweeter.

'What on Azure upset you so much?' Pearl asked.

'I found what I was searching for.'

'Was it something awful?'

'It was music. Music is beautiful.'

'What is music?'

'It is the secret that was hidden. I was right. It is sounds. I made a song for Cosmo. It scared him away. Perhaps it is impossible to share music with Cosmo. Or with anyone.'

'Impossible? You thought it was impossible to find what you sought. But you have succeeded. Nothing is impossible. One day you'll show us all what music is.'

'Music is meaningless if I can't share it. If I die now, music dies with me.'

'So don't die Ripple. Make another song. Make it for me or for Echo. Don't give it to some strange boy dolphin you hardly know. Stay alive and be a lovely auntie for Aroha's baby.'

'Oh Mother, I can hardly wait to meet Aroha's baby. I just hope I can give it a song.'

Without their knowledge, a seraph passed close between them. A shimmer of its prescience clung briefly to their spirits and Pearl said . . .

'Ripple, I don't even know what a song is but in my heart I believe that one day you will give one to Aroha's baby.'

Ripple was comforted.

'And your music will resonate through my own future.'

Ripple grew suddenly cold.

My mother's future? Why does that chill me?

~~~

A kilometre below them the nest of anacondas squirmed and lusted for Ripple's warm blood. Erishkigal was aware of the dolphins recovering far above in the light of the sun. Hundreds of deep-sea fish in all their fantasy shapes swarmed to the bloated monster to be consumed.

We looked down on this horror and marvelled at the diversity of Azure.

Soon Erishkigal was so distended she could eat no more. Her writhing stopped, the vibrations slowed and she drifted motionless, a shadow blacker than the deep except for the blue light radiating softly from the tip of each tentacle.

~~~

'Nasty creature,' Sterne said.

'Nightmare!' I agreed.

The seraphim surrounding us had continued their frightened whimpering since the first moment of Ripple's glissade. I wondered why. They were not normally such timid spirits and Erishkigal couldn't harm them. I comforted them as best I could and shepherded them away behind me out of Sterne's way the better to let her concentrate. But the seraphim were not easily comforted that day. As I fussed with them, I wondered for the ninetieth time, how Sterne would possibly manage without my guidance and support in this great Azuran mission of hers.

~~~

15
TEACHERS

Was the problem just with Cosmo, Ripple wondered? Or would all dolphins be as deaf to her music as he was?

I'll create a song for Mother. If Mother cannot hear my music, no dolphin can.

Ripple became lost in the task of creating the second song. She worked in solitude beyond the edges of the main school. No one saw her except a lone scout who passed close as he patrolled the outer edges of the school. She didn't notice him but he picked up her working thoughtstreams.

'She's deranged,' he thought.

~~~

Aroha was discussing a work problem with Pearl: a youngster was disturbed after witnessing a blackfin take his newborn baby brother. In such cases Aroha used all the skills and resources her training had provided. She also sometimes made use of her mother's wisdom. They were deep in discussion when Ripple bounced up in a dazzle of spray.

'Mother! I've made a song for you. Perhaps you too will misunderstand it; but please, listen anyway.'

'Of course dear,' said Pearl. 'We'll give you our honest impressions.'

Aroha focused on Ripple. What on Azure is this about, she wondered?

Ripple played the song right through, thoughtstreaming it to her sister and mother. She streamed each note of the music distinctly, aiming for perfect clarity. She danced gently as it played. The song finished. It took her a few moments to escape the spell cast by the beauty of the new song. Then she turned to face them. Aroha and Pearl looked at her blankly.

'Darling, are you all right?' asked Pearl. 'What is confusing you so terribly?'

Ripple clearly heard Aroha wondering if she should forget her other patients and sort out the madness emerging in her own family.

'Can't you hear the music?' Ripple smacked the water with her flukes. 'Listen harder and you must.'

She played the music again, more slowly this time and even more clearly. But it made no difference.

'Stop!' Pearl cried. 'This chaos must upset you.'

Aroha said, 'Ripple, can you stop?'

Ripple stopped immediately.

'That's a relief,' said Aroha. 'If you can control it at will the problem can't be too serious. We should be able to help you before you get any worse. Mother, has she had any shocks lately? Has something upset her?'

'I'm not upset!' Ripple thoughtscreamed. 'There is no chaos in my mind. There is only music. And you're too stupid to hear it!'

And having caught an echo of what they had been discussing before her arrival, she added . . .

'I hope you both get eaten by the biggest blackfin in the sea!'

She swam away in search of solitude.

Pearl called after her, 'Ripple! Are you alright?'

'I'm angry. Don't follow me.'

Once alone, she was surprised to feel her spirits rise.

Now at least I understand why Cosmo swam away. Normal thoughtstreams don't work with music. But what on Azure can I do about it?

Did I really say that to Mother and Aroha?

She sent them a distance thoughtstream: 'I'm sorry. I didn't mean it about the blackfin.'

'We know dear.'

'But Aroha, I forbid you to try and heal me. I don't need to be healed.'

Ripple played the new song again through her mind. It banished the last shreds of anger. Soon she was leaping and dancing like the windblown spray, listening to her music, refining it, utterly alone, but fulfilled. Half an hour later, Pearl accompanied Aroha back to her work-zone. They passed Ripple dancing with her chaos and noticed she was unaware of them.

'She's not safe like this, Mother' said Aroha.

Pearl scanned the ocean and found no danger for the moment but she knew Aroha was right.

~~~

'Dreaming all alone,' said Pearl to Ripple's teachers as they swam with flukes to the setting sun. 'Dreaming happily but with chaos raging in her brain.'

'In her first day in my poetry class,' said Tercet, 'I observed some confusion in her thought patterns, though I wouldn't call it chaos.'

'Her previous confusion only intensified into chaos after her discovery,' explained Pearl.

'Discovery?'

'Yes. She calls it music but it's intellectual chaos.'

The sky held a spectrum in pastels in a gradient from horizon to zenith. The light was changing as daylight faded and the east awaited the moon. Wavelets slapped and whispered with the passage of the dolphins.

'Does my Ripple have a handicap or is she a kind of genius? What are your thoughts as her teachers?'

A brilliant star appeared on the eastern horizon. It was the centre point of the uppermost edge of the rising moon.

Axis, the mathematics teacher replied. 'She shows a complete lack of interest in my subject. We should be concerned about this dreaminess.'

The moon-star had expanded into an arc. The dolphins accepted its invitation by swimming up the pathway of light it cast.

'I notice no dreaminess in Ripple,' said Mio, the cultural history teacher. 'She memorised the entire history of the "Alien Waves" after hearing it just once. She can name every one that's swept the oceans of Azure including all those existing in our time. I wouldn't be surprised if she chose a branch of history for her life's work.'

Mio's words soothed Pearl until Delph the astronomy teacher spoke.

'How can Ripple progress far as a historian if she has no ability in mathematics and little interest in astronomy? No historian's education would be complete without them. And since you mention "Alien Waves," how could she ever understand these beings without knowledge of the galaxies they came from?'

All the dolphins paused to think with reverence of the Alien Waves. Meanwhile the moon inched upwards to become circular with only the lowest point of its rim in contact with the horizon. It broke loose from the sea and ascended as Delph spoke again.

'Two nights ago I had a night session with Ripple's class. They were learning the stars of Orion. I noticed Ripple drifting in both body and mind. I detected traces of the chaos Pearl has described. I called her back. Her only explanation was that she'd tried to think of the stars but had instead thought of the spaces between them. Then she thought she could hear the spaces between the stars and had swum off to listen better. I detected no dishonesty.'

A pale wash of light from the vanished sun remained in the sky behind them and the sea was dark in all directions but towards the moon. The red super-giant Antares in Scorpius was low in the sky. Higher, Crux hid itself in a veil of cloud while the blazing pointers swinging from its short axis remained visible below.

'As though she truly believes she's listening to the spaces between the stars!' added Tercet. 'A lyrical concept is it not? She has a rare poetic talent for one so young. Perhaps her interest in history lies in its inspiration for poetry.'

Pearl considered this with a little more hope dawning. Crux, flying high in the sky between south and the zenith, emerged from the cloud. The visible arm of the home galaxy was a river of light across the upper sky. Zuben the gymnastics teacher spoke for the first time.

'I think there's a good chance of Ripple choosing gymnastics as her life work,' he said. 'Her physical skills are vastly superior to others her own age and older. And no-one who hunts as well as she does could have any kind of handicap. If it's a choice between that and genius Pearl, I'd be thinking genius.'

'I worry about her safety,' said Pearl. 'She becomes so absent during her times of chaos, like the astronomers. We all know how vulnerable they would be without their minders but Ripple has no-one to guard her.'

After a moment of thoughtful silence, Delph said, 'I wonder if she could work with an astronomy group. It's possible she could operate alongside them. I'll keep in touch with you Pearl and let you know when circumstances permit a trial.'

~~~

16
BESIDE THE ASTRONOMERS

Cosmo heard the scuttlebutt as he arrived for history.

'They say her mind's in turmoil.'

'She's such a loner.'

'We swam right by her. Her crazy brainwaves deafened us, but she never even knew we were there!'

'Ssssh. Here she comes . . . and Mio too.'

Ripple bounced into class. Cosmo saw her look around and pick up the sudden hush and half-hidden sniggers of her classmates. She sank below the surface and stayed two body lengths down, mind heavily veiled, surfacing for breaths as rarely as possible. Mio arrived and launched into the history lesson.

Cosmo heard no chaos from Ripple that day, though the mind-barriers stayed firmly in place. Just like me, he thought. Can't blame her for that. At least she can hide it, whatever it is. Maram couldn't. I hope she doesn't think it was me who spread the rumours.

Later the same day, Cosmo and the other four members of the junior practical astronomy team, turned up to their meeting with Delph, to find that Ripple was also there. Delph observed their reactions with interest. Ripple kept her distance from the boys.

'Why's the oddball here?' asked Givan.

Delph made an announcement.

'Today you'll have Ripple among you. Welcome to class, Ripple'.

'Is she an astronomer too?' asked Quin. He didn't look at Ripple.

She's sidelined already, thought Delph.

'She needs your minders while she's engaged on her own pursuits,' he said.

'What would they be, I wonder?' said Givan.

'That's enough thank-you.'

'Today your bodies will be in a state of torpor, so you'll do an hour of physical drills first. Please include at least a hundred high leaps each with plenty of air-spinning, at least two deep dives over ten minutes duration, and some high-speed surface swimming on both straight and curving courses. Ensure that each of you takes their turn at leading. Ripple, you may as well follow – exercise is good for everyone.'

Normally the five young males would have warmed up first, but this time they took off at top speed, straight-lining. Ripple followed but kept well back. Delph observed from a distance.

He messaged her, 'Try to match them, Ripple!'

She maintained her distance from the boys. Delph watched carefully.

The gap isn't increasing, he thought.

Because of her distance behind them, the boys didn't notice that she was easily swimming at their speed. Nor did they notice that when they leapt she leapt higher and when they dived, she dived deeper. But Delph, watching from afar, noticed and he laughed. Fit, skilled, and strong for an oddball, he thought, and he went off to meet the minders.

At the end of the hour, Ripple closed on the boys again as they returned to their work spot.

'Get a bit left behind did we?' jeered Givan. 'We've big work to do today. You'd better keep out of our way and let the minders look after us.'

'Do you think I'd want to follow at your flukes?' Ripple said.

'We don't know what you want,' said Givan. 'From what we hear, you don't either!'

'I've got better things to do than follow you around.'

'Yes. We've heard how you're searching for something.'

Rush, Quin and Flip sniggered. Cosmo looked away.

The way he said 'searching' made Ripple want to attack. But she controlled herself, needing all the restraint she'd learnt from Pearl. She swam away trying to suppress her anger so the boys wouldn't pick it up. A little further off Ripple stopped and whacked a wave with her flukes. She saw Cosmo watching her and knew he had read her mood.

Who cares what he thinks!

Delph arrived back, punching through a steep westerly chop with the two minders, Hadar and Pollux. They were older dolphins and like most minders they had experience of practical astronomy but no longer worked at it.

'I'll allow Cosmo to travel with you today since you are not going beyond the moon,' said Delph. He gave them a few last-minute instructions and sent the boys on their mission.

Ripple remained beside Delph and the minders. She watched the boys make a V formation with Givan in front at the point, Rush and Cosmo to his right and Flip and Quin on the left. They sprinted and slowed, keeping perfect formation, which helped to co-ordinate their minds. The complexity of their moves increased as they settled deeper into their group mind and body alignments, each one taking a turn at controlling the moves. Once they were fully prepared for take-off, they slowed.

They're ready, thought Ripple . . . any moment now . . .

The five dolphins made one final co-ordinated leap and . . . Ripple could almost see it happen as though their minds had leapt higher than their bodies, and gone on their way, without physical encumbrance. Their bodies slowed, with only essential brain areas operating. Ripple stayed close to the group as Delph had recommended. Hadar and Pollux took up their positions around the now-absent boys. When one began to drift too far away, Pollux gently nosed him back to the others. When one seemed to have gone too long without breathing, Hadar guided him to the surface and used penetrative sounds to stimulate his breathing zones.

Ripple waited alongside Delph. She suddenly felt left out and almost regretted that she hadn't studied astronomy well enough to be allowed to join in such an adventure.

Love those sounds the minders make to get them to breathe. They could be useful.

'I'm leaving now,' said Delph. 'You're permitted to swim with the absent ones and let their minders keep you safe in your own work.'

Ripple watched Delph departing and wanted to chase after him.

Hadar said, 'Feel free to start your work. Delph has asked us to give you the same care we give the boys.'

Still she hesitated.

'My work is different from theirs. I don't travel away in mind.'

'We've been told your mind becomes as lost within you, as theirs becomes lost in space, so don't swim away. You'll be safer here.'

'My work is chaos to others. You may be bothered by it.'

'You can relax with us. Hearing unusual brain activity is a normal part of our task.'

It reassured her. She calmed a little and looked at the world around her.

The southeast wind is fresh, a cross current making the waves leap; hear them hiss. Listen to the heartbeats of the absent dolphins . . . slow . . . slower . . . someone breathed; little Flip I think.

She began to re-arrange the sounds including the distant boom of the surf on the beach of a nearby island. She was sliding at last into working mode.

Her emotional relaxation deepened. She swam near the astronomy group but not among them. The first few quiet notes entered her mind and she arranged them into trills and flurries which grew gently into flowering fountains of sound as she surrounded herself with music of her own creation.

The minders noticed that she seemed more comfortable working apart from the boys, so Hadar took it upon himself to watch her, leaving Pollux to concentrate on the others.

'I'll be within call,' he said to Pollux.

As Hadar followed her, he soon noticed the chaotic brainwaves building and fading. He wondered what was going on in her mind. Was it madness as the rumours suggested or was it just something no one understood?

Then he noticed an aspect of her work very different from the ways of the astronomers. Their bodies moved slowly while their minds were far away, but this girl went through various phases of movement ranging from slowness very like the astronomers, to highly energetic displays of gymnastic skill. No wonder she preferred to keep separate from the boys. It was dazzling.

With chaos pouring from her mind, Ripple flung herself into a fantasy of fluid movement, leaping as Hadar had never seen a dolphin leap; spinning and rolling in rhythmic patterns of grace and power.

His years of practice at dealing with preoccupied minds helped him to cope with the task of guiding without distracting her, so that her gymnastics did not take them too far away.

After an hour the minders exchanged roles.

~~~

On this first day of Ripple's working alongside them, the boys travelled a short astral voyage mostly within the confines of Azure's atmosphere. They circled the globe in various directions, flying in and out of night and day to practice navigation skills Delph had taught them. They crossed blazing deserts, mountain ranges, steaming rainforests and both the frozen poles. Navigating was Givan's responsibility but Delph expected all five to understand the process. Givan as leader was also responsible for the overall care of the group. The boys included a quick trip into inner space orbiting the moon once before returning to Azure over a northern hemisphere landmass. They soared in a curving southward course back to the Northern Islands where their bodies waited. The whole session took no more than two hours.

Once he knew the boys had returned, Hadar informed Delph by distance thoughtstream. Pollux, being truly adept at his task, interrupted Ripple without causing stress or shock. He swam back with her to rejoin the others for the wind-up of the day's activities. Delph was there already and discussing their trip with the boys. In late afternoon sunlight, the eight males set off towards the main school with Ripple listening in close behind.

'We had a race with the daylight!' said Flip. 'We raced the sunrise over a whole continent and then we turned on our flukes and went back into the night to see what the animals did on land in the dark. Some scurried into holes and some lay on the hard ground, (that must feel so bad!) and some started hunting, just like we do at sea.'

'Well observed, Flip,' said Delph. 'I promise you most land creatures would be almost as frightened in the deep ocean at night as you would be to lie on the hard ground. What did you all think of the moon trip?'

'Journey score one hundred percent. Destination, two percent,' Quin said.

Delph laughed. 'Dolphins rarely find much to admire in a lunarscape. How was the navigation Givan?'

'It went smoothly. Quin's data was spot on and we took turns, as you required.'

'Cosmo?' said Delph.

Cosmo had never been into space before and was still not quite ready to speak of the experience, but he rallied at Delph's query.

'This was the highlight for me.' He shared a picture of the blue planet floating huge against a background of space and stars.

Ripple felt a wave of music rise at the scene he'd painted on her mind. She crushed it down. This was no time for disruption.

'Well done all of you. And Ripple? How did your work go?'

She hesitated.

'I was very satisfied with what I created. '

'Hadar streamed me that your methods were visually spectacular and you showed commitment to your mysterious task.'

Delph dismissed them and he and Ripple swam away to their families. The boys did not immediately split up.

'What was all that about?' said Rush.

'No idea,' said Givan, 'What commitment does she have?'

'Her task is certainly mysterious,' said Rush, 'He was right about that.'

Cosmo was also puzzled by Delph's comments but his curiosity was aroused. How could a girl like her have been 'spectacular' enough to impress a minder who'd travelled to the stars?

~~~

Months passed. Ripple worked alongside the absent bodies of the astronomers, becoming relaxed and productive under the care of the minders. Her music developed well. During the workouts that preceded the astronomy sessions, Ripple stayed out of the boys' zone sensing their need to bond without distraction from anyone outside. Even Delph now rarely trained with them in person for this reason. She usually swam out of sight in an opposite direction, returning for the start of the main session. She didn't begin her work until the boys departed astrally, to avoid unsettling them.

The daily physical training was not as vital to her since she worked hard physically during her work sessions. She soon came to think of it as free time and often picked up a snack. The boys came to accept her presence, once they realised she wasn't likely to push herself into their working zones.

Outside of the astronomy class, the boys had other classes to attend and so did Ripple. Having found her vocation, she was not a perfect student, often skipping classes that interested her little, such as mathematics. She did continue to take interest and achieve well in poetry, history, and home-based astronomy since these enriched and inspired her music.

The boys suspicion of Ripple dissipated but their understanding of her had little chance to grow. The nature of their work meant that although they worked side by side they could hardly have been further apart.

Delph required all the boys to take a turn as minders. He was now occasionally sending them to inner space to explore other parts of the solar system. Cosmo was not allowed beyond the moon's orbit, so when the team

took these more distant routes he stayed behind as extra minder alongside
Hadar and Pollux. At these times, Cosmo hid his disappointment well.

~~~

17
IO MISSION

Givan, Rush, Quin and Flip soared through the dust rings of Jupiter on course for Jupiter's moon Io, in orbit beyond the rings.

Io expanded before them; about the same size as Azure's moon but without craters; just a rocky surface of pitted plains dotted with towering mountains. The only liquids were lakes and rivers of boiling lava. Quin became absorbed in estimating the temperatures of features he saw. Rush translated Quin's figures for Flip's benefit:

'Hot enough to turn a whale to cinders.'

'Colder than the South Pole.'

They cruised above Io's surface. Its harsh colours contrasted with the soft caramel swirls of Jupiter covering most of the sky above.

'The crust of this world is thin,' said Givan. 'And the tides so strong, they drag the land around. Look!'

An area of rock bulged visibly.

'Is it a tidal bulge?' asked Flip.

'No, it's volcanic action, caused by those tides though. It's about to blow. This'll be a story to take home.'

~~~

Back on Azure, Hadar and Cosmo kept their eyes on a group of sharks prowling nearby. The sharks were non-threatening, cruising deep and seeking smaller prey than dolphin. Nevertheless, they kept themselves between the sharks and the absent astronomers.

Pollux arrived back and Cosmo went to take his place guarding Ripple a few minutes swim away. That was when the minders noticed a change in the sharks' behaviour. They were now moving in lazy circles, rising slowly, directly below the dolphins. Time to recall the astronomy team.

~~~

The bulge on the surface of Io swelled upwards. Rocks tumbled and bounced as the crust stretched like a mountainous monster trying to escape an underground prison. A great fissure ripped across the bulge, an evil mouth opening to grin at them. It vomited red-hot rock in vertical rivers that jetted past them into the sky. Clouds of soot from the lava fountain blackened the colours of Jupiter above. The volcano couldn't harm them in their bodiless state, but Givan knew it could endanger them emotionally. He began a hurried team-check.

'Rush, rock-stable as always, Quin, hardly distracted from his calculations. Flip? . . .'

Givan felt a sudden tug. Something was dragging at him.

'Recall!'

The fires and volcanoes of Io vanished in an instant and Jupiter became a fleck of light in the black sky. Cool water lapped their skin as they thumped back into their bodies on Azure.

~~~

We were impressed by the speed of the dolphins' response to the emergency, both on Io and on Azure, but we'd noticed a problem they had not yet picked up for themselves; a problem more worrying than sharks, and the absence of Delph and Cosmo.

~~~

'Where's Cosmo?' said Givan.

'He's bringing Ripple in,' said Hadar.

Rush located Ripple and Cosmo approaching from the north-east. They arrived, a bewildered Ripple still clearing veils of music from her brain.

'We've called for fighters to back us up,' said Pollux.

'We may not need them,' said Givan. 'No point fighting now we're together. We can out-swim them; let's go.'

A large shark chose that moment to charge. Ripple leapt in fright as it lunged past her towards Flip.

'Flip!' shouted Givan. Flip did not respond. Givan deflected the shark just in time with a clumsy sideswipe.

If this is how they defend themselves, thought Cosmo, I'll have no option but to help out.

The minders rushed to Flip's side.

'He's not back!' said Hadar.

~~~

Sterne and I were glad someone had noticed at last. Flip was alone beside an Ionian volcano while sharks targeted his body on Azure.

~~~

The discovery gave Givan no option.

'We can't leave Flip,' he said. 'We stay and fight!'

'We have two minders, three astronomers, one untrained female and Cosmo,' said Quin. 'Will that be enough until the fighters arrive?'

'One less,' said Givan. 'I have to go back to Io for Flip.'

'We're not allowed into space alone,' Rush reminded him.

'No choice,' said Givan. 'Failed recall shock could kill Flip at any moment. He and I need the rest of you to protect us until we get back. Ripple and

Cosmo, first priority is to evade sharks that approach you. Help to fight if you can. At least try not to get in the way.'

Cosmo did not respond.

Givan positioned his body beside Flip's and attempted to return to Io, but his survival reflexes kicked in. The shark threat made it impossible for him to relax enough to escape his body. The harder he tried the more he tensed. Quin thumped away a shark that approached open-mouthed from beneath.

'I can't get away!' said Givan.

'Give me the navigation figures,' said Cosmo. 'I think I could manage it.'

Givan glanced at the hungry sharks and shook off his hesitation.

'Give him the figures, Quin.'

Cosmo felt the data bullet thump into his brain.

'Once you're on Io, the volcano is easy to find,' said Quin. 'It's the only one erupting in the leading half of the subjovian hemisphere.'

Cosmo employed the fighter's technique of relaxing the mind to control the body under stress. It was the work of a moment. He over-rode the survival reflex and took off for Io. It was clear to all of them that he'd gone.

'How could he do it when I couldn't?' asked Givan as he turned to face the fray.

The astro team were strong and fit but had only rudimentary training in the arts of defence and attack. Ripple had none whatever and the minders were old dolphins; cunning but no longer as efficient as they'd been. And now there were two absent astronomers to guard.

More sharks arrived. Ripple evaded one that charged her. The sharks had not yet noticed Cosmo's absence and were still targeting Flip. Quin deflected another hit on Flip at the same moment as both Givan and Pollux evaded interested sharks. No blood flowed so battle pace was slow.

The dolphins split into two groups. One contained Flip, Quin, Givan and Pollux; the other had Ripple, Rush, Hadar and Cosmo.

'We must protect ourselves,' ordered Givan. 'But co-operate to protect Flip.' He streamed a message across the gap. 'Rush, your lot do the same for Cosmo.'

At first the sharks seemed more interested in the group containing Flip. But they quickly noticed Cosmo's vulnerability. Cosmo's group soon had as many sharks circling them as Flip's. Rush dodged a charge and deflected an attack on Cosmo. Cosmo began sinking. Ripple nudged him upwards and made sure he took a breath while a shark swam close below both of them. Her flipper touched its gritty skin as it passed. The speed of the sharks' open-mouthed charges increased.

~~~

From our vantage point in The Hereafter we divided our attention between sharks threatening dolphins on Azure and events on Jupiter's moon Io.

~~~

Cosmo navigated into the zone of Io's orbit of Jupiter. He found Io, then easily located the erupting volcano which created a beacon so perfect he had no need of co-ordinates. Molten lava still roared from the gaping fissure on Io's surface. He sent out wide-range thoughtstreams to locate Flip. There was no response.

Recall shock must have stunned him, he thought.

He sent stream after stream into the ash-blackened space over Io's surface.

'Flip! Where are you? Wake up!'

At last he heard a weak response from a dense cloud of volcanic ash close to the eruption. There it was again – a wisp of intellectual existence trying to assert itself. Cosmo entered the cloud and homed in on the signal. Flip was half-conscious, but trying to drag himself awake. Cosmo streamed reassurance. Moments passed before Flip's first blurry thoughtstream.

'Is . . . is someone there?'

'I'm Cosmo, come to take you home.'

'Cosmo!' Flip revived. He was the team-member who'd always been most ready to trust Cosmo. That could save him now.

Cosmo drew Flip to a calmer region away from the smoke and sulphur; a dim clear place on the edge of the Ionian night where it was easier to imagine an ocean below. Flip calmed as Cosmo streamed images of clean water and cool Azuran air into his mind. Cosmo screened his knowledge of the physical danger surrounding their bodies at home.

~~~

Back on Azure, a big shark headed straight for Cosmo. Ripple and Rush charged in from different directions. Ripple's hit deflected the shark one way but Rush's pushed it back again. Each hit would have worked better on its own. The blows failed to keep the shark from Cosmo but were just enough to convert a mortal hit into a glancing slash on his right side. The cut began bleeding. Every shark in the area smelled the blood and turned towards it, losing interest in Flip now that blood flowed elsewhere. Cosmo now was in the greatest peril. The young astronomers defending Flip left him in the care of Pollux and moved towards Cosmo.

~~~

A flash of pain from Cosmo's body on Azure crossed the abyss of space to strike at him.

Shark hit, thought Cosmo. Not serious, but probably bleeding badly.

He hesitated and it took all his self-control to screen this event from the younger dolphin. To save himself and Flip he must ignore it, make sure they stayed calm and trust the dolphins at home to protect them. He managed it with difficulty. Flip recovered rapidly.

Cosmo judged Flip ready for take-off and the two of them departed Io, which shrank to a black speck against the bulk of Jupiter. Jupiter itself spun away into space as they swept towards Azure. They travelled at the fastest speed that allowed Cosmo time to prepare Flip for the scene that awaited.

'You were recalled because we're under shark attack,' he said. 'But there are fighters on their way and the others will hold the sharks off until they arrive. Just be ready to protect yourself as soon as you're back.'

~~~

Flip leapt sky high to let them all know he was home safely. From the air he saw groups of sharks closing in on Cosmo. A shark passed by him on its way to the blood-cloud. As Flip re-entered the water he turned and jabbed it in the gills, hard enough to banish its hunger.

Cosmo arrived to stinging pain, the taste of his own blood, and several sharks coming for him. Ripple, Rush and Hadar were nearby, Quin and Givan were racing to join them, hitting and deflecting sharks as they came. Beyond them, Flip was already leaping and fighting. But there were too few dolphins. Further away, he could see shadowy shapes of more sharks arriving.

He breathed and relaxed again.

The first shark lunged. He slipped down out of its path at the last moment.

Others arrived from several directions and entered the blood cloud together. He waited beneath it. A heavy shark swam blindly through the bloodied area with its mouth open. With a carefully judged shove, Cosmo shunted a smaller shark up into the path of the gaping jaws. The shark bit down near the caudal fins of the smaller one and fresh blood bloomed around them. Cosmo moved out of the large blood-cloud though he could not avoid taking some of his own smaller blood-cloud with him. He flashed around and between the sharks, shoving here, pushing there, each move designed to cause one shark to bite another and maximise their confusion. The more blood flowed, the more frenzied the sharks grew until they lost all judgement and ate anything within reach. Jaws snapped, tails thrashed, bodies twisted and lunged. The newly arrived sharks charged into the blood-zone, jaws gaping and grabbing; ripping and crunching, eating and being eaten.

Cosmo swam to the sidelines and joined the others still jabbing at the sharks on the outskirts of the feeding frenzy.

'No need for that,' he said quietly. 'They'll sort themselves out.'

The dolphins withdrew to a safe distance to observe the sharks' crazed consumption.

'Look at Cosmo,' said Givan. 'He hasn't even raised his heart-rate. We should call in a few more shark-packs to give him a decent workout.'

Cosmo read Givan's undisguised respect and it was not just for the fighting.

'Yep,' said Rush as the fighters arrived. 'Here come the troops, but who needs them? We've got Cosmo.'

The fighters joined them and watched the mêlée until the last few sharks had followed the blood trails left by the remains of their companions as they sank into the deep.

Later, Givan asked Cosmo how he'd managed to leave his body.

'Just a fighter's trick I learned in the Southern School. I can teach you.'

'I didn't know you were a fighter.'

'I started fighting, very badly, when I was two days old. The Southern School taught me to do it properly.'

'A trained fighter! Why didn't you tell us?'

'Because I came here to learn astronomy.'

'Today you saved us by using both.'

~~~

A senior dolphin representing the fighter dolphins of the Northern School visited Delph the following day accompanied by a respected school elder.

'We've come to inform you,' said the elder, 'that in view of events yesterday, the school has decided to bestow a high rank in our defence hierarchy on the dolphin Cosmo.'

'He may not be pleased to hear that,' said Delph.

The sou-westerly whistled and whitecaps hissed through the long pause that followed.

'This honour is not offered lightly,' said the senior fighter. 'It would be a valuable opportunity for the southerner to carve a prestigious position for himself in our school. We came expecting a grateful response. Fighting is obviously the vocation of his choice.'

'Not so,' replied Delph. 'A dolphin of his quality will appreciate this honour. But he is a practicing astronomer and cannot also be on call as a fighter.'

'With his skills? How could this be?' asked the elder.

'This expertise must not be wasted!' said the senior fighter. 'He is obviously the cream of the southern school's fighters. There are plenty of young ones aspiring to astronomy. Why should we miss out so you can have one more trainee?'

'I admit even the southerners regarded him as their best fighter and they were sorry to lose him,' Delph explained. 'But they had no practical astronomy classes available for him. His motivation drove him to swim for days for a chance to learn astronomy. He has demonstrated promise in practical astronomy as far above average as his fighting skills.'

'That must be considered,' said the elder.

The white-caps hissed through another pause. Gannets wheeled and cried and the swoosh of their dives indicated nearby fish.

'We wouldn't force him to a vocation not of his choosing,' said the senior fighter, 'but our trainees could learn much from him. How would it be if all we asked was a little teaching when it suits his commitments with you?'

'If that was all he may be happy to oblige you,' said Delph.

Later that evening, Delph went into the sea alone and transmitted the story of the Io mission to Zenith in the Southern School.

~~~

Givan met privately with Flip, Quin and Rush. At Givan's initiative, the team decided to ask Delph not only to include Cosmo on all missions in future no matter how distant, but also to allow him to travel as their leader.

'He's proved he can do it,' said Givan, 'and I prefer navigation alone to navigation and leadership.'

Delph agreed and commended Givan for his maturity.

~~~

18
WONDER ATHLETE

White puffs of cloud cruised on the blue. A gentle easterly barely ruffled the surface where the bodies of Cosmo's absent team drifted like logs. Hadar and Pollux floated among them.

The rings of Saturn faded as the five young intellects slid homewards across inner space towards Sol and Azure. Blue and gold light expanded around Cosmo as his body rushed to meet him. The water of his planet encased him in cool silk. Cosmo swirled his flippers and flexed his caudal muscles. He rolled upwards, breathed, shot away underwater, then rocketed into the air three times his length. Rush and Givan were airborne with him. They re-entered the water just as Flip and Quin leapt skywards. The five played until the water boiled and spray hissed across the shattered surface. Cosmo smacked the sea enjoying the strength in his flukes, the foam fizzing on his skin and the blood pumping through his veins.

You appreciate your body so much more when you've been without it awhile, he thought. Then the hunger hit him.

Hadar and Pollux laughed at the spectacle of the return of their charges

'We'll let you wake Ripple from her work today,' said Hadar. 'She'll need feeding too. Wake her carefully.'

The two minders swam away.

Ripple was dancing nearby, lost in her work.

'More baby-sitting,' grumbled Givan.

The boys cruised over until they were close enough to feel her noisy brainwaves thundering around them. Givan snorted his distaste. Cosmo thought of Maram. He shivered and crushed the memory.

'Ripple. Wake up,' he called.

She continued working as though she was as far away as he'd recently been.

'I'm hungry,' shouted Givan. 'Wake up, you lunatic.'

'Is she even on the planet?' asked Flip.

'A planet of her own,' said Givan. 'Rowdy-Ripple WAKE UP Rowdy-Ripple WAKE UP,' he chanted.

Flip and Quin joined in, swimming around her in a tight circle. Cosmo was suddenly anxious watching his team-mates teasing the girl. Rush stayed alongside Cosmo.

For Ripple the ocean sang, the wind rushed, the birds called and the music played.

'Rowdy Ripple WAKE-UP.'

Her music collapsed like a wave on a rock. Cosmo saw that she had returned.

She flew up and out over their heads higher than they'd ever seen or would have believed possible. Had she taken wing? The boys followed her flight, their heads moving from right to left in unison. She re-entered the water, impossibly far from them, and swam away. They were awed into silence by the sheer power of her flight. Yet she had leapt to escape them not to impress them. Rush was the first to react.

'Well, you woke her.'

'Good. Now we can hunt,' said Givan, shaking his head to clear the image.

They set off in search of food, except Cosmo who'd forgotten his hunger for the moment. He followed Ripple, intending to apologise for his team. He swam quickly but the gap between them increased. He didn't know any dolphin his age that could outpace him, yet she was racing ahead. He accelerated to full speed and was gaining on her until she noticed him and smoothly pulled away. In the end, he turned and retraced his course back to his classmates in the hunt.

'I couldn't catch her,' he admitted.

'You couldn't catch up to a girl?'

'Who is she? What is she?' asked Rush

'I don't know . . . but she's really something,' said Cosmo.

'Something weird,' muttered Givan, 'pretending to be so weak and useless but she can sure move when it suits her. You sound like you're interested Cosmo. She's cracked, you know.'

'No wonder, if everyone treats her like we just did. How do we know what's in her mind?'

'We've heard it. It's turmoil.'

'Or maybe beyond our reach, like her swimming and jumping.'

'You got it bad, Cosmo.'

'I detest her chaos more than you do. A dolphin with thoughts like hers beached himself in the Southern School.'

'Why would anyone choose to die that way?' asked Rush, shivering.

'I don't wish to speak of it. He was insane. Ripple can control her chaos. We saw how quickly she snapped out of it just now. So from now on, let's give her "work" whatever it is, the same respect she gives ours. That's if she ever comes back.'

'I wouldn't care if she didn't,' said Givan.

'What've you got against her, Givan?'

'My dad says it lowers our status having that oddball around.'

'And my dad says status has to be earned,' said Rush. 'How could Ripple prevent us earning it?'

'Delph sees no problem with her being around us and that's good enough for me,' said Cosmo.

'She should be an astronomer,' said Flip, 'She's strong enough to take her body along. Maybe Givan's scared she might take his place on our team.'

Givan whacked Flip with his fluke. Flip corkscrewed downwards with closed eyes and open mouth as though dead. Rush mimicked a shark arriving to clean up the carrion. His efforts to swim with the side-to-side shark action were too much for Cosmo and he laughed at last.

'Stop it you lot, I need food. Let's hunt.'

~~~

Ripple swam alone.

I'll never work near them again; I'd rather have Erishkigal's company. And why was Cosmo following me like that? I'm glad I beat him. Astronomers and fighters and gymnasts are all the same. They think the rest of us can't swim.

~~~

Some hours later, with hunger pangs appeased, the boys met with Delph to make a full report of their mission. Afterwards, Cosmo remained behind and told Delph of the incident involving Ripple.

'I wanted to apologise, but she swam too fast for me.'

'This surprises you?'

'I thought I was faster than all others my age in the school. Why's she not training to be a gymnast or astronomer?'

'Because she has chosen neither as her vocation.'

'Are her skills to be wasted then?'

'Perhaps, but I must tell you Cosmo, that while you were among Saturn's rings, I came by to check on you. Ripple worked nearby. She seemed just like an astronomer, observing some chaotic alien culture. She could have been one of you except for one big difference.'

'What difference?'

'You astronomers descend into physical torpor on your missions. Ripple does too, but sometimes she keeps moving. Today as she worked, she romped in the air above the sea like a bird. The minders have seen her keeping it up for hours.'

So that's where the fitness comes from, thought Cosmo.

He saw again the effortless flight of the leap she'd made to escape them; then shivered at the memory of the chaos.

~~~

In the evening, Delph met with Rigel at an arranged location one hour's swim north-east of the northernmost island. By then the story of the events surrounding the Io mission had already circulated, greatly increasing the boys' prestige. But Delph was unsurprised to discover that Rigel hadn't heard it as he had been away in the Tectarius galaxy while the scuttlebutt was rippling through the school. He gave Rigel the full story.

'I don't know Cosmo,' said Rigel, 'Which family is he from?'

'He has no family; he was orphaned after birth. Cosmo came to us from the Southern School to receive training in astronomy.'

'It's good to know there's one coming along with such leadership potential. He could be destined for greatness. Rare to hear of one so young, who's a talented astronomer and a skilled fighter. His fitness must be excellent.'

'There are no boys in the school who can touch him for physical speed and skill. But he has been shocked to discover there's a girl who can outpace him and she's no older than he is.'

'Who is this female wonder athlete?'

'She's your daughter, Ripple, whose sanity has often been questioned.'

Rigel gaped, spluttering slightly. He was speechless for a long moment and then began to laugh. His laughter grew until it infected Delph and they laughed until the sea around them quaked.

~~~

Delph didn't allow the boys time to enjoy the glow of their newfound fame. They were almost ready to journey beyond the solar system so he stepped up their workload. There was no shortage of destinations of value to explore within the home galaxy and much to do to prepare. So it was a few days before Cosmo finally found the time to speak to Ripple. She was near the southeast edge of the main school when she spotted him swimming in her direction.

Is he coming to speak to me? Yes, he's looking at me and swimming this way.

She glanced at Echo and saw that she'd seen him. With the safety of the school around her and the security of an older sister, she felt no compulsion to swim away. He swerved alongside giving her his slipstream.

'Ripple, I've been looking for you.'

Why would the famous shark-fighter and star of the Io mission be looking for the biggest misfit in the school?

'I only chased you the other day because I wanted to apologise. I'm ashamed of how we behaved.'

There was an uncomfortable pause. Echo had melted away.

'Your work is a mystery to us all, but Delph told me that if you wished to be a practical astronomer or fighter or gymnast, your physical skills are good enough.'

'I'm not interested in any of those vocations. My father is an astronomer. My mother says I get my speed from him.'

'Your father is an astronomer? What's his name?'

'Rigel.'

'Stars of Dorado!' He performed a corkscrew leap. 'This will shut Givan up. No wonder you swim like the wind. Rigel has the speed of a hurricane.'

Cosmo and Ripple edged away from the school. Many body lengths lay between them and the nearest dolphin. A brisk westerly had blown the sea into a short steep chop that glittered in the sun.

They were swimming downwind, cruising easily on the faces of the waves. She remained in formation with him and they breathed in unison.

'The day in Cascade Cove,' he said, 'I thought you were warning me off, so I left. Then I thought you might be sick so I told your mother.'

They swam for a few moments in silence, Ripple gliding in his slipstream. Gannets worked nearby, whooshing and splashing.

'You were right to tell my mother. She . . . helped me on that day.' (She'd almost said 'saved.')

'Were you warning me off?'

'No. I was trying to show you music, but that was how I first found that others cannot hear it; they hear only chaos.'

'What's music? Why can't I hear it?'

'Music is sound. Thoughtstreams are ideas not sounds. I searched for music all my life but it was only when you came that I found it at last. I wanted you to hear it first.'

He leapt over a wave and she followed. Then she moved forward to give him her slipstream.

'I wish I could hear the music as you do. I prefer to fight a hundred starving sharks than hear chaos from an intelligent mind, so it's good to know it's not chaotic to you.'

Cosmo was enjoying her lead style, the graceful almost flickering movements he'd seen in the surf, and the way her emerald skin glowed deeper underwater and flashed brilliantly in the sunlight.

The gannets finished hunting and moved away towards the west. White clouds drifted east sending patches of shade across the ocean.

'Will you return and work near the astronomy team again?'

'I'm happy to work alone.'

'I want you to come back.'

'I can't.'

'Will you be safe to work alone?'

'I'll be careful.'

'Ripple, will you promise me something? If ever you find a way to communicate your music, will you show it to me first, as you intended before?'

She tensed and there was a very long pause as she considered her reply.

He doesn't know what he's asking. Could I ever try again with him?

She stared at the ocean, seeking a guiding signal. Eastward, a blue whale surfaced and blew, its great back arching from the sea. The tail rose and Ripple saw the sunlight glinting from the waterfall that drained from the trailing edges of the vast flukes as they swept forward, then back and propelled it downwards, a harmony of power. She saw the spreading smoothness on the surface at the place where it had been and followed its magnificent descent. Her spirit calmed at the vision. Her muscles relaxed.

'I promise,' she whispered at last.

~~~

Ripple worked alone, away from the main school where she hoped her thoughtstreams would not bother anyone. A few days passed and she encountered no danger, so her confidence grew. She continued skipping lessons, except those that provided her with musical inspiration: poetry, history and home-based astronomy. One exception was gymnastics which she attended because she enjoyed sharing her dance moves with others.

They love my moves. If only they knew how much better it is when the music plays.

Ripple set many poems to music and created some herself. Others came from her favourite Azuran poets and some from distant worlds, including the Fragrant Planets.

~~~

Even though there are dozens in your own galaxy, you humans know nothing of the Fragrant Planets, where flowering plants have evolved beyond belief. But even in Ripple's day, the dolphins of Azure knew of the millions of whale-sized, long-lived flowers, all with intelligent minds, sharing and blending their essences and intellects to create perfumed poems powerful enough to heal epidemics, create wealth, and prevent wars. The flowers loaded their aromatic songs daily onto the winds for distribution throughout their worlds.

Ripple's music was like the perfume building inside the closed night-time flowers of the Fragrant Planets, but she could find no way to release her own gifts on the morning wind.

~~~

19
KNOWLEDGE LOST TO MEMORY

The seraphim were restless that day. They darted around, invading our auras and dragging at our aural wings in a most annoying manner.

~~~

Ripple followed the flight of a wandering albatross as it rode the steady easterly. She called and it cried back. It wheeled to see if she herded fish and then soared away.

This bird is alone like me. How suited he seems to his solitude. I long for such strength.

She felt the internal stirring which she now recognised as the impetus for the creation of new music. The bird evoked continuous soaring sounds, pure and strong, with a slow underlying wing-beat. Ripple concentrated, forgetting the ocean. She transformed a bird in the sky, into music she could carry with her everywhere. It was a song of searing loneliness but it imparted the bird's strength as solace to the lonely.

~~~

The seraphim gathered above the sea between Ripple and the bird. Deep beneath her we could see a shadow stirring; vast tentacles slowly coiling, flickering blue. Ripple, lost in albatross music, was unaware the shadow had detected her.

The Shadow Queen hung there, bag-like, hungry and calculating, red eyes staring upwards.

The seraphim radiated a frantic hysteria which the dolphin could never detect. Did they think they could warn her? Why did her fate bother them? They were never anxious seeing other creatures of Azure approaching violent death.

~~~

'What is that I see above us,' asked Erishkigal.

'It is a young female dolphin,' replied Vipa. 'The very one we were cheated of once before.'

'Quiet, you fool!' hissed Lashette. 'She will hear you. Do not even think too loud or she will be gone.'

'No,' said Malevine. 'She is unheeding; lusting for some bird in the sky. She does not notice us. But we must be stealthy if we are to provide our Queen with the meal she deserves.'

'So my daughters,' whispered Erishkigal. 'We shall rise as silently as poison moves through blood. Allow not the slightest vibration to disturb her reverie. I shall not exude one drop of ink lest she detect us by our delicate perfume. Veil your very thoughts, as Lashette has suggested. If we are patient I shall feed on warm flesh this day and all of us will be stronger for it.'

'My Queen,' whispered Vipa. 'Let me make the strike. I will not let you down.'

'You may, O Most Murderous of my deadly daughters. Keep your timing razor-sharp and be generous with your sweet venom.'

So the Shade Erishkigal, Nightmare of the Southern Seas, with her tentacles floating silently around her, stole upwards from the darkness towards her prey.

~~~

Again and again, the seraphim trailed their electric veils over Ripple's rostrum, her eyes, her dorsal fin, her flukes, but they could never reach her.

~~~

If she'd focused her mind downwards, Ripple would have easily detected Erishkigal and her minions rising, hairsbreadth by hairsbreadth, towards her. She would've caught the red glare skewering her in their sightline. She might even have seen the blue tips glowing, though they were fainter than phospho-slime.

But Ripple looked up.

Clouds, she thought, their thunder could add drama to my albatross. She played with thunder for a while but found it too dominating for the mood she was trying to express. She moved on to the hundreds of different sounds of wind interacting with water and worked with some that had suggestions of the land, hoping she might find one to suit the bird. On and on she worked, absorbed in the creation of music, oblivious to the danger.

Vipa's tip was closer now.

Fifteen metres . . . twelve . . .

Rain on rocks, thought Ripple, and held that sound in her head; then moved the falling rain from hard rock to wet seaweed, comparing and blending the sounds, trying them against the bird like a colour to see if it matched.

Ten metres . . . seven . . .

Ripple's mind focused on a single feather pressed on the wind, effecting a sweeping turn among the hissing spray against a backdrop of tumbling clouds.

~~~

In the space above the dolphin, the electric particles of the seraphim's bodies began quaking. The quaking gradually accelerated into a shivering vibration.

~~~

Four metres . . . three . . . Erishkigal almost had Ripple in her grasp. Digestive juices pumped into the cave behind the double row of dagger teeth where the monster anticipated ripping flesh. Vipa reached out towards the prey, her tip stretching like an evil finger delivering a curse. Venga and Lucifina followed her closely. Venom engorged the fangs creating a blue shimmer on the tips of each tentacle.

~~~

Sterne could barely bring herself to watch. Looking back on that moment, I sometimes wonder if she might have been tempted to make the grave error of interference if I had not passed my restraining wing within her aura. Ripple had uttered no prayer, had made no demand upon us; this was no time for divine intervention. The nearest thing to prayer I detected from that ocean came from the tentacles of the Shade but Sterne wasn't inclined to answer such 'prayers'.

~~~

The bird rested on pillows of wind, almost asleep. Ripple wondered what the sea would sound like coming up to it from below. The thought made her switch her own attention to the sounds of the surface.

Two metres . . . one metre...

~~~

The seraphim froze above the sea like a suspended iceberg.

~~~

'I will have you soon my darling . . . . I will take you now!' Erishkigal lunged. Vipa's tip, loaded with venom, slid backwards to gather force, then flicked forwards to strike at the target; Venga and Lucifina followed.

~~~

The seraphim scattered. They darted into the Hereafter and hid themselves among the most distant constellations of Koru. Sterne half-closed her evergreen eyes and groaned.

~~~

Shwsst! It was no louder than any other wave swishing by. The whipping sound was so faint Ripple almost missed it, but she heard it and erupted skywards on a lucky diagonal as Vipa, Venga and Lucifina lashed in, fangs extended, venom pumping.

Venga and Lucifina missed by hairsbreadths, but Vipa's tip made contact as Ripple descended from her upward leap, spinning madly. The tentacle touched Ripple's face and glanced off, one fang scratching her slightly leaving a film of poison-blue slime over the scratch. The sea washed it off as she re-entered the water.

As though attempting to stay out of the same ocean that held Erishkigal, Ripple departed flying-fish style. She was passing out from suffocation by the time she remembered to breathe. She looked back once only; to see two red orbs surrounded by a boiling mass of blue-flashing tentacles stabbing at sea and air. She didn't look back again, afraid the fiend was somehow following supernaturally at her flukes. But that glimpse showed her the one vengeful corner of the monster's brain still giving it satisfaction; Vipa knew she'd made a contact so Erishkigal believed they'd made a kill.

Ripple did not stop leaping and swimming until she'd returned to the school and the comfort of Pearl and Echo.

I'll never leave my mother's side again. If I live, I'll forget music and become an ordinary good dolphin.

Pearl and Echo were among a group feeding co-operatively on a vast sphere of anchovies.

'The Shade has touched me!'

The dolphins stopped feeding. The anchovies escaped. Suddenly the world went dark, sounds drifted into the distance and the pain came. Pain as though the sea around began to boil. She cried out, ceased breathing and writhed, longing for the coldness of the deep. She tried to dive down but Pearl prevented her.

'Call Nimbus!' cried Pearl.

Ripple could feel them stimulating her to breathe. She felt Echo tracing the scratch on her skin on the left side of her rostrum where it joined her cheek.

'It's inflamed,' said Echo, 'and the skin is peeling.'

Ripple had been touched by the Shade; nobody in living memory had survived any brush with that monster. Nimbus arrived, looked at the suppurating scratch and immediately sent helpers to collect special seaweeds. Rev was among those on the medication mission and was the first to return with long green streamers trailing from his mouth. He passed them to a dolphin standing by and gave one to Nimbus. She crushed it in her teeth to release chemicals then draped it over the wound while Pearl supported Ripple. Echo pressed the weed gently against the wound with her rostrum to encourage the release of the cooling chemicals.

Pearl, Nimbus, Echo and others, applied the herbs to soothe the scratch. They worked in shifts, keeping Ripple at the surface, stimulating her to breathe, but she remained semi-conscious. She took no food and faded with dehydration.

The pain continued, coming in waves as though all the fluid in and around her kept heating up, then slowly cooling. At first the intervals between each wave was long – several minutes of coolness – until the next wave sent her spiralling into torment. At the pinnacle of each wave she writhed and cried out. The pain waves lengthened and the intervals between them shortened. Ripple was tiring.

Nimbus read Ripple's pain. Never, in all her years of tending sick and injured dolphins, had she seen such pain.

~~~

We deities heard Pearl praying that every particle of poison and every shred of pain could pass from her daughter's body to her own.

'She cannot really want that pain! Why does she pray for it?'

'It is a negative prayer surely? You could ignore it.'

'No. It is mother love. Nothing could be more positive. She has spread much light during her life on Azure; perhaps her spirit deserves release.'

'Not yet. Not yet. The time is not right.'

~~~

In a moment of clarity, Ripple felt vibrations of escalating fear from Pearl, Echo and Nimbus. They think I'm dying she thought. Perhaps I am. The clarity faded as the fluids boiled within her again, blurring everything around her, voices calling, fading, drifting in and out of focus, bodies coming, going, actions, orders, desperation, while the heat continued.

Then came the heat that did not fade, searing beyond boiling; a wave of intensifying colour, white, yellow, orange, to a red which darkened to the colour of the throat of the megalodon where stars the size of a thousand suns consumed her to blackness.

And she was dragged up through the dark, up away from her home on the sea, looking down at the ring of dolphins far below, surrounding her dead body.

'Breathe Ripple,' she heard them from afar, 'breathe . . .'

~~~

But she left them behind, left herself behind and stumbled out alone into our divine presence. Sister Sterne reached out and captured the scattered ellipse of Ripple's spirit as it spun towards us. She cradled it, soothed it, unified it. I watched a disappointed Sister Sterne regarding the little spirit.

'She has failed again,' I said.

'She hardly had much chance; she was barely full grown. She at least achieved a partial success. She believed she had found what she was looking for.'

'What use was that if she never communicated it? It has not helped the universe one jot. But no more lives, Sister Sterne. She is completely spent.'

'Are you sure she has finished this one?'

'Her body on Azure is no longer breathing. Her heart has stopped. She is dead! Her sentence is over. Her spirit is here with us. It is like a worn-out rag.'

'I disagree, Father. Her spirit light is very different from when last it rested here within my aural wing.'

'You must not re-sentence her; not to Azure, nor any other world. This time I insist she be granted however many aeons of rest she needs for complete recovery.'

'Shall we ask her?' said Sterne. 'To be sure that is what she wants.'

'I will ask her myself. She will beg for rest. She has begged before and you have always ignored her. We will give her what she asks this time.'

'I will do as you say.'

'Ripple,' I said, 'If you wish to be released from pain we will release you. You need no longer struggle with your music. We will find you a place where you may rest long, in coolness, peace, and beauty, surrounded by love. Is this what you want my dear?'

'I want to go back.'

Sterne responded. 'Are you aware of the pain still to be endured back there?'

'I am.'

'Your struggle will continue. It is far from over.'

'I know.'

'You have lived many lives since you last wished to return to any of them, little one,' I interrupted, 'even when there was no pain awaiting you there.'

'This time, I want to go back.'

'Sterne, I am astounded! She truly deserves to succeed.'

'Well, Father? Do we still agree to give her what she asks?'

'She has chosen Sister. She has a will of iron. Send her back, poor spirit, though it is hard to see her suffer.'

Ripple screamed in agony as she descended to the ocean into the heart of her fire once more.

'Her spirit, it seems, will survive anything,' Sterne said, 'but I must provide powerful medicine to help her physical body through this ordeal.'

'Your compassion is blossoming at least,' I replied, 'I will be interested to see how you manage it.'

I continued watching, as Sterne's revolutionary work with her Azuran charge continued.

~~~

Squelch's alien mind worked overtime as he watched the dolphins desperately trying to save Ripple. He floated star-like, with only a few suckers of one tentacle attaching him to Rev's dorsal fin.

'I saw her heart beat.' cried Echo.

'There it goes again,' said Nimbus. 'Incredible!'

'Thank the stars and the planets and every atom in the universe,' said Pearl. 'I thought she was dead.'

'But she might die any moment,' said Nimbus, 'She can't continue like this. The heartbeat is very faint.'

Squelch knew there was nothing his clever tentacles could do for Ripple, but was there perhaps some vital piece of information in his five-day memory that might help? He trawled through every cell in his limited supply, searching for some fragment that could be of use.

Suddenly his eyes lit up. 'I have an idea,' he said to Rev, 'I don't know what made me think of it. Take me to Nimbus.'

The pair approached Nimbus and Squelch communicated his idea to her. Nimbus listened intently, then questioned the octopus briefly. Echo listened.

'Then go!' said Nimbus abruptly. 'Go now! She must have it immediately. I don't think she's dead after all, but she can't last the hour.'

Squelch now firmly attached himself to Rev who carried him away in haste.

The dolphins around Ripple waited.

'But Nimbus, will it work?' Ripple heard her sister ask. 'This could poison her even worse.'

'It could. But it might work. She'll die anyway if we don't try something. We have only this one chance. The octopus has an effective brain and he's sure of himself.'

Ripple endured wave after wave of fire as the minutes crawled.

Breathe Ripple . . .

Beat heart . . . beat heart . . . beat . . . beat . . . beat . . .

Another burst of activity – someone arriving. She heard Nimbus and her brother Rev.

'Have you brought it?'

'It's here.'

'Why were you so long?'

'These creatures are rare. Squelch had trouble finding it.'

Pearl and Echo balanced Ripple with her head above the surface. Nimbus was close by, bearing some glowing living thing that swirled on her body and pulsed with paua-coloured iridescence. Soft tentacles caressed her; a living tube entered her mouth. Honey trickled down her throat. She'd never tasted anything like it, but it reminded her of The Shade, The Shade in reverse, bright for dark, kind for cruel, cool for fiery . . . and she slipped into a coma.

Breathe Ripple . . .

Beat heart . . . beat heart . . . beat . . . beat . . . beat . . .

The coma alone would have killed her by asphyxiation if it weren't for the minds of the surrounding dolphins stimulating her to breathe.

~~~

'Sister Sterne, you are beginning to impress me after all; that was beautifully managed. She is cooling already.'

'It was nothing. All her Azuran friends requested it. I only answered their prayers in the most obvious way. Knowledge lost to memory is sometimes redeemable, even in a five-day octopus.'

20
MIDDLE OF THE SCHOOL

The waves of heat were shorter now and less intense. Ripple drifted towards wakefulness and felt the presence of her father. The strength of her parents pressed mental ice against every overheated blood cell in her body.

Rigel and Pearl battled within her mind, moderating the pain. The medicine from the phosphorescent octopus worked in her blood to counteract the poison. That indomitable spark burning through the light of Ripple's own soul fought the spiritual battle. Ripple could at any moment have escaped into the cool of the Hereafter but her spirit remained resolutely in her body, fighting the inferno. Another thread of strength helped to weave the healing spell; he was coloured midnight blue. She sensed his nearness.

~~~

'She could still die any moment from dehydration,' called Nimbus. 'Bring food.'

A call went out. 'Bring food for Ripple! Small squid to start with.'

It was daytime, when squid swam deep, but dolphins brought them at Nimbus's call.

She felt a tiny one in her mouth and swallowed it. Some minutes passed. Another squid arrived, her favourite food, the lemonade of the sea. Good fluids began circulating in her blood, diluting the poison. Squid kept arriving as though by magic in her mouth but Nimbus carefully controlled the intake. The cool intervals between the pain spells grew longer.

Nimbus requested other fish and larger squid. Cosmo and Rush hunted hardest for Ripple. Nimbus found she could rely on these two alone to bring enough food for Ripple and her carers.

'I don't think there's much practical astronomy going on right now,' thought Echo. 'I wonder why those two are so attentive.'

Soon Ripple was turning the fish in her mouth for herself.

My strength is returning, she thought. The poison is retreating.

Nimbus studied Ripple's internal organs by ultra-sound, observing the signs of dehydration fading.

'She's healing,' she announced to Pearl. 'But there's organ damage. It will repair itself slowly but she'll be weak for a long time.'

'Will Ripple always carry the terrible scar on her face?' asked Echo.

'The scar on her skin will fade to a thread but see how the welt has penetrated to strike its mark on the skull? The bone-scar will outlive her. Echo you've been a great help. Continue nursing your sister. Bring her back to health. If you succeed I'll be happy to teach you my vocation.'

'I'll make her so strong she's invincible!' Echo squeaked.

Her tone caused Pearl to glance away from Ripple for the first time in days to regard her middle daughter closely. Pearl recalled Echo's concentrated strength working with herself and Nimbus through these dark days. She felt a glow of pride and knew that Echo had found her vocation at last.

~~~

As soon as Ripple was well enough, Echo asked her how the attack happened.

'I was working, not thinking of the sea around me. I can stay safe when I'm just playing my music, but this has proved I'm not so safe when I am creating it.'

'And why weren't you in the care of the minders as Delph arranged?'

'The boys never really wanted me there. One day they teased me so I stopped working with them. Cosmo told me he wouldn't let it happen again, but still I didn't feel right about going back among them.'

'Must you do this "work" Ripple?'

'Right now I can't imagine ever making music again.'

'Two boys in the astro-team seemed to take some responsibility for what happened to you.'

'Who?'

'Cosmo and that beautiful jade-green one called Rush.'

'Rush is beautiful?'

'I think so.'

'Echo!'

'But I'm not impressed by the rest of the astro-team. I might have a few words with them.'

~~~

Ripple no longer needed full time care but she swam close by her mother and sister and if neither was near, she swam among the crowd to avoid the solitude where nightmares slithered up out of the abyss. She wouldn't dive for food because of the darkness in the deep, so Echo and Pearl fed her at times. At night the dark was everywhere and she could not escape it.

Azure is savage. The Shade is not the only danger. The blackfin hunts the lonely too. The tiger shark, the tail-biter, the megalodon and his ilk, all think of me as a mid-morning snack. Now I'm so nearly well, I don't want to die.

She tried to bring her music back but her inner world had fallen silent. She listened to the continual chatter of the school and the thoughtstreams of the others sent their comforting noise through her brain. All was friendly, safe, even stimulating sometimes, so she didn't miss music too much.

'Why did I ever bother myself about it? I must seek out a 'normal' vocation. I'll see less of Echo now that she's found her calling. I'll be so lonely without her! I must go back to school, and find a new direction.'

She looked out at the world hoping for a bright new future to unveil itself. There was only rain, seeping from a grey sky onto a leaden sea. Even when she closed her eyes the greyness remained. Pearl arrived at her side. The rain shone suddenly silver, as though a light shone from her that lit up the sea.

As Ripple's strength returned, she began attending normal classes, but more regularly than before. Pearl was pleased at this change. Ripple was quickly star of the gymnastics class again and enjoying the admiration she received for her skill. Soon all her classmates were copying her as before. Ripple gradually learned to dive for her food again, as long as she had friends beside her so that she didn't have to face the deep alone.

Pearl was tired after Ripple's illness. Her appetite waned and she wasted a little. She asked Echo to look at her organs and Echo noticed some discoloration on her liver.

'You must rest mother,' said Echo. 'I'll ask Nimbus what weeds might help. Let Rev hunt for you. He'll love any excuse to do extra.'

~~~

Ripple worked hard to catch up on all she'd missed throughout her illness and previous negligence of her studies. Maths was the biggest difficulty. She'd missed so much, the class had outstripped her. She made some effort but only because she knew how much Pearl wanted her to do her best.

Whenever she hunted, she took food to her mother who was still unwell. Rev was feeding her also; Pearl's anxious offspring cosseted her. Nimbus checked Pearl carefully and sent Rev to collect weeds that grew on the rocks near the islands. Echo fed these to her mother over a few days, insisting that Pearl chew them and suck their juices, though dolphins' teeth are not suited to such food. Pearl soon announced she felt much better. Echo was pleased to observe the liver stain had almost vanished.

'Great remedy!' she thought.

~~~

Once Ripple and Pearl had both recovered, Echo threw herself into her new work with Nimbus. The sisters saw less of one another, as Ripple had foreseen. However, Echo made time to pay a visit to the boys of the astronomy class. They'd just returned from a short interplanetary journey and were about to begin hunting.

'Hey, look who's coming,' said Flip.

'It's Ripple's good-looking big sister,' said Rush. 'Wouldn't mind her in the astronomy class.'

Cosmo looked up. 'I think I can guess her errand.'

Echo arrived in a graceful swoop, scattering swathes of spray.

'How's Ripple doing?' Cosmo asked.

'Fully healed, thank-you.'

Cosmo checked his team to ensure no one was considering a swift departure.

'I came to tell you that Ripple was attacked by Erishkigal because she was working alone and unguarded. You'd teased her so she no longer wished to work near you. There was good reason that Delph allowed her to make use of your minders.'

'I thought that might be how it happened,' said Cosmo. 'I tried to persuade her to work with us again.'

'At least you tried to undo the harm done, Cosmo, before it was too late. And you, Rush, helped those who worked to save her after the attack. You other three still need to admit your part in what happened. Or did you choose to ignore it?'

There was a mumble of apology from Flip, Givan and Quin. Flip's shame impelled him to close his eyes and dive deep.

Echo swam away leaving them subdued, but she was satisfied they acknowledged their contribution to the disaster that had almost killed Ripple.

Suddenly Rush left the group and raced after her. He pulled up alongside and a little in front, giving her his slipstream.

'Echo I knew it was a mistake when we teased her that day. Cosmo did too. We're all happy to have her with us again, but if there's anything else we can do to help, just let me know.'

'Ripple and I would be happy to hunt with you and Cosmo any time.'

'I'd enjoy that Echo, and not just because of Ripple. The whole school is talking about the fantastic job you did of caring for your sister.'

'She's my sister! What else could I do?'

'You wouldn't leave her, not even to find food.'

Echo laughed and leapt skywards, 'Lucky for me we had you and Cosmo on hunting detail. We'd more food arriving than Ripple alone could ever have eaten. Perhaps you helped to save my life as well as hers.'

'I'm glad,' said Rush. 'See the birds working ahead? Shall we hunt there now . . . together?'

'Looks like good kahawai. Let's go.'

~~~

Cosmo and the others waited for Rush to return.

Flip surfaced at last.

'Where's Rush?' he asked.

'Can't you guess?' said Givan.

'He could do a lot worse!' said Cosmo.

'That's 'cos you fancy her psycho sister.'

'And who do you fancy Givan?' asked Cosmo.

'Happy with whichever piece is closest when required.'
They set off to hunt but without their usual playfulness and the catch lacked its flavour that day.

~~~

Ripple was where she most liked to swim at that time, smack-bang in the middle of the main school. White clouds towering on a blue sky beguiled her, stimulating old memories. For the first time since her illness, a song awoke within her; a cloud-song. An elderly couple overheard her thought-streams.

'Whatever's that distortion?' said the old female to her husband.

'It's her chaos.'

'How can she hunt, eat, and communicate, with such turmoil?'

'I've heard she calls it music.'

'That must just be her name for chaos!'

'They do say she's mad.'

'But look at her. She's swimming like the windblown spray! Do you remember that poor dolphin who was born deranged? He moved with the grace of a tail-less seal.'

'I remember. In the end he was taken by a blackfin who mistook him for just that. I can't imagine a predator mistaking this girl for an injured creature.'

'I've heard she suffers ridicule from the thoughtless ones among us.'

'Teasing is easy to deliver, but never easy to receive.'

'The way she's swimming now reminds me of cloud formations. Her mind is a mystery but her movements make me wonder if perhaps she should be protected from ridicule.'

Ripple came back to herself with a jolt.

'My music is back!' She tasted the sweet tang of the breeze, heard the rush of foam, saw Azure's colours intensify and felt the ocean stroking her skin like a lover.

'I'm very sorry!' she said to the elderly couple who looked shocked.

'That's alright dear! We don't understand but we don't mind.'

'All the same,' she thought, 'I can't be unsettling others like this.'

~~~

21
VIA THE BLACKFIN

Rigel swooped in to super-charge his offspring. He found the three youngest on full action-alert, with only Aroha remaining calm, as stately in her movements as her mother.

Rigel prodded Ripple in the side with his beak, behind her flipper. She giggled. He insisted the family swim together with Ripple leading, so his youngest could show him how her paces had returned. Then he let Rev and Echo take turns in front. They finished with a family romp with all three younger ones trying to outdo one another and their father in displays of high-flying exuberance.

Rigel was keen to become acquainted with Squelch, the famous octopus who'd saved his daughter's life. Rev led them to Squelch's cave. He let the octopus ride on everyone in turn. Afterwards, the family swam south to a shoal area rich with food, where they hunted and played together for days. Rigel told them of his travels in the universe and his many strange encounters there.

He took the opportunity to swim alone with Ripple.

'You're very good at keeping your mind veiled, my dear,' he said. 'If I didn't know better, I'd think you were no more than an empty-headed frothy.'

Ripple did not reply, so he continued.

'Pearl has spoken to me of this music of yours. Is that what you hide?'

Ripple leapt and dived and he entered her slipstream, finding her moves original and satisfying to follow.

'Music felt like the focus of my life,' Ripple said. 'But I've decided to look for some other vocation, because music cannot be communicated and it led to my brush with the Shade.'

'Show me this music.'

'You'll see only chaos.'

'I'm expecting that. It won't bother me.'

He watched as she relaxed her mental barriers to reveal a rich intellect flowering behind them.

'I'll play you a song about the constellation containing the star you're named after.'

During her performance, he kept his reactions to himself.

'I see why your mother's worried,' he said, when she'd finished. 'But you say it's not chaos to you? So what is it like?'

'It can be sad, happy, or majestic, but always beautiful. It makes me want to leap and move. There's no chaos. How might I make others hear it as I do?'

Rigel considered this. Father and daughter continued swimming, with Ripple choosing the moves and Rigel in her slipstream. Suddenly he seized the lead and his powerful wash dragged her along. He laughed when he heard her wondering if even death could stop such progress, but he swam on, considering everything he knew of his daughter.

'You must continue with this task alone,' he said, 'since there are none to teach you. You must not give up but you must study widely in case you find the key to communicating your work within one of the other disciplines. Mathematics is vital to many tasks. Could it hold the key to your problem?'

'I detest mathematics!'

'Why?'

'Calculations are boring. Numbers have no emotion. My work is all about emotion and sound. How could mathematics have anything to do with it?'

'My work is all about mind power,' Rigel countered. 'How could physical fitness have anything to do with it? The body plays little part in our journeys. We leave them behind like unwanted luggage. But only the dolphins with the strongest and fittest bodies ever make it to their first mission beyond Azure. There may be some field of expertise, as vital to music as physical fitness is to astronomy, and as seemingly unrelated.'

'But how shall I recognise it?' she asked, diving beside him under one of the short steep waves driven by the fresh westerly.

'Learn, learn, and learn, until the answer comes. Mathematics is a good starting point. Give Axis your full attention in future.'

He let his lead evaporate and she lost her rhythm, but recovered in a heartbeat. He followed in perfect synchrony, pleased to observe how smoothly she accepted the lead he'd offered.

~~~

Ripple took her father's advice. She studied widely, struggling at first in some subjects, particularly mathematics. He'd advised her to continue her music. She did want to of course but thought it unfair on other dolphins in the main school. Working alone had proven too dangerous; besides, her mother forbade her from ever working alone again.

There was one alternative; she could go back to work in Delph's astronomy class. Cosmo had promised to protect her from teasing. She'd heard the boys were already journeying beyond the solar system.

They're all so famous now; they won't want me hanging around them smirching their glory.

Echo had passed on the apologies of the boys. Even Givan sent her a sincere message. Still she couldn't bring herself to turn up to class as though nothing had happened.

~~~

Ripple was setting off to hunt when she saw Cosmo, Echo and Rush approaching. She swam to meet them. The girls performed a unique dual whirly-spin of their own invention.

'Your Shade-scar has almost gone,' said Cosmo.

'You're the only dolphin with a Shade scar!' said Rush, examining the now thread-like scar, 'but I can hardly see it.'

'Who's hungry? Let's eat!' said Echo and they shot away to find the nearest shoal of fish.

The next two hours were a blur of sunshine, food and laughter.

Then Cosmo asked, 'Ripple are you working with your music again?'

'Yes, my songs are coming back to me. I'm even upsetting elderly dolphins in the main school with them.'

'Time you got back to astronomy class then. Can you come tomorrow?'

'Are you sure the others won't mind?'

'Even Givan's fine with it. You should've seen his expression when I told him who your father was.'

'Well then. I'll be there.'

Before Cosmo left he said, 'Can we hunt together after class tomorrow?'

She laughed. 'I'll look forward to it.'

The four performed a few last spiral skyjumps in formation and then the boys headed away.

Echo turned to her sister. 'I'm sure he likes you, Ripple. They're all saying he's the best young astronomer the school's produced for years. Do you like him?'

'I love him, but he fears my music. Do you like Rush?'

'More than internal organs, blood circulation and skeletons.'

'So we're both in love.'

Ripple returned to the astronomy class and began working at her music. The minders were pleased to see her and the boys polite and even welcoming.

~~~

But the orbit of Azure had passed the point where her tilt kept her southern oceans closer to the sun. The dolphins felt Sol's rays weakening in strength. The days shortened, dark clouds gathered and cold currents swirled up from the south.

'The weather adepts,' announced Delph to his students, 'are already predicting a hard winter. I doubt that classes will continue much longer.'

One grey autumn dawn a call went out for the school to assemble. Dolphins arrived, hailing old friends and catching up with the scuttlebutt. The concentration of dolphins in the area of the main school increased throughout the morning until there were thousands circulating there. It was the first full assembly Ripple had witnessed and the crowd amazed her. She arrived with Cosmo, Rush and Echo and they joined Pearl, who'd come in with her old friends Breeze and Nimbus.

Ripple saw her father cruise in with the senior astronomy team. She noticed the respectful glances and gestures he received from dolphins as he passed. Rigel spotted them and changed his course to bestow caresses on Pearl and his daughters. Ripple and Echo bounced excitedly at receiving his attention.

Ripple saw Cosmo watching Rigel's every move as the astronomy team took up a position in the crowd nearby.

By mid-day the assembly was ready. An elder called for order. Ripple noticed Aroha's mate Matangi among the elders and wondered why he was there.

The elder used a wide-range thoughtstream to reach the entire crowd.

'This assembly has been called on advice from the weather adepts.'

A buzz of curiosity spread through the school. Weather adepts had not called in the school in the lifetimes of the oldest dolphins there. But to Ripple it explained Matangi's presence among the elders, weather being his vocation.

The elder continued. 'They have asked us to inform you that we're soon to enter a hard winter. The first of many brutal fronts will sweep in from the west and will continue through the darker months bringing frequent gales. Thicker cloud cover will bring heavy rains and allow less heat and light through. The sea will be colder than we've known it. Food supplies will diminish. Predators will be hungry and unpredictable.'

A hush fell on the crowd. Ripple felt Echo's flipper brush against her and she returned her sister's caress. Dolphins comforted one another throughout the crowd. Older dolphins looked towards the sky in resignation as though they saw their fate written on the clouds.

Ripple, Cosmo, Echo and Rush bunched themselves so closely they could detect the warmth of each other's bodies even through the cold water. Cosmo stroked Ripple as Echo had done. His touch calmed her.

'We recommend the school disbands,' the elder said. 'There's no hurry; the first severe fronts are still fourteen or fifteen days away. But after that we can't stay and compete for food in the same area. Families and social groups should stick together, hunt far and wide as necessary and re-group here again in the spring. Until then we recommend that all classes and organised activities be cancelled.'

Ripple overheard Rigel speaking to his team.

'It's fortunate we still have some time,' he said. 'Enough to forewarn our contacts in Tectarius of our absence over coming months.'

The dolphins were in no hurry to disperse after the assembly, appreciating the camaraderie of the main school now they knew it would soon vanish.

Many felt the need to reach out to old friends and make contact again before the coming weeks of darkness.

Twelve days later the weather closed in. Thick cloud hung above like a roof of grey mud, blocking the sun and deepening the chill of the sea. Food thinned. Dolphins gathered their families and the school began to disperse.

~~~

Late on the twelfth afternoon after the gathering, Pearl realised that her illness had returned. This time she hid it carefully, but she felt a rapid deterioration of her body as though she'd swallowed a poison. Could she have eaten a fish which had in turn eaten something dangerous? She tried to disguise the illness by swimming energetically but within a day or two she knew she could no longer pretend. She did not ask Echo to look at it this time but went direct to Nimbus who carefully examined her inner organs and circulation. Nimbus confirmed Pearl's suspicions that the old liver stain had returned and spread. She also told Pearl that poisons in the liver were now leaking through her blood. It was a rare but swift-acting illness for which there was no cure. Pearl was not surprised since by this time she was having difficulty moving; even breathing had become an effort. Nimbus called Breeze, who arrived within moments. Alone with these two, Pearl was relieved to finally abandon all efforts to disguise her condition.

The three older females cruised away together slowly, Nimbus and Breeze supporting their old friend. Many private messages passed between them.

Later that evening Nimbus and Breeze returned without Pearl as a series of vicious southerly squalls swept freezing rain across the ocean heralding the beginning of a winter which was to prove more terrible than any in living memory. Pearl was never seen again on the oceans of Azure in that life nor in any subsequent ones.

Even in dying, Pearl, out of compassion for a hungry young blackfin, intentionally gave it one less reason to deprive a vulnerable baby dolphin of a joyful life dancing across the oceans of Azure.

~~~

22
DARK WINTER

Nimbus and Breeze arrived as Rigel was concluding a final meeting with his astronomy team, before they returned to their families for the winter.

'We'd like to speak to Rigel alone,' said Nimbus. All but Rigel disappeared in seconds. Nimbus felt Rigel delving their minds; piecing things together.

'It's Pearl,' he said. 'What's happened?'

'She's gone from Azure. We were with her. Your children don't know yet.'

It was as though the fluke of a whale had struck Rigel. He withered before their eyes. Nimbus hadn't been aware Pearl meant so much to him. Like others in the school she'd allowed the characteristic physical separateness of this couple to cause her to misjudge the depth of their attachment.

'What took her?' he asked finally.

'She chose the predator herself – a young blackfin.'

'She chose? Why?'

'An affliction of the liver. There was no hope. She wanted her children to witness neither her death nor her decline. We supported her in her choice.'

'Pearl asked that you watch over the children,' said Breeze, 'at least for the winter. She was most concerned for Ripple. But she also asked you to be near Aroha at the time of the birth of her baby in the spring. I'm to assist with the birth. Pearl wanted you to pass on her love to all the children and to tell them she was ready to move on.'

There had been other females in Rigel's life besides Pearl, but she was the only one who'd been truly part of him. His body was as skilled and strong as ever, his intellect as sharp, but a driving force within him was extinguished just as winter took its grip. Rigel joined with his three youngest offspring and the girls' new male friends. For Echo, Rev and Ripple it helped to have their father near now that Pearl had gone, and Rigel took comfort from their presence. Only Aroha was not among them since she chose to remain with Matangi and his group.

Winter roared in under a blanket of mud-like cloud which shut out sun and stars and released storm after storm. Thousands of dolphins scattered themselves in small groups across a vast area of ocean surrounding the Northern Islands. Food was short and predators hunted voraciously, preventing many dolphins who'd played in the main school that summer from returning to it the following spring.

~~~

Where's Mother, thought Ripple? Is she on the other side of this enormous wave? Yes, surely I can hear her. I should see her any moment. But the troughs are so dark, I can't find her. She's always beside me if I'm frightened in the dark. Mother! Mother!

She searched from the mountainous crests to the blackest troughs of every wave, but though she heard Pearl's voice murmuring all around, her mother did not appear.

My father is here, and Echo and Rev. I can feel the touch of their flippers. Pain billows around them like the evil ink of Erishkigal. Why do they feel pain? They must know where Mother is. Why don't they bring her to me?

Is it true what they say? Is Mother dead? Is it because of my music? If the Shade had never touched me, would Mother still be alive? How much more harm will come upon us because of my music? I must never make music again. Mother can never understand it now anyway. I wanted her to hear my music. Instead it has killed her. I have killed her!'

'Ripple! Stop that!' said Rigel. 'Your mother's death was not your doing.'

'Father's right,' said Echo, 'You can't think that way. It will destroy you.'

'How can I be sure she didn't die because of me?'

'Nimbus couldn't have hidden such an idea from me!' Rigel said.

Ripple tried hard not to think that way but the vibration of the thought had sunk deep within her where it worked its poison. She expelled the thoughts from the surface of her mind and replaced them with other thoughts of her mother.

I remember the day when Mother found me in the abyss. She drew me back to the sunlight. Though she had no idea what music was, she said, 'Your music will resonate through my future.' But now she has no future.

Ripple remembered how the idea had chilled her. Now it was a faint source of elusive hope, but try as she might she couldn't work out why.

Cosmo was beside her all the time now but Ripple hardly knew he was there; they all seemed so distant in the darkness. She felt the touch of their flippers and their comfort wafting around her like a warm current, but the freezing seas reached through and chilled her.

Cosmo brought fish for her. Sometimes he gave it to her with his own mouth. Sometimes he gave it to Echo to feed her.

'As if I can't catch it for myself!' she thought. 'If I felt like hunting or eating!'

~~~

Rigel noticed how Echo buried her own sorrows to nurse the shattered family. He saw her giving food when they needed it even when she needed it herself. He saw her organising Rush and Cosmo to hunt for those who couldn't face hunting and he hunted with them though she didn't ask him to. It seemed Pearl lived on in the shape of this daughter. He made sure he found food for Echo if he thought she'd sacrificed too much.

Even if the weather had cleared and his astronomy team had called him away to the stars, he wouldn't have left his family now to answer that call.

Rigel chose a moment when his three children swam close together and Rush was off hunting. He steered Cosmo away to speak privately without losing sight of the group.

'How do you feel about the chaos Ripple carries in her mind?'

'It frightens me. But I haven't noticed it for a long time. Perhaps she's healed.'

'Healed?' Rigel was silent for a time. 'Think back to a time when you remember hearing my daughter's chaos. Picture her as she was then in your mind. Share that picture with me.'

Cosmo pictured Ripple as he'd seen her in the summer, capering oblivious to her surroundings, with chaos pouring from her mind.

When Rigel was satisfied with the picture Cosmo had sent him, he allowed them to return closer to the others.

'Compare her then with what she is now,' said Rigel.

They observed Ripple who was swimming between Rev and Echo. She moved in an undeviating rhythm, communicating with no-one; her mind distant, her spirit cold. While they watched, Rush arrived with a small fish which he gave to Echo. Echo gave it to Ripple who declined to eat it at first though Echo eventually coerced her. She ate as though it tasted like sand.

'Well?' said Rigel.

'She grieves,' said Cosmo. 'She's not herself.'

'She's hardly healed,' said Rigel.

Cosmo looked towards her but though she was close, all sight of her was suddenly obliterated by a howling squall. He wanted only to return beside her. Still Rigel prevented him.

'Your own teacher, my old friend Delph, has told me that you're an astronomer of great promise. Astronomy is a vocation, which can utterly absorb you, yet I'd renounce astronomy forever if it would bring Pearl back for one minute.'

Cosmo was silent for a long time while the wind-driven foam hissed around them.

'I take your warning,' said Cosmo at last. 'But I hope one day to emulate my own father who put my mother before himself to the last moment of his life. When they died, I was so young I had few memories of them. An older dolphin gave me all her own memories of my parents. It's in my power to do something similar for you.'

Rigel received a vivid memory from Cosmo showing Pearl and her children all together, as he'd seen them on the first day he had entered the

Northern School. Rigel saw Rev's apparent disease, resolving into a passenger octopus and Ripple's welcoming leap against the sunset. He saw Pearl's health, her grace and beauty, the warmth and fulfilment of her motherhood, and how happy she'd been that day to have all their own children around her.

'This is a gift beyond all expectation,' he said.

The two swam in silence until they saw Rush setting off again to hunt and went to help him. Rev joined them and the four males swam deep and hunted long, expending much energy, eventually providing a meagre meal for them all. Echo tried and failed to feed Cosmo's first offering to Ripple, who insisted she was not hungry. In the end Echo ate it herself, which pleased Rush.

All that night the squalls continued. The six stayed close. Dawn came at last, with no glimpse of the sun, just a brief grey day during which they fed on the little they managed to find. There followed a dreary succession of long violent nights, dismal dawns, and cold hungry days.

During that time, Cosmo found many chances to make use of his fighting skills defending them against predators. The others there learned much from him, even Rigel.

~~~

Many weeks later, on a howling black morning when vicious sou-westerly squalls lashed the sea as they seemed to have done forever, Rigel led the group of six beside an underwater cliff face. Rev recognised the spot.

'Squelch's hole is just over there,' he said and hurried towards it. Rigel sensed his son's spirit lifting at the thought of reunion with his old friend. But as Rigel had expected, the hole was empty. Squelch's natural term of life had run out months ago. Rigel recognised that for all his children, the discovery of the passing of Squelch was the darkest moment since the death of their mother. Their world for now was as black and empty as that hole in the rock, and all laughter a thing of the past.

'Will this winter ever end?' he wondered to Cosmo and Rush, but at that moment the mouth of a low-slung cloudbank opened, vomiting horizontal rain and gale force winds across the sea. The worst storm of the winter had begun.

~~~

As Rigel wondered if the winter would ever end, two hours away to the north-east Matangi announced that it very soon would. Aroha had continued all winter in the care of Matangi's family. The loss of Pearl had taken away her desire to hunt or eat; partly because of her condition. Her health had deteriorated and there was concern for the health of the baby she carried. Matangi and his strong family had nursed her, bringing food to her, though like the males in Rigel's team, they'd often been hungry themselves. They had also guarded Breeze, keeping her from harm and minimising her hunger, grateful for Aroha's sake that Breeze had wintered with them.

Aroha understood that if her baby lived, it would never meet the most beautiful grandmother it could have known. Surely presenting Pearl with a grandchild was the main reason for having a baby in the first place. So what point was there now? She was angry with Pearl for breaking her promise to help with the birth. But it was Pearl herself, living on in Aroha's own memory and imagination, who helped in the end. She urged her firstborn daughter to remember the stars in the clear summer skies, the birds soaring in warm ocean breezes, the surf thundering towards the shore, to encourage the life within. As the time approached, Aroha noticed a lightening of heart and a kindling of anticipation.

When Matangi announced the coming of spring, Aroha suddenly thought of her sisters. Her longing to see them grew as the storm faded.

~~~

23
SPARKLE OF ENERGY

The height of the waves diminished and their speed decreased; rare fingers of sunlight touched the queasy sea. Rigel's group was still near Squelch's old hole, feeding on reef fish which seemed more plentiful. Other dolphins appeared from various directions as the main school began to re-group.

A long-distance thoughtstream arrived in Ripple's brain. She glanced at Echo and saw that she'd received it too. It was from Aroha.

'Echo, it's the baby!' said Ripple. 'Where's mother? Oh, we must help Aroha ourselves.'

'Aroha, we're coming,' streamed Echo.

The girls reported Aroha's message to the males and all six set off at full speed to the north-east.

'You might be of some help to her, Echo,' said Ripple as they swam. 'But what use will I be? She needs an aunty like Breeze. What if Breeze didn't survive the winter?'

Echo messaged Aroha. 'Who is with you?'

'Breeze is here,' came sifting back to them. Ripple calmed.

They arrived at Aroha's side two hours later.

'You've changed, Echo,' said Aroha. 'You remind me of Mother.'

'You're to be the mother now,' said Echo.

Aroha is thin, thought Ripple. Her eyes are dull and she's lost her vigour like all of us.

Breeze was coaching the baby.

'Does it know what to do?' asked Echo.

'I'm confident she understands,' said Breeze.

She, thought Ripple.

'Not long now,' said Breeze, 'Guard please? We need vigilance.'

The four males from Rigel's group joined Matangi's family and all dispersed on predator patrol.

The warning note in Breeze's voice reminded them all that the first drop of birth blood would bring every winter-starved shark for miles.

We're lucky to have Cosmo's skills today, thought Ripple. I hope he's careful.

The females watched and waited. Ripple scanned Aroha's body and saw the baby positioning for birth.

Pearl was not there, but Ripple felt her presence in the sunlight shining through a thin mist of cloud onto a silvery sea. She breathed and let the cool air blow through her, let it lift the corner of a dark veil inside her. She looked again at the unborn baby.

A baby, she thought, a new dolphin who did not exist before. A miracle.

'What's a miracle?'

Ripple gaped. The question had come from the baby!

'May I speak to her?' she asked Breeze.

'Certainly,' said Breeze, 'This baby is almost as bad as you were for wanting to communicate.'

'What's a miracle?' asked the baby again.

'You are,' said Ripple.

'I thought I was a dolphin!'

'You are a dolphin and you're a miracle too. A miracle is something so wonderful you can hardly believe it's true. Are you ready to be born?'

'Breeze has told me everything. But there's too much to remember.'

'Relax and listen. All will be well.'

The baby's tail appeared soon enough. Aroha kept swimming for some time while the baby emerged little by little and then all in a rush. Once free she shot to the surface, squeaked and complained about the light, wriggled and bounced, was sternly reminded to breathe, insisted she'd already breathed, got confused about who was her mother and followed Ripple by mistake. Ripple laughed for the first time in weeks and swam about with the tiny one in her slipstream. She steered her back towards Aroha. All the females were absorbed in the new arrival.

Within minutes they heard the vibrations of their nearby guards fighting off sharks which had smelled the blood. The guards must be doing well; no trace of fear or pain escaped from them to worry the birth party.

'What will you call her, Aroha? Who shall inform Rigel he has another female descendant?'

Aroha named her baby Rikoriko, for the sparkle of energy she emitted. Rikoriko was appreciating her spacious new world.

'Miracle!' she squealed, 'Miracle! Miracle! Everything's a miracle!'

Ripple had never seen anything so perfect as this miniature dolphin, so smooth and flexible, with eyes and spirit clear and clean. Rikoriko's own freedom from grief and sorrow banished such burdens from all those who looked at her. Ripple wanted to keep her for herself, but Aroha was also healed by the arrival of Rikoriko and would not allow Ripple to abduct her daughter, although it seemed as if Rikoriko would've been happy to be kidnapped by Ripple. That faded when she tasted her mother's milk.

'Miracle!' said Rikoriko at the first sip.

It became important for Rigel's family group and Matangi's to stay together, since Ripple and Echo wished to stay near Aroha for now. It was not difficult; the entire school was now re-grouping, spring having arrived at last, bringing warmer currents, softer breezes, longer days, and ever increasing food supplies.

Many dolphins had departed Azure during the winter. It was a smaller school that gathered around the Northern islands that spring.

As the days rolled by, dolphins grieved and slowly healed, classes and vocations resumed. Rigel reunited with his old team who began planning new assaults on the universe.

Cosmo's junior astronomy team was also meeting regularly and Delph set much revision. But soon enough he was allowing the boys to make short interstellar voyages within the home galaxy. Then whole days would pass without Ripple or Echo seeing anything of Rush and Cosmo. Meetings, when they happened, were quieter than of old.

Echo was working hard at her new vocation. She was now in full training with Nimbus so Ripple saw less of her. Ripple's old classes recommenced but she did not yet join up with the astronomy team to create music. Since her mother's death she'd returned to the same strange blank music-free world she'd inhabited after her Erishkigal illness.

Others noticed this. 'That youngest one of Pearl's is not as cracked as she used to be,' they said, 'The shock of her mother's death must've snapped her out of it. Pearl would be pleased to know her daughter's becoming normal at last.'

Aroha no longer saw it that way, however.

'Much as her music bothered me, I preferred the old chaotic Ripple to this incomplete version,' she thought.

Ripple filled the gaps in her life by spending every possible moment with Aroha and Rikoriko.

Very occasionally Ripple would spot a soaring bird, or hear the rush of foam flying on the wind and she'd think of music and feel a momentary longing to be alone and listen to it. But a poisonous vibration inside her always prevented it.

~~~

Soon even Aroha began to take on a little of her old work. One day she went to help another family, which like her own, was having trouble recovering from the loss of loved ones over winter. Matangi had travelled south with his weather team to collect data on currents, so Ripple and Rikoriko were left alone in the main school for a while.

'My favourite slipstream!' laughed Rikoriko as she slid into Ripple's.

Ripple performed a dance routine she'd invented to entertain her niece who loved the unpredictability of Ripple's lead. Rikoriko did her best to copy.

'Ripple, what's music?' Rikoriko asked suddenly.

In her surprise, Ripple belly-flopped. Rikoriko did too.

'Who told you about music?'

'I heard you thinking about it this morning.'

'You little busybody!'

'But I like music.'

'I don't believe I just heard that.'

'I like what you like, and you like music.'

'If not for music Rikoriko, my mother might still be alive and you would have a loving grandmother.'

'I don't need someone else to love me. But how could music hurt your mother?'

'Because I was making music heedlessly, a bad creature crept up and poisoned me. My mother had to nurse me and she got sick herself and died.'

'Mother told me my Granny died because of something poisonous she ate.'

'Perhaps Aroha's right.'

A tight knot, deep inside Ripple, loosened slightly.

'So music is not bad and you can teach me.'

'I can't. It's locked inside me. '

'How can I learn then?'

'The sound games I played at your age are a little like music. Perhaps they'll do you no harm.'

'How could sounds harm me? Teach me.'

'Listen to the sounds of Azure. Play with them in your mind and see if they form patterns. What can you hear right now if you close your eyes and listen really hard?'

'I heard a rude noise from that boy over there.'

The eternal joke did not fail to amuse Ripple. But Rikoriko showed the greater maturity on this occasion and was soon describing all the other noises.

'I can hear your heartbeat . . . wind in the froth . . . bubbles popping . . . dolphins scanning for fish . . . a gannet diving.'

'Now try and mix the sounds, to make patterns that are interesting or pretty.'

Rikoriko closed her eyes and concentrated so hard Ripple could imagine her little brain heating up. 'You need to relax, Listen easily and let the patterns form. Don't force anything.'

Rikoriko relaxed and Ripple knew she was really playing with sounds. But she detected no dangerous longing to seek out some elusive goal, like that which had driven her to discover true music.

'You're doing well. Keep enjoying the patterns in the sounds around you. That's a kind of music.'

Rikoriko promised to keep practising what she'd learnt but Ripple was a little worried about how Aroha might feel about her daughter taking up an activity so closely linked to insanity in the minds of many. So she urged Rikoriko to learn everything her mother wanted her to learn and only to think of music as a hobby. Surely that was harmless enough.

Strange, thought Ripple later, I gave the first music lesson ever, to a child who has never heard a note of music in her life! I hope I haven't corrupted her.

~~~

A few days later, Aroha found the first opportunity to leave her baby with Breeze, and after a short consultation with Nimbus, collected Ripple and swam out alone with her.

'Rikoriko has been telling me that you think Mother's death was because of you.'

'I worry that she died because of my illness. So I do feel responsible.'

'Ripple, I've just spoken to Nimbus, who was with Mother at the end. She's sure you had nothing to do with the sickness.'

'Father said that too, but I still worry,'

'These illnesses happen from time to time. It's the turning of the universe. It could've been something she ate, or it could've been something else. Everyone has to die of something. You can't go on thinking like this. It will stop your life from progressing.'

The tight knot inside Ripple loosened a little more.

'I want to help you,' said Aroha. 'There are therapies I can apply but you must do exactly as I tell you.'

'Will your therapy do anything to my music?'

'Trust me Ripple. I'm only working with zones of your mind I understand well. I only want to clear you of unnecessary negatives. Are you ready?'

'I'm ready.'

'So . . . relax . . . drift . . . breathe . . . let your mind wander . . .'

Ripple followed every instruction and suggestion as Aroha sent her specialised thoughtstreams weaving into her sister's subconscious with practiced ease. Ripple floated away from herself and saw the oceans stretching far and wide around them and the school swimming nearby. She saw clouds below, between her and the surface of Azure, and although it was daytime she saw stars and the arm of the galaxy swooping above and all around her until Sol became a tiny speck among millions of other stars. It reminded her of the departure she'd experienced during her illness. Then came a moment of sudden but smooth release, as the knot inside unravelled completely and she soared more lightly through the universe . . . gliding . . . drifting . . . until she heard her sister's voice calling from far away and she turned in a great arc back towards Azure.

Ripple's body leapt to wakefulness.

'Aroha! What did you do?'

'Just a simple therapy. I should've used it on you weeks ago. How do you feel?'

'I feel like . . . making music! But I'm too hungry. Let's hunt.'

'Good, let's hunt. We can pick up Rikoriko. And I'd best sort out any issues the rest of my family may have. Strange to think I've been helping other families and left my own to fend for themselves. Why don't my family do as other dolphins do and just ask for help when they need it?'

As they swam Aroha said, 'Ripple, this might surprise you but I'd really like to think you were making music again. I've learnt that you are more whole when you have music in your life.'

'But Aroha, Rikoriko heard me just thinking of music and she asked me to teach her. Don't worry! I can't teach her much, since it's incommunicable. Do you worry I might corrupt her with it?'

'You said "worry" twice then. I thought I'd healed you of it.'

After this, Ripple began to think more of the conversation she'd had with her father about links to music in unlikely fields of learning. Strangely, the unwelcome subject of mathematics demanded space in her thinking. She made sure she was on time for every mathematics lesson and drank in every detail.

There was a little spare time at the end of the lesson.

'Any questions?' asked Axis. 'Ripple, was everything clear?'

'Yes, thank-you. Echo's been helping me catch up, but I have a question, May I see you afterwards, Axis?'

'Certainly.'

Axis had noticed a difference in her since her illness. Not only had she been present in body and mind at every maths lesson but had displayed aptitude. He responded to a last question and dismissed the class.

Ripple and Axis swam away from the main school towards the deep sea.

'My father thinks mathematics could solve my problem,' she said.

'His views are worth taking seriously. What problem?'

'Something I wish to share with others. I call it "music" but to others it's chaos.'

'This music . . . what is it exactly?'

'It's patterns made from sounds. But I can't communicate it by thoughtstream.'

'Not surprising. To communicate a sound we must make the sound or describe it. We send ideas by thoughtstream.'

'Shall I demonstrate?'

'Go ahead.'

She streamed a few seconds of sunrise music.

Axis had heard of her chaos, but was surprised by the reality.

'I'm sorry,' he said, 'It is as chaotic as they say.'

'But now,' Ripple said, 'I wonder if it might be possible to describe my music mathematically – by its levels of volume, pitch and timing of the sounds – then use this to communicate it?'

Axis digested this. They swam on under bright blue sky with towering summer clouds. The sea was as clear as the air above it but deep sapphire in colour. He spoke at last.

'I don't see why it wouldn't work. If you can make accurate descriptions we could use a formula to compress it into a "data bullet" which would be either thought-streamed or passed on as a compressed physical sound. Thoughtstreaming would be ideal for long-distance communication but a compressed sound would work within hearing of the sender. A number unlock key would allow it to play in the mind as perfectly as it did in the mind of the sender.'

'It sounds as though you've done this before, Axis.'

'Often. Our astronomers use data bullets to navigate their astral journeys. The information they need is too vast and complex to carry any other way. If it works for them, it should work for you.'

'I've neglected maths in the past believing it wasn't relevant to music. Now I'll work at it with all my heart. If I succeed in preparing music will you help me to apply the compression formula and attach the unlock key?'

'I'd be more than happy.'

He was silent a moment and seemed gloomy.

'One thing bothers me – when students take an interest in mathematics only because they've found something it can do for them, instead of seeing the beauty of mathematics for its own sake. You're no worse than the astronomers in this respect and they're accorded more respect than the mathematicians whose calculations are the true force beneath their flukes.'

'I'll try to see the beauty in maths,' she promised.

Axis laughed, 'Keep that promise and I'll do my best to see the beauty in "music" when its time comes.'

He spun around, breached to the east, and raced off towards his waiting family.

In the days and weeks that followed, Ripple's mathematical prowess accelerated. Never before had Axis seen a student improve so rapidly.

~~~

Ripple sought out Rigel later that night, under a moonless but starlit sky. By a stroke of luck he was home on Azure and free to talk. She described her conversation with Axis.

'My dear, I've had faith in you since the first moment I heard your "problems" mentioned by Delph, the old fusspot. He wanted me to cosset you, but look at how you're working out your own course without me.'

There was a time when Rigel would have laughed to remember the day of Delph's rebuke, and a more recent time when it would have given him a stab of pain. But Aroha had ministered to all her family by this time and he was almost whole again. He looked Ripple over.

'It's good to see you recovered so well from that dark winter.'

'You too, Father. I still miss Mother but I'm enjoying my life on Azure once more. Rikoriko and Aroha have revived us all.'

Rigel sighed. 'Daughters, daughters, and now grand-daughters! What would I do without them? But why are there so few males? It's splendid news that Rev has finally dedicated himself to a worthwhile vocation. Strange to think of my only son becoming a substance adept – a specialist in the inks of rare octopuses! He never showed the slightest interest in following my vocation, which disappointed me. But now I'm well-pleased that my youngest daughters look likely to bring two of the best young astronomers on the planet into the family. Any grandchildren you both produce will have more than their share of astronomers' blood.'

Pleased at these words of approval for Cosmo and Rush, she performed a high-flying corkscrew spiral back-flip she'd invented herself. He had never seen anything like it but he copied and the sensation tickled him until he laughed as he used to when Pearl was alive.

'You're refreshing company after those serious astronomers. But I see fear within you still, and it's a barrier. That fear may need to be faced.'

He did not explain further. She continued swimming while puzzling over his prediction until a rumour of food nearby arrived in their minds by wide-range thoughtstream.

Father and daughter dashed off to the location given. Cosmo arrived to join in the hunt, as did several other hungry dolphins. It was squid, large, lazy and sweet, rising towards them in streams, a gift from the abyss. The dolphins fed until the juice of the meat drenched their blood with fresh energy.

~~~

24
I KNOW YOU'RE OUT THERE

Maths became Ripple's focus. She soaked up everything in class and sometimes requested extra help. She only once worked with the astronomy class and that was to create a 'maths' song. She hoped one day to deliver it to Axis. In her free time she applied what she had learnt. Little by little the descriptions of the music came together. At last a day came when she was ready to take a piece of music to Axis for the data compression process.

They worked together for several evenings. First, he showed her the processes used by mathematicians and astronomers to compress navigation data and they modified it to suit Ripple's data. Then he taught her how to apply it to her own material, and finally how to create, transmit and activate a numerical unlock key.

She made sure she was alone for the first test. She cleared her mind and centred the compressed 'bullet' in her consciousness. She breathed, relaxed and applied the unlock key. The music played.

~ ~ ~

'What's that new cacophony she's made?' Sterne asked.

'More noise she has cobbled together.' I replied, 'Hmmm; it seems not quite as bad as the usual bedlam.'

~ ~ ~

Ripple was disappointed. The music played but the new process had distorted it horribly. This was nothing like her true creations; it was chaos in comparison.

Chaos? That's the word everyone uses. Now I begin to understand. If this is like what they've been hearing, no wonder they thought I was mad. Poor Mother.

She forced herself to listen again.

Yes, it's awful. But faintly recognisable in places. Enough for hope?

She told Axis.

'Refine your mathematical descriptions; improve their accuracy,' he advised.

Ripple worked on, calculating her songs, week after week, her head full of music and numbers. She hunted little and rarely socialised.

At last she was ready to compress and unlock for the second test. She listened carefully to the result. It was still not perfect, but suddenly she knew!

I need only keep at it to succeed. Father was right. Mathematics! My perfect solution all along.

That night she hunted with Echo, Rush and Cosmo and told them of the progress. Cosmo swam alone with her afterwards.

'Ripple, we both know how much your music has alarmed me but I'm curious to have it clarified at last.'

'I've not forgotten my promise to give the first song to the one who inspired it.'

She was amused to hear him wondering what a 'song' was.

~~~

Ripple immersed herself in her task through days and nights.

'Strange' she thought, 'how I can do this work alone and remain perfectly aware of the ocean and any dangers it might hold. Mathematics is far safer than creating music.'

One or two hungry sharks took an interest in her when they sensed her solitude but she evaded the danger.

Measuring, quantifying, organising, calculating; I watched with sister Sterne as Ripple worked on hour after hour, stopping only for the bare minimum of hunting. For a dolphin who didn't like mathematics, she'd come a long way.

When the work was complete, she decided for her third test she'd use a different piece of music, start from the beginning and go through the whole process.

She started at first light on a morning at the height of summer. The piece she chose was about three minutes long. It was one of her earliest songs; a song of hope inspired by sky-colours she'd seen one misty pre-dawn, shortly after her discovery of music.

Using her new processes it took about an hour to create and calculate the mathematical description of the song. She applied the compression and the resulting thought 'bullet' was ready to communicate by thoughtstream. That would be an instantaneous action. She created an unlock key, cleared her mind and applied the key, just as the sun was rising.

There were other dolphins in the vicinity and mindful of her promise to Cosmo, she veiled her mind while the song played.

~~~

We of the Hereafter could have listened but we chose to respect her barricades.

Sterne even banished the seraphim to the far side of the universe to ensure Ripple's privacy.

'Don't come back for an hour,' she warned.

They were back in ten minutes but by then the test was over.

~~~

Ripple lay drifting in a daze of unveiled thoughts.

Not a note too high or low. Not a note too long or short. Every pause, perfectly timed. The melody, the chords, every beat, every trill, every subtle vibrato, every sweeping glissando, exactly as I intended.

Ripple streamed a thought to her niece playing far off beside Aroha in the main school.

Rikoriko, you'll need to work hard at your maths if ever you wish to make music.

Ripple allowed herself to be hypnotised by the surface patterns around her, light glancing through water, tilting this way and that, ranges of miniature peaks linked by shining curves. She pressed her tail gently against the muscle of the sea, propelling herself forward; lacy patterns of bubbles brushing her eyes; the water parting cleanly around her body.

She drifted down then looked at the surface glimmering above. Shafts of sunlight spread gradients of colour from deep royal to light jade-green through the sea. She released diamond pebbles of air and followed them to the surface where she breathed and still carrying this strange calm within her, cruised towards the main school.

Ripple knew she was approaching a turning point in her life, but somehow it did not delight her to know her secret would soon be out.

It's been my own for so long. Do I really want to share it? Do I want to hear others talk about my songs as they talk about weather and hunting?

She sought Delph and asked after Cosmo and the boys.

'They're away on a mission,' he said, 'and unlikely to return before late tomorrow.'

A reprieve.

Ripple spent the rest of the day close to the main school, processing and compressing song after song, stacking the song-bullets neatly in her mind until many of her favourites were ready to share. Her efficiency grew as she worked, so that each song was processed quicker than the one before. She visited Aroha and told Rikoriko that she had a big surprise for her soon.

Rikoriko turned many cartwheels. Ripple joined in pretending she couldn't help being sucked into lopsided acrobatics by the tiny slipstream. Aroha stayed out of their nonsense and kept her poise, laughing at them all the same.

'So,' said Aroha, once their antics had calmed, 'I gather from your mood, you've solved your problem.'

'Yes. Father recommended mathematics. It was the right advice.'

'When do we get to experience music then?'

'I've promised Cosmo he's to be first, but he's away, so you must wait.'

'You seem calm. Is it hard to be patient?'

'I can hardly wait to share it, especially with Rikoriko. But a part of me is sad to unveil something which has been private for so long. Perhaps Rikoriko will become my first apprentice musician. Will you mind?'

'That's difficult to answer without knowing what it is she is choosing. But I think she would want your vocation even if you were a bubble counter. She's mad on maths at your suggestion.'

Ripple laughed, 'Counting bubbles does come into music occasionally.' The afternoon passed and night drew on.

Ripple sought solitude to enjoy her music while it was still hers alone, perhaps for the last time.

'I know you're out there,' she whispered, as she gazed at the stars and played music of starlight. She listened with half her mind while the other half monitored her surroundings, but nothing disturbed the peace of her ocean that night.

The next day dawned overcast and gloomy. Cosmo's team was due back late afternoon. Ripple made herself busy. She prepared a few more songs for communication by thoughtstream. She attended a mathematics class and informed Axis that her project had reached a successful outcome and that she'd demonstrate it shortly. He congratulated her. She spent time with Aroha's family, hunting a little and playing with Rikoriko. It rained. The sadness of the seeping rain made them swim slower and closer together. They compared the sharp empty taste of the raindrops to the rich salt of the seawater. Around them, the ocean lay eerily muffled beneath a thickening blanket of cloud.

In the afternoon Ripple attended a poetry class with Tercet.

Two boys misbehaved during the lesson. They hadn't learnt the poems, the discussion was beyond them and they became bored. They interrupted and tried to distract other students. Tercet ordered them to stay behind after class. Ripple overheard him muttering.

'Why is it that there are always some who don't respond to poetry the way others do?'

Ripple thought she had swum too close to an iceberg.

Always some who do not respond to poetry? Will music be like that too? Why should Cosmo care about a bunch of sounds I've arranged?

Tentacles of fear squirmed in her mind like shadows of true madness.

~~~

25
THE UNIVERSE CHANGES

As the afternoon drew on, Ripple moved towards deeper water to find the astronomy team. Raindrops patterned the smooth swells and ripples arrowing from her dorsal fin complicated the pattern. By the time she reached the team the rain had stopped but the cloud remained, colouring the sea silver-green.
Delph arrived from the opposite direction. The five empty bodies lolled in the water with the more active shapes of the minders close by.

'We're expecting them back shortly,' said Hadar.

Only a few minutes later the five bodies leapt to life as the travellers returned. Ripple thoughtstreamed Echo to let her know Rush was back.

The boys calmed a little then gave Delph an outline of their mission. They'd visited a planet partially covered with flame and had met fire-sprites, a strange life-form which had evolved at high temperatures.

'The fire-sprites pitied us when we described our watery home,' explained Rush. 'To them Azure is a kind of hell. They didn't believe us when we said water even falls out of the sky.'

'You need to hunt now,' Delph said, 'Tomorrow you transfer your material in full to historians for storage. I'll attend that meeting and learn more of your voyage then.'

The team was free to go. Ripple swam with them to nearby feeding grounds and Echo romped in from the south. By the time they'd eaten their fill it was night, the cloud was breaking up letting a few stars shine through. Ripple and Cosmo headed out alone. She gave him her slipstream in recognition of his tiredness. She told him of her success with the song bullets.

'Have you tested it yet?' he asked.

'Only on myself.'

'Ripple, will you show it to me now?'

Her stomach twisted. Live tentacles coiled inside her.

'You're tired,' she said. 'We could leave it until tomorrow.'

'I don't wish to leave it one second longer.'

She began swimming erratically, trying to fight off the clutch of the tentacles and to hide them from him. But he'd seen.

'Stars of Dorado Ripple! What's the matter? Is that music?'

'It's fear.'

'I won't ridicule you even if it's still chaos.'

'I'll give you the first song now.'

She tried to thoughtstream the song bullet but the tentacles strangled its flight. She tried again. The same thing happened.

~~~

I turned and spoke to Sister Sterne.

'This is a dark moment, as though all the flowers of the Fragrant Planet have locked their perfumes away from the morning wind at the moment of greatest need.'

Sterne did not respond, so intent was she on the events below us in the ocean.

~~~

Ripple turned from Cosmo and the awful silence surrounding them. She sought a deeper silence she could wrestle with. Cosmo followed her, though she was hardly aware of him.

This is the fear father warned me of.

She stopped moving forward and sank below the surface. Deep into the dark.

Cosmo stayed alongside, saying nothing. He brushed a flipper along her body, a calming gesture. She tensed a little at his first touch then her muscles relaxed. She drifted. The tentacles inside her released their grip slightly. She swam up, surfaced and breathed the midnight air. At the surface, he stroked her again. She felt a picture slide from his mind into hers; the moonlight rainbow. She knew it had helped him in his own time of crisis. Now it shimmered for her – a vision of hope and reassurance. She calmed until her mind was clear enough to recognise the tentacles for what they were: the last vestiges of Erishkigal's poison.

She asked him not to follow and swam away carrying the rainbow with her. Alone over deep water she conjured a picture of the monster so real she could smell its stench and hear its teeth grinding. She stared for a long time into the evil eyes glowing in her brain. Their lust would have defeated her, had it not been for Cosmo's rainbow shining beyond. Then at last, although the monster was nowhere near, Ripple cried out;

'Erishkigal - Shadow Queen
Vipa, Venga, Malevine,
Lucifina, Sadistine,
Fera, Lashette and Clawdine,
Go down now!

The ocean was her mother, whose silken caress enfolded every particle of her skin. She looked up. Last wisps of cloud were dissolving, revealing a blaze of stars and the arm of the galaxy candescent above her. Azure's sweet atmosphere moved softly on the ocean. It carried a faint perfume tonight.

Land-flowers, she thought.

The tentacles evaporated.

She returned to Cosmo's side and effortlessly streamed the song-bullet to him. Cosmo felt it thunk into his head.

It feels exactly like a navigation data bullet coming in from Delph, he thought.

Next he received a number from her; the unlock key.

'I'll trigger it for both of us when we're ready,' she said.

Strangely, he was the nervous one now.

'I'm no longer afraid,' she said, 'but the fact remains, you may not respond to music. Understanding may develop later, or not.'

It must be something obscure and difficult, he thought privately, since she's worked on it alone all her life. I'm tired but I must try to understand no matter how murky it seems. It must help her to offload this burden. A mathematical description of sound, she says? I hope I grasp it. I don't want her to think I'm stupid.

Later he was glad he'd veiled those thoughts.

He moved into her slipstream and prepared his tired brain for an intellectual effort. They swam slowly forward. She whispered in his mind.

'Are you ready Cosmo?'

He tossed his beak to signal assent.

'Then we'll breathe together now, so we won't need to breathe again until the song is well started; it starts very softly so we need to listen carefully at first.'

They both breathed. She triggered the unlock.

The music began, lilting gently; feathers of sound brushing the waves, but building slowly; its power mounted, until the chords swept over Cosmo like the wind and the lyrics rode on the wings of the melody.

Under a moonlit rainbow
Through the flying spray
Who did you leave behind
When you came my way?

The dolphins breathed and the music continued.

She danced. He followed. His tiredness vanished as he spun and spiralled after her across the surface of Azure with the stars of Koru blazing above. The first love song ever was playing right here on his own planet. Cosmo could hardly believe this was happening to him. Nothing in all his travels had prepared him for the experience.

'My life will never be the same. No dolphin's life will ever be the same. The universe has changed forever. Lonely little Ripple, my Ripple, has done this for all of us. How blind and deaf we've been!'

Carried in the midnight silk
Of starry currents in the seas
I listen to the rising wind
That sings to you of galaxies

It sings to me of you,
Stranger from the blue
And will you take my music
To the galaxies with you?

Under a moonlit rainbow
Through the flying spray
What were you fleeing from
When you came my way?

The last notes trailed away and the first song was over. Cosmo was silent for a long time, but spoke at last.

'Ripple?'

'Yes?'

'Is this what your "chaos" has been?'

'Yes and many dolphins have wanted to cure me of it. Even those who love me.'

'What on Azure should we do?'

'I could play you another one.'

'There are more?'

'There are dozens ready to share and dozens more to be processed.'

'Dozens? How could you carry all this within you? I can't bear to think of how we treated you like a freak! How can you ever belong to me alone?'

He swam in silence, surfacing more frequently than normal to breathe. Ripple fussed alongside him, also agitated.

'I'm sorry,' Cosmo said. 'I'm . . . thunderstruck.'

'You like it?'

'I do.'

'Then enjoy another song.'

After many more songs, he said, 'You've written my life's work. Clearly it's my task to circulate your music to the stars. It will repay a hundred-fold everything those distant cultures have given Azure.'

'But not the first song. Take my other songs beyond Azure but let's keep the first song to ourselves.'

The first song of all time . . . was given to me alone, he thought.

He saw Ripple as the central point of a beginning spiral, new as a baby seashell, ever expanding until its arms matched the spirals of the galaxy and all existence beyond it.

Ripple nudged him with her beak. 'Just enjoy the music,' she said. Then she shared some more songs and he enjoyed them as he'd never enjoyed anything before.

~~~

There were no barricades in Ripple's brain this time. Deities and seraphim of the hereafter listened in with Cosmo. All of us heard what he heard. Like Cosmo, I knew without any doubt, that a new phase of the universe had begun. The future directions of no less a deity than Father Clement MJS (Most Joyfully Sublime) were permanently defined by the actions of one young female dolphin on the planet Azure. Music was my own destiny, I was certain of it.

Sterne silently observed the two dolphins. Then she became absorbed in watching the seraphim. They changed as they listened. They've never been the same since. Music completed them at last. The first chords of the song calmed them as though true peace descended for the first time. They expanded and flowered. We watched as Ripple's music exalted the race of seraphim into the race of angels, and in return they devoted themselves to music for eternity. Their auras intensified in colour and stretched into wings of power sweeping the universe. When the last notes faded the angels hovered transcendent, at the dawn of their perfection, almost too bright to look upon.

After their metamorphosis, even Sterne viewed them with respect she had never shown towards their immature form. I suddenly recognised them as a vast source of latent musical abundance awaiting ignition. The newly exalted angel host remained over Azure for many weeks. I arranged them into choirs and they listened to Ripple's music alongside me. They sang with her though she did not know it. Some of them returned with me to the Sacred Galaxy. Under my guidance, they commenced their new but everlasting task of musical praise and musical creation. They returned frequently to Azure to exchange places with angels who had remained there learning from Ripple.

In recognition of Sterne's achievement, I did not hesitate to recommend her advancement in the Divine Hierarchy. Sister Sterne DS (Developing Sublime) became Mother Sterne MLS (Master of the Light of the Spirit) for her work with Ripple alone, of all the billions of spirits under her care. I graciously encouraged her to share her revolutionary methods of measuring the worth of a soul by reading the light of its spirit.

My own new task of guiding angels in their pursuit of music, allowed me to spend much time among the dolphins of Azure. I too was honoured with a new title: Father Clement MJS MAC (Most Joyfully Sublime and Master of Angelic Choirs).

Later I thought back to the time when Sterne and I had listened to the first music. How strangely calm she had been; as quiet and still as the snow that lies on the poles of Azure. Not a tear escaped from her eye, though many poured from mine.

Was it modesty? I was soon to discover the real cause of Sister Sterne's strange calmness.

~~~

26
RIGEL'S PRAYER

Cosmo explained to Delph that he needed some time free to support Ripple in something that would soon become clear. Then Cosmo accompanied Ripple on a visit to Axis to give him her song of mathematics.

'Music might have stayed inside me forever if not for you, so I've created this to thank you.'

They listened to the song. Axis was almost as astounded and appreciative as Cosmo had been. He played it over and over again and they left him there gently dancing to the music.

Then they visited Aroha and Rikoriko.

Aroha laughed after hearing her first song. 'How fortunate I didn't cure you of music as I once hoped to.'

'Instead you were the one who revived it in me,' Ripple reminded her.

Rikoriko was not surprised to receive music. She'd never expected anything less from her favourite aunt. She demanded to become Ripple's first apprentice and now had the full blessing of her mother. Rikoriko became the second dolphin ever to choose music as a vocation.

Cosmo went to the elders, leaving Ripple to share her music with her relatives. He explained that Ripple had made a discovery more valuable than anything ever discovered by astronomers in the universe. He asked they call an assembly so she could reveal it to the school. The elders began arranging the first music concert for later that day.

Ripple first gave them a lively piece in praise of the glittering oceans surrounding the Northern Islands in summertime. All over that very sea, thousands of dolphins leapt and danced to the melody. It was a smash hit.

~~~

As I looked upon that first Azuran celebration of music, my attention was captured by the familiar golden shape of Rigel swimming deep in the crowd. I lacked Sterne's finer skills but even I could see the light of his spirit expanding with pride, so great was the aura surrounding him. Rigel's mighty intellect used all its power to convey a simple prayer.

'Come back to us Pearl. Come back and see what our daughter has created!'

161

No-one on Azure heard Rigel's prayer though its energy resounded through the Hereafter. But Pearl was dead and her spirit had moved on to a galaxy impossibly distant. She could not come to him.

Ripple shared a dozen songs at the concert.

The demand was enormous and she circulated other music pieces afterwards by passing them to smaller groups of enthusiasts who circulated them from mind to mind. Ripple was correct in thinking that some would not respond to music as well as others. There were a very few who found it merely pleasant. Most felt as though they had been starved all their lives and Ripple had provided their first food. Dolphins born after that day could hardly imagine Azure without music.

Many wished to talk to Ripple, to thank her, or to apologise for their former misunderstanding. Cosmo and Echo had to shield her when sometimes their attentions almost overwhelmed her. Cosmo decided this was a good time for a holiday in the hope that the initial frenzy would calm down while she was away. He collected a group consisting of Ripple, Echo, Rush, Flip, Quin, Givan and himself, and the seven of them took time out to travel to his old school, near the Southern Islands. They shared Ripple's music with the Southerners who received it as enthusiastically as the Northerners. Cosmo took great pride in introducing Ripple to his friends from childhood, including his old teacher Zenith. The seven visitors from the north were welcomed joyfully and shown the best hunting and surfing during their stay.

A few weeks later on their return to the Northern Islands, the school had indeed recovered sufficiently to remember their manners so that Ripple was allowed to concentrate on her own work, including her new task of teaching Rikoriko. Many others soon wished to learn to make music. Ripple selected a small class to begin with and launched into the task of creating musicians capable of becoming teachers, to allow the new skills to spread. Delph offered to assign minders as required for musicians working at composition.

Rikoriko proved the most adept of all Ripple's students; she seemed to have been born to follow her aunt. Although the youngest in the class by far, by the time she was two years old she was making music comparable with Ripple's.

Cosmo returned to work with a clear mission. He and his team spent the rest of their lives transporting music to distant planets within Koru and far beyond.

~~~

We deities can tell you folk of Azure today, twenty million years later, that music was the contribution above any other for which your planet is renowned. Initially spread throughout the physical realm by Cosmo and his team, it has rolled further through space and time than even he could ever have imagined, carried on and on by others in later generations and distant worlds, down the millennia.

I still remember the day, not long after it all happened, when I discovered the reason for Sterne's icy composure on the day of the first song.

Surrounded by a phalanx of angels performing a stirring waltz in my praise, I sailed up to the recently promoted Mother Sterne (MLS) in the Sacred Galaxy, the rhythmic movements of my approach in perfect time to the waltz. With such music surrounding me, I felt that I must once again express my appreciation.

'That was a resounding success of yours, Mother! I will thank you for it eternally.'

'I've had a few successes lately Father Clement. To which of them do you refer?'

Her aura dazzled brightly but lacked fluidity, having tightened up noticeably as we arrived.

'Bit grumpish today eh? I'm talking about that tired little spirit you sent to Azure – who invented music and through love found the perfect way to release it to the universe.'

'Oh yes, it was a success I suppose, if you like that kind of thing.'

'But Mother! It's an absolute hit. Every angel of the Hereafter has mastered the trick. They're sitting about on nebulae, singing away like . . . well, like angels I suppose.'

'But it goes on day and night. It's given me a headache. I think I preferred the silence we had before.'

'You'll have to move with the times, girl. This music thing is here to stay. It's all over the universe. Makes you want to skip and dance as though you were young again.'

'It's inescapable, I'll give you that. But the main thing is the little spirit was fulfilled at last. That's my only concern. And I can put up with music if it makes the universe happier.'

'Good lass, that's the spirit!'

I danced on my way, immersed in glorious music, with the colours of my aura shimmering around me, billowing in time to the majestic chords of the waltz.

Sterne, poor thing, was tone-deaf. Yes, it's true; even we deities have our imperfections, though I can't think what mine could be. I thought back to the day when we had listened to Ripple's first song and understood that Sterne had only been able to understand the magnitude of Ripple's achievement by observing the metamorphosis it inspired in the seraphim.

~~~

Ripple bore three children to Cosmo. Neither parented children with other dolphins. Their love mirrored that shared between Kismet and Mimosa, who'd died so long ago for Cosmo. Ripple and Cosmo produced only boys to Rigel's delight. It was inevitable that with the blood of Rigel and Cosmo in their veins, two of them became master astronomers and followed their revered father and grandfather travelling between the stars. Only one became a musician. He was great in his day, but Ripple's musical legacy flowed most powerfully through the spirit of her niece Rikoriko. For hundreds of years it was common to refer to both in one breath.

'A song worthy of the era of Ripple and Rikoriko.'

~~~

Towards the end of their lives, Ripple and Cosmo decided to bequeath 'The First Song' to the ocean. They knew it was too precious to die with them so they gave it to their children for release after their death.

Twenty million years later, dolphins still sing the love song she gave to Cosmo. Known everywhere as, 'The First Song', it's the most beloved of all the songs she created, though all remain as treasures within ocean mind.

Winter was lashing the ocean when Ripple and Cosmo reached the end of their phase on Azure. They made a decision to give their worn-out bodies to a group of hunting sharks that were threatening their own newborn great-grandchild and other newborn dolphins in the area. The sharks were satisfied and the newborns survived. Cosmo and Ripple escaped their Azuran bonds together.

~~~

We of the Hereafter wished to recognise their contributions during their lives on this planet. Mother Sterne took the spirit of Ripple and cradled it in her aural wing, as she had done before she had sentenced it to life on Azure. I drifted alongside her supporting the spirit of Cosmo.

'Look at the change that has come over this spirit,' she said. 'Remember how pale and faint it was? We almost believed it was ready for aeons of rest. Now it has become strong and fulfilled. Do you still feel it should be withdrawn from its spiritual path Father Clement?'

'I most certainly do not! You once read strength within that spirit, Mother Sterne, which I admit I did not see myself back then.'

'Thank you, Father. But what do you suggest we do with them now?'

'I believe both are now ready to step up to those levels which allow past-life memory.'

'Agreed, but shall we reward them in any other way for their recent lives?'

'I think we should allow them to meet in the Hereafter between all their future lives so even when they are temporarily separated by life sentences, they will know their love remains eternal.'

'An excellent plan. You are kindly, Father Clement. I might never have thought of that. And let's allow them to stay together for a goodly rest before they commence their first separation.'

'Such a suggestion, Mother Sterne, illustrates to me that your compassion is advancing at a pace with your other special strengths.'

~~~

In the twenty million years since the life of Ripple, music in the ocean has progressed far beyond even her wildest dreams. Dolphin music now has the power to heal any disease, heal any physical or emotional scar, display tales across the mind in moving pictures, carry a spirit into the past or the future, sweep the listener away on astral voyages and transport spirits into the Hereafter to visit lost friends. Dolphin music has also allowed the dolphin brain to evolve into an organ capable of splitting into two parts, one of which can stay present in the physical world while the other part is asleep or away on an astral or musical voyage of discovery. Minders are no longer needed.

So you humans have now heard the story of Ripple.

But you may be wondering why Mother Sterne was so keen for you to hear it. Why did she insist old Clement go to the great trouble of translating everything into your human speech? And why now?

To answer that, let me take you away from your unimaginably distant past and into your not-so-distant future to show you where Azure is heading, now that humanity is on the scene . . .

~~~

27
MARCUS'S JOURNEY

When Marcus Evans rose for a 5am piano practice on that wintry Thursday morning in the year 2257, he experienced an unusual headache. It alarmed him for a moment but passed so quickly he soon forgot it. He saw nothing to indicate that this would be the last piano practice of his life.

Marcus threw on a warm robe and thick socks and crept to the music room, activating full sound-proofing to avoid waking the family. He settled at the instrument, un-brushed hair sticking up on end, hedgehog style. He warmed up with scale passages and then let his fingers lead him through some familiar pieces. As always he was absorbed and uplifted. For Marcus there was no world beyond the music as it travelled its route from page to eyes to mind to hands on keys, and from the keys through the workings of the machine, to make the sounds pouring into the room. He did not think of its complicated route. He was only aware of the music.

There were other things he was unaware of as he played: the slow spread of magenta light in the eastern sky as sunrise approached; the eerie silence in the oceans washing the borders of his island home; and the tiny tumour growing aggressively in his own brain.

The last piece he played that morning was 'Dolphin Nocturne.' He'd discovered it in a folder of old sheet music borrowed from a friend. The melody intrigued him. It had a light-heartedness which suited such playful animals. Since the piece was not too challenging, he was considering including it in the performance. The fact that he played it at all that morning was an odd co-incidence as it turned out; one he wouldn't forget.

The piano practice was necessary since his skills were rusty and he'd agreed to perform at a local community fundraiser only a fortnight away. Evans was an excellent musician when he practiced, but not a professional; his day job was scientific research in the field of sound. However the organisers knew that if Marcus Evans turned up to play, they would have a good turnout. Marcus had obliged, being community-spirited, even though he knew it would mean weeks of sacrificing early morning exercise. He'd become more inclined to jogging or cycling than music of late; it meant he could eat what he liked and stay lean. But piano practice was acceptable on such wintry mornings even if it did mean cutting down on food a bit.

At 7am, practice over, he closed the piano, entered the kitchen where coffee was by now wafting in the wind. He fought his way around the smaller breakfast-seeking family members, cooked and ate a couple of poached eggs on toast, regretfully skipped his usual follow-up of toast and marmalade, drank two mugs of coffee without sugar, (groan) showered, dressed, and made his way to work.

On the ten minute, 50k trip in the transporter, he listened to modern classical, which raised his spirits and relaxed his mind for the day's work ahead.

So far, so good. No black cats crossing his path. No angel feathers descending in his vicinity. No warning signs of impending life-changing phenomena.

He walked into the lab, greeted his colleagues and progressed through a normal day until after lunch when the new equipment arrived. Like school kids being introduced to new gym-gear, the scientists gathered round and listened hungrily as the technician explained the operation and uses of the machine. They were the first laboratory to test the technology. Its function was high-level mathematical analysis of sound.

Marcus booked the first trial session for 5pm when the others would be leaving. He wanted to try it out in the solitude of an empty laboratory to assess it without distractions.

When the time came, he dug out an old recording of sounds from nature. He started up the machine, positioned the earpieces, inserted the memory cell and read its menu on the screen. It had birdcalls, an amplified recording of an earthworm wriggling across paper, wind on water, weather sounds, animal calls, the rattle of a rattlesnake etc.

Marcus liked animals, so he selected the sound of a cat meowing. The original sound played first – it lasted about one and a half seconds. The machine automatically analysed the sound and played out its complete interpretation. The interpretation lasted ten seconds and sounded completely different from the original sound – more complex, with a far greater range of tone and pitch. There were even tiny breaks in a sound which had seemed continuous in its original state.

Sounds almost like a human language, thought Marcus. Amazing!

After playing the interpretation, the machine presented visual data in the form of figures, notes and graphs to explain how it had arrived at its analysis. He studied the material and couldn't fault it, though he'd worked in the science of sound all his working life. His interest in the new machine was increasing. He looked at the menu again. There were a few cetacean sounds. Cetaceans had made all sorts of interesting but meaningless sounds that people felt compelled to record: clicks, whistles, squeaks, booms, horn-like noises. Marcus chose a dolphin sound that interested him as much as any other. It was a three-second whistle. The original played and the interpretation began.

Marcus's whole body stiffened with shock. After just a few moments, he stopped the programme, consulted the guides, and re-checked everything to make sure he had made no errors with the process. He went through the start-up again using the same sound-clip. The interpretation began again.

Sweat appeared on his forehead. His mouth dropped open and his hands moved slowly from the arms of his chair to the sides of his head. He stared at the machine in disbelief. Gradually the shock gave way to ecstasy. His hands dropped down again slowly. The sweat dried but tears flowed instead. He was looking at a machine, but you'd have thought from his expression that he was looking into the eyes of an angel. Marcus was listening to music! This sophisticated machine was telling him that dolphins had created music that could send all human music straight to the trashcan.

The machine's interpretation of the three-second dolphin squeak lasted sixty-five minutes. Though he'd listened to most of the world's masterpieces, he had never heard music the quality of this. A bird who had suddenly progressed from flapping like a chicken to soaring like an eagle might have understood what happened to Marcus during those sixty-five minutes.

It was woven from sounds that seemed to have come from a planet in a different galaxy and time. Chords swept from unknowable instruments, carried him away as though on Arethusa's dreams, over surging tropic oceans through cerulean despair. They swept him up into midnight, and out between oscillating constellations that spun him to the ends of the universe where the spirits of the ages set him adrift in eternity, to wander back, unified, through a million lifetimes to his own reality on Earth.

All inside sixty-five minutes or a three second dolphin squeak.

From this time, all his interest in human music was lost but he was spiritually recharged as though he had physically travelled on the journey the music described. What he did not know at the time was that this recharge was to be life-long. The powers within the dolphin's musical journey had permanently altered his brain cells. They rendered benign the malignant tumour, which had grown aggressively in his brain for the last two months. It began to dissolve from that moment.

When the interpretation was over, Marcus Evans took a little time to adjust. The tears he'd shed streaked his face with salt and made his vision unreliable, but he glanced around, re-established his whereabouts and brought his scattered thinking under control. He tottered to the bathroom and sluiced his face with cold water. The rough-soft texture of the towel on his skin helped to re-ground him.

'Dolphins!' he muttered, 'What in this world were they?'

He recalled something he'd read about the dolphin brain having ten times the sound processing capabilities of the human brain. If we already knew that, he wondered, how could we not have guessed?

He returned to the machine and sat with his head in his hands for a moment or so. Then he stared at the mathematical data the machine had provided. One look was enough to tell him he would need to commit serious time to studying it if he was ever to understand a tenth of it.

'I'll listen to the music again. Second time might be easier.'

By the time his colleagues arrived for work fourteen hours later, Evans had heard the interpretation of the dolphin squeak twelve times. He didn't hear them enter.

'Hello! Evans is still here!

You been here all night buddy?

Ain't you got a home to go to?'

Marcus groaned, 'Omigod its morning!'

'Friday morning - Woohoo!'

'Jack,' said Marcus, 'know much about dolphins?'

'I know they're all dead.'

'Seen pictures of them,' chipped in another.

'You think we're all palaeontologists, Marc? What the hell have you been doing all night! You look like death.'

'They died out suddenly between 2207 and 2217,' said an older scientist. 'About the time of the Great World Famine. I was still a kid. Humans were starving so new fishing methods were developed and cetaceans lost their food supply. The fish saved millions of human lives but all whales and dolphins were lost.'

'Yeah, it was before I was born but I heard about it. Weird to think there were warm-blooded mammals that lived their whole lives at sea. The extinctions upset some folks for a while, but they were only animals; we had to put human survival first. And no real harm came of it in the end. Why everyone . . .'

'I know that,' Marcus interrupted. 'I mean research. Ever heard of research on dolphin sounds – using our modern tools?'

'Haven't heard of any. Interest in those animals pretty much died when they died.'

'Then I suggest we start researching now.'

A weird exhilaration glowed from beneath the exhaustion that stamped the face of Marcus Evans.

'You'll understand when you listen to this.' He tapped the menu item on the machine, heaved himself to his feet, walked out, rode home and slept.

Later that day he arranged to replace his slot at the fundraiser with dolphin music. The committee promoted it, played it to the community and staged many extra performances to cope with demand. Marcus received recognition and gratitude from the community for providing such a financial boost.

He reverted to jogging in the mornings in preference to music practice. It felt less futile and meant he could eat toast and marmalade as well as poached eggs for breakfast and go back to putting sugar in his coffee.

~~~

RIPPLE – THE POEM

Tentacles that suck and strangle
boiling in the deep
Dolphin! Listen to the stars
that shout and laugh and weep.

The world is young, a sapphire
Floating soft in solar space.
Jewel of the universe,
what pure ellipse you trace.

On the ocean's perfect mirror
one sweet raindrop fell.
The monster's heartbeat thundered
but she heard the tiny bell.

The stars were silent in her ears
bubbles giggled endlessly.
A million tiny beating hearts
The rhythm of the rolling sea.

In the music of the ocean
where the monster hunted long
In the shadow of its bloodlust,
She has sung the world's first song!

The monster longed to rip her flesh.
The song leaped up to certain death.
Searching in the stars above
alerted by a scream of love
Beyond the grinding teeth.

She danced so curving, lissom,
like the laughter of the song,
She sent resounding into space
and down the ages long.

~~~

AFTERWORD:

HOW YOU CAN HELP DOLPHINS AND WHALES:

- ✓ Never pay to view captive dolphins or whales. It encourages the practice of imprisoning them. Dolphins are born to be surrounded by their families and chosen social groups. They need deep water beneath them and the freedom to swim hundreds of miles of open sea whenever they choose. Many captive dolphins die young and some commit suicide by ceasing to breathe.
- ✓ Never stay at any hotel that keeps captive dolphins for the entertainment of their guests and be sure to tell the hoteliers why you are rejecting their hospitality.
- ✓ Reduce your usage of plastic and always dispose of all your rubbish, plastic, and chemical wastes thoughtfully, to be certain these items never end up in the ocean where they can kill dolphins and other sea creatures.
- ✓ Think carefully before eating any seafood. Be sure it was caught using sustainable fishing methods. If in doubt, refuse to eat seafood unless you have caught it yourself. We are land animals. Dolphins do not steal our fruit and grains. We should not steal their fish.
- ✓ If you have money to invest in energy resources, make sure you invest in those which are renewable, clean, and safe for our oceans.
- ✓ Reduce human populations. Honour childlessness as a blessed sacrifice. One child between two is next best. Once human populations are down to sensible levels we can eat as much sustainably-caught seafood as we wish.
- ✓ Do everything you can to reduce your own use of non-renewable energy and encourage others to do the same.
- ✓ View the documentary "The Cove" and encourage others to view it also.
- ✓ If Ripple has changed your attitude to dolphins and whales, be sure to recommend the story to your friends at home and around the world. The more people who become aware of the true possibilities of these magical creatures, the less likely they are to die or suffer at the hand of man.

ABOUT THE AUTHOR

Strangely enough, Tui Allen lives inland, in the Waikato of New-Zealand, which is the ideal location for the cycling and country walking she enjoys these days. But Tui grew up in an Auckland sailing family and her first marital home was a small wooden yacht, the classic H28 design Patricia. In her early married life, she sailed the South-Pacific in Patricia with her husband Bill Simpson and came face to face with many cetaceans who inspired the story of Ripple. Tui has worked as a primary schoolteacher and a web designer. Her previous published work consists of stories, picture books and poetry for younger children, articles for newspapers and magazines, mainly on sports topics and of course many web sites. Tui is very motivated about conservation issues particularly marine conservation.